ANDROMEDA RISING

JAMES RAMSEY

This book is an original work of fiction. Names, sponsors, characters, and incidents are the product of the author's imagination and are used fictitiously. Any resemblance to actual events, locales, or persons, dead or living, is coincidental.
The opinions expressed in this book are solely those of the author.

Andromeda Rising

Published in the United States of America

www.james-ramsey.com

http://jamesramsey09.blogspot.ca/

Twitter: @jamesramsey09

Facebook and Goodreads: James Ramsey

Editing: Maxann Dobson—The Polished Pen
www.polished-pen.com

Proofreading: Christina S

Cover Art: Lindsay—CoverLure www.coverlure.com

Interior Design and Formatting: Angela McLaurin—Fictional Formats www.facebook.com/pages/Fictional-formats/578230928856597

Blog tour: Jena Gregoire—Pure Textuality PR
www.puretextualitypr.com

Table of Contents

The Wiccan Rede	1
The Charge of the Goddess	5
Chapter One	7
Chapter Two	18
Chapter Three	43
Chapter Four	64
Chapter Five	82
Chapter Six	105
Chapter Seven	124
Chapter Eight	142
Chapter Nine	161
Chapter Ten	173

Chapter Eleven	189
Chapter Twelve	196
Chapter Thirteen	216
Chapter Fourteen	235
Chapter Fifteen	250
Chapter Sixteen	263
Chapter Seventeen	272
Chapter Eighteen	281
About the Author	291

Dedication

With much love to my Grampy,
who started and fed my book addiction.

And Mom, who always encouraged my imagination.

For my loving husband, Cary, who said I could.
And Max, who said I should.

The Wiccan Rede

Bide within the Law you must, in perfect love and perfect trust.

Live you must and let to live, fairly take and fairly give.

For tread the circle thrice about to keep unwelcome spirits out.

To bind the spell well every time, let the spell be said in rhyme.

Light of eye and soft of touch, speak you little, listen much.

Honor the old ones in deed and name, let love and light be our guides again.

Deosil go by the waxing moon, chanting out the joyful tune.

Widdershins go when the moon doth wane, and the werewolf howls by the dread wolfsbane.

When the Lady's moon is new, kiss the hand to Her times two.

When the moon rides at Her peak then your heart's desire seek.

Heed the north wind's mighty gale, lock the door and trim the sail.

When the wind blows from the east, expect the new and set the feast.

When the wind comes from the south, love will kiss you on the mouth.

When the wind whispers from the west, all hearts will find peace and rest.

Nine woods in the cauldron go, burn them fast and burn them slow.

Birch in the fire goes to represent what the Lady knows.

Oak in the forest towers with might, in the fire it brings the God's insight.

Rowan is a tree of power causing life and magick to flower.

Willows at the waterside stand ready to help us to the Summerland.

Hawthorn is burned to purify and to draw faerie to your eye.

Hazel-the tree of wisdom and learning adds its strength to the bright fire burning.

White are the flowers of apple tree that brings us fruits of fertility.

Grapes grow upon the vine giving us both joy and wine.

Fir does mark the evergreen to represent immortality seen.

Elder is the Lady's tree burn it not or cursed you'll be.

Four times the major sabbats mark in the light and in the dark.

As the old year starts to wane the new begins, it's now Samhain.

When the time for Imbolc shows watch for flowers through the snows.

When the wheel begins to turn soon the Beltane fires will burn.

As the wheel turns to Lammas night power is brought to magick rite.

Four times the minor sabbats fall use the sun to mark them all.

When the wheel has turned to Yule light the log the Horned One rules.

In the spring, when night equals day time for Ostara to come our way.

When the sun has reached its height time for oak and holly to fight.

Harvesting comes to one and all when the autumn equinox does fall.

Heed the flower, bush, and tree by the Lady blessed you'll be.

Where the rippling waters go cast a stone, the truth you'll know.

When you have and hold a need, harken not to others greed.

With a fool no season spend or be counted as his friend.

Merry meet and merry part bright the cheeks and warm the heart.

Mind the Three-fold Laws you should three times bad and three times good.

When misfortune is now wear the star upon your brow.

Be true in love this you must do unless your love is false to you.

These Eight words the Rede fulfill:
An Ye Harm None, Do What Ye Will!

The Charge of the Goddess

Listen to the words of the Great Mother, who was of old also called Artemis; Astarte; Diana; Melusine; Aphrodite; Cerridwen; Dana; Arianrhod; Isis; Bride; and by many other names.

Whenever ye have need of anything, once in a month, and better it be when the Moon be full, then ye shall assemble in some secret place and adore the spirit of me, who am Queen of all Witcheries.

There shall ye assemble, ye who are fain to learn all sorcery, yet have not yet won its deepest secrets: to these will I teach things that are yet unknown.

And ye shall be free from slavery; and as a sign that ye are really free, ye shall be naked in your rites; and ye shall dance, sing, feast, make music and love, all in my praise.

For mine is the ecstasy of the spirit and mine also is joy on earth; for my Law is Love unto all Beings.

Keep pure your highest ideal; strive ever toward it; let naught stop you or turn you aside.

For mine is the secret door which opens upon the Land of Youth; and mine is the Cup of the Wine of Life, and the Cauldron of Cerridwen, which is the Holy Grail of Immortality.

I am the Gracious Goddess, who gives the gift of joy unto the heart. Upon earth, I give the knowledge of the spirit eternal; and beyond death, I give peace, and freedom, and reunion with those who have gone before.

Nor do I demand sacrifice, for behold I am the Mother of All Living, and my love is poured out upon the earth.

Hear ye the words of the Star Goddess, she in the dust of whose feet are the hosts of heaven; whose body encircleth the Universe; I, who am the beauty of the green earth, and the white Moon among the stars, and the mystery of the waters, and the heart's desire, call unto thy soul. Arise and come unto me.

For I am the Soul of Nature, who giveth life to the universe; from me all things proceed, and unto me must all things return; and before my face, beloved of gods and mortals, thine inmost divine self shall be unfolded in the rapture of infinite joy.

Let my worship be within the heart that rejoiceth, for behold: all acts of love and pleasure are my rituals. And therefore let there be beauty and strength, power and compassion, honor and humility, mirth and reverence within you.

And thou who thinkest to seek for me, know thy seeking and yearning shall avail thee not, unless thou know this mystery: that if that which thou seekest thou findest not within thee, thou wilt never find it without thee.

For behold, I have been with thee from the beginning; and I am that which is attained at the end of desire.

Chapter One

The quartz pendulum swung back and forth across the map in a never ending routine of futility. I had been at it for hours. Looking at the clock, I realized it had been more than a few hours; it had been almost a full day. Each time I concentrated with everything I had, hoping the crystal would start to swing in a circle, hoping that this time I would get a positive response.

It was always the same answer. No.

I threaded my fingers through my hair and pulled in frustration. I couldn't understand it. The spell had always worked before. I had found dozens of people this way. But this time, try after try, map after map—Seattle, the northwestern states, USA, Canada, Mexico—farther and farther out, I expanded my search until now I was looking at a world map. Nothing. It was like Tonesha Johnson had vanished. I started to feel desperate.

Angrily, I swiped my arm across the coffee table, scattering the piles of maps and my atlas all over the floor. Damn it! If magick wouldn't work, I would do it the old fashioned way. Grabbing my bag and favorite hat, I headed for the bus stop. I would find that little girl. Her parents would know what happened to her.

Rubbing my eyes, I fought back the tiredness creeping over me. After spending hours combing the streets and talking to dozens of people, I wasn't any closer to finding that little girl than I had been, and now it was late and I still hadn't found my most reliable informant. The narrow back alleys around Occidental Park weren't the place to let fatigue dull my senses. Only a few blocks from the Union Gospel Mission, it was a good place for the homeless to panhandle during the day. Picturesque in the daytime, at night it was a very different story.

I re-adjusted my hat over my hair and swung my waist length mahogany brown braid to hang over my chest so the strap of my shoulder bag didn't pull it. My boss, Jimmy, always said I looked more like a college kid than a private investigator. My normal work wear consisted of worn jeans, a long sleeved white T-shirt with some kind of band T-shirt layered over top, beat-up Converse sneakers or boots, and a wool pea coat or jean jacket paired with my canvas messenger shoulder bag and a military cap to shade my brown eyes. It being summer, I had switched out the long sleeved shirt for a tank and jeans for cargo capris. I looked like any busy university student around town. I didn't like to stand out.

Keeping my head down but my instincts sharp, I kept an eye on the prostitutes and their hovering pimps, the johns and the dealers. I wasn't here for them. Miraculously, I wasn't hassled, most of them seeming to look right through me as I wound my way through the darkness.

"Psst! Joss! Over here." A sharp whisper came out of the dark dank alley on my right.

I tilted my head to the side masking the startled darting of my eyes. You never wanted look like you had been scared. Seeing a grimy face peering from around a dumpster, I relaxed a bit. It wasn't the face I had been looking for, but it was just as good.

Stepping into the alley, I looked down at the small boy who had found me. "Hey, Jacky. Whatcha got for me?"

A gap-toothed grin gleamed out of the darkness and the dirt covering his olive skin. All the street kids in Seattle knew me. They were my network of informants, my lost tribe, and I was their friend, occasional meal ticket, and sometime savior. They trusted me.

"Heard you was lookin' for Pete." His eyes held a mischievous glint.

Pulling a Jolly Rancher out of my pocket, I flipped it to him with a smile. "You heard right. You know where he is?"

He caught it but instead of a cocky grin, his mouth turned down and his eyes held a world of worry. He nodded. "Not s'posed to tell you though."

My heart sped up a bit. The only time these kids didn't tell me things was when one of the others told them not to. It was a close-knit group of survivors who relied on each other when the mean streets would chew them up without a thought. The only reason I was included was because I had been one of them once. They looked to me as a role model, someone who had walked in their shoes and not only lived, but thrived. If

Pete had told the younger ones not to find me, he was in real trouble. The kid had a chivalrous streak a mile wide, uncommon in a street kid.

"Where is he, Jacky? How bad is it?"

Chewing his chapped lip, the kid, who couldn't be more than seven, contemplated breaking a code stronger than the vows of the priests in the Catholic church not ten blocks away. "He'll be mad."

"Just tell me where to find him. I won't say who told me." Flipping him another Jolly Rancher, I hoped he'd cave.

"The building at Washington and Third. In the back there's a wood path where you can see the train tunnel behind it. He's hiding under there." He mumbled out the location, and I knew he wouldn't be repeating himself.

Reaching into my bag, I pulled out a wrapped sub sandwich and a juice box, passing it to him with a smile. "I didn't hear it from you."

He snatched it out of my hand in a blink, the hardened little waif clutching it to his chest. "Thanks, Joss." His eyes darted back and forth for a second before he lunged forward and gave me a quick hug. "You's good people."

Swallowing around the lump in my throat, I reached out and ruffled his greasy hair. "You know how to find me if you need me." I knew better than to try to pressure him to get off the street.

He nodded and darted off into the darkness.

While there were lots of great foster homes out there, the risk of being sent to a bad one was sometimes too great for these kids to gamble on. Sometimes life on the streets was better, at least in the summertime when it was warm. If I tried to *preach* at them, tried to convince them that a life in the system was better, they'd stop talking to me—stop trusting me. I wouldn't be able to handle that, so I offered them my understanding and prepaid burner phones with my number taped to the back. I knew the phones often got traded for food or goods, but sometimes the kids would call me for help or to offer information in exchange for money or something to eat. Whatever they needed, as long as it wasn't drugs, I gave it to them. Some caseworkers hated me, called me a bad influence and an enabler. They could stuff it. Most of them hadn't lived in the system. The kids trusted me, and I helped them whenever they'd let me.

Sighing, I headed east towards the hideout Jacky had pointed me to, worried about what I would find.

Peter Barrie was the last kid I had helped before I aged out of the system. It was a chance meeting at the Youth Crisis Center. He was in the secure wing of the Center, having just been rescued from his parents' highly abusive home, and I was attending some kind of life prep counseling course that was supposed to prepare me for *adult life*. Peter was an old soul in the body of a six year old. Cynical and jaded, he was angry at everyone. The mistake the social workers made was talking to him like he was a child. He wasn't. You couldn't be after everything he had seen.

We had bonded over our hatred of garbage bags. See, whenever they were in a hurry to move you from place to place, they'd give you a garbage bag to put your clothes in. It was easy, cheap, and held a lot. What they failed to realize was it made us feel like *we* were garbage. Disposable – something to be placed on a curb and picked up to be shuffled off to the next place where they most likely wouldn't keep you for long. The older you got, the less likely they would keep you.

At a few weeks short of my eighteenth birthday, my time was ending. His was just beginning.

I gave him my backpack full of essentials. A bar of soap, travel toothpaste and toothbrush, a towel, a warm hoodie, a couple of pocket books, and a flashlight with some spare batteries. I told him to never keep anything valuable in the bag because it was likely to get stolen, to make sure he got an education, to trust his instincts, and to give people a chance, but if something felt off–it most likely was. He was also the first kid I gave a burner phone to.

Ten years later, and I was dreading what I would find.

Easing up to the dark hole that was the underside of a wooden boardwalk, the gravel crunched under my feet as I skirted the fences separating the tracks from the parking lots of the buildings above. The rail lines ran underground here, and many of the city's homeless took shelter in the overpasses of the streets above. The darkness was an impenetrable wall in front of me, a menacing presence that promised unseen hazards lurking between me and my young friend. I gripped my unlit flashlight, nervous of the dangers hovering around me. Wetting my lips, I whistled the first seven notes of *Twinkle Twinkle Little Star* and then waited.

For eight deafeningly long heartbeats, I was frozen, worried, and scared all at the same time. From the darkness came three flickers of light: one long, two short. I sighed in relief. Switching on my own light, I flickered the reverse pattern—two short and one long burst of light—before turning it back on and making my way around the wooden supports. Up, stuffed way in the farthest recesses of the dirt embankment, was a lump of motionless rags with dull pinpricks of light staring out of them.

"Pete?" I whispered.

"Joss." The voice was gravelly and the effort was obvious.

When I got close enough, what I saw broke my heart. "Peter, what happened?"

His wheat blond hair was matted with dirt and blood, his face a painted mess of bruises and clotted with blood. His clothes were torn, and he clutched at his ribs enough that I thought they might be broken. Amazingly, all these years later, he still had the backpack I had given him.

"Who told you I was here?" he whispered hoarsely.

"Pfft!" I snorted. "Please, like I need help to find you."

His head fell back, thunking against the concrete wall behind him with a wince. "Jacky-boy."

I gave him a look of disbelief I didn't think he bought. "That kid skip out on *another* home?"

Peter rolled his eyes. "Cut the crap, Joss."

Shrugging off my bag, I sat beside him. "He's just worried about you. You look like hell."

He cracked open an eye at me. "You paid him off with Jolly Ranchers, didn't you?"

My braid caught on the button of my jean jacket as I shook my head. "He would never sell you out so cheap!" I smiled. "It was the sub sandwich that got him."

Pete chuckled but let out a painful hiss.

"So you gonna tell me what happened?" I asked. I dug another juice box out of my bag and offered it to him. He really didn't look good. He was always pale, but his skin under the bruises looked like parchment.

Wincing as he shrugged, he took a measured breath. "You shouldn't be here. The streets are too dangerous right now." He took a long draw of the juice and smiled his thanks.

My eyebrows rose. "I know just how dangerous they are, kid. Don't lecture me."

Peter looked at me seriously in the dim light of the shielded flashlight. "Not like this." He swallowed hard. "We haven't ever seen stuff like this before."

At seventeen he was on the verge of adulthood, but now he looked decades older. "Something weird is going on. Our lost tribe of young ones is disappearing."

Years ago, I told him the story of Peter Pan and the Lost Boys, the ones who lived in Neverland with no home, and the name had sort of stuck. Only we called it our lost tribe—a group of boys and girls alike who formed their own family when society failed them.

I sucked in a breath. "What are you talking about?"

"I've been trying to get the youngest off the streets. There are people out there looking for our kids. The ones who are the youngest, the weakest." He looked at me with anguished eyes. "They tried to take Jacky two nights ago. They were nice at first, talking about a new life and some kind of religious crap. When Jacky tried to leave, they grabbed him. I managed to fight them off, and Jacky got away but..." He stopped, trying to breathe and, I suspect, not cry.

A chill ran down my spine when he mentioned the religious crap. "But they didn't take you..." I half asked the question.

He shook his head. "They only want the young ones. It seems like after about the age of twelve or thirteen, they don't want them. I have the older ones scouring the city and dragging the brats back but things are scary right now."

"It's not just the lost ones, Peter," I whispered. "I came looking for you because my newest case is a nine year old girl. She disappeared walking home from school." And they had almost taken me when I was her age.

His jaw clenched as he swallowed. "I convinced Jacky to go to the Mission and turn himself in to the people there. I can't protect him like this. I thought he'd be safer in a home."

I knew how much it would have cost Peter to do that. He hated the system. "He looked to be headed that way when I saw him," I offered, my brow shifting into a frown, worried that he may not have made it. But even the loving home that Tonesha had come from hadn't protected her.

"How many?" I whispered.

"Two." He choked on the word. "Ray-Ray and...and little 'Shell."

I gasped. Little 'Shell was actually Michelle Fraser. She was eight but only looked about six. Her blonde hair and blue eyes made her a beautiful little magnet for trouble, and I knew Peter had adopted her as his *street sister*. They were tight and if you didn't know, you wouldn't guess the two weren't related. This would be just about killing Peter.

Peter's head rolled to look at me, the bruises—both physical and emotional—weren't hiding the pain. "Sing me better?" he whispered.

I nodded and reached into my bag. After cleaning his face the best I could, I took him in my arms as I had so many times before and began to sing softly.

"Flower bloom and grow,
release the sun inside,
heal what has been hurt,
love in the Mother's kiss reside.
Mother hear my song,
your child is hurt and wronged,
guarded by the strength of He,
safe in your arms, blessed be."

When I pulled back I saw a lone tear escape his eye. "I missed you, Joss," he whispered.

"I missed you too, bud. You could have called. You didn't have to do this alone." I cupped his young face with my hand.

"I'm not a kid anymore," he murmured, the lingering protest of the child ringing through his tone.

"No, you're not. But even I ask for help when I need it." I tapped my finger against his temple to get his attention. When his eyes met mine in the darkness, I continued. "Will you trust me enough to let me help you? Will you let me take you someplace safe?"

His eyes were troubled, but he didn't hesitate before nodding.

"Thank you," I whispered as I pulled out my phone. "I'll help you find them, Peter. I promise."

Chapter Two

God I was tired. Physically, emotionally—every way a person could be tired. It was close to three in the morning, and I was *finally* on my way home. I was tired and hungry and wanted nothing more than to collapse into my bed, maybe have a good cry, and sleep for a week. A cup of strong coffee sounded heavenly, but I wanted to be able to sleep when my head finally hit my pillow.

The humidity of the hot August night weighed heavily on me, almost as much as my heart, and seemed to add to my overall exhaustion. Mentally kicking myself for thinking the bus was less conspicuous than my Jeep, I hitched my heavy bag higher on my shoulder. As my sneakered feet plodded against the pavement, I thought about the crappy day I had and the reasons I was dragging my carcass home so late.

My *day* had actually started two days ago. From the minute I saw her gap-toothed grinning face and offset braids in the picture her parents had brought, I knew I had my work cut out for me, but I was determined to find that little girl. Tonesha Johnson's parents had gone to the police, but because she had a history of running away and came from a less than affluent neighborhood, Mr. and Mrs. Johnson felt that the police weren't taking it as seriously as they should, so they called us. How someone nine years old who chased an ice cream truck once and got lost had a "history of running away," I couldn't figure out.

After thirty-eight hours of tough leg work and my best magick, I still couldn't find her. None of my tried and true methods worked. *Nothing* I tried worked. I had exhausted all my sources. It was like she vanished into thin air. Normally, I was able to at least locate a grave, but my best guess this time was that she was dead and there wasn't enough left of her to find. And now there were more kids missing. But how was someone missing if no one knew they were gone?

My boss was going to be pissed. I had never come up short before. Of course no one knew about the magick and spells—that was a secret that I guarded with my life.

After dropping Peter off at the best place I knew of so he could heal in safety and maybe find a safe sanctuary as I had, I was looking forward to going home. Nothing had gone the way I had wanted it to today.

My miserable defeat and depression over even more missing kids had quickly turned to disgust when I had gotten a phone call from a friend of mine on the Seattle police force. I wanted to go home, get some sleep, and then get back on the trail with fresh eyes and more energy, but my dumb-ass figurehead of a boss had screwed up the one assignment he had begged me for and blown his cover with the wife of a client we were supposed to be following. Again. Instead of just identifying himself as a private investigator, he tried to make up some lame excuse and landed himself behind bars for stalking.

So instead of going home to bed, I had to spend a couple extra hours to go down to the local precinct and convince my friends that as incompetent as Jimmy was, he was in fact my boss and the woman was his case. And I needed to do it all without seeing him. Maybe getting Jimmy out of jail would soften the blow when I told him, for the first time, I wasn't able to complete my own assignment.

The boys at the precinct all suspected I did the actual work at Mackenzie Investigations and helped me out when they could. It wasn't the first time something like this had happened, so getting him out of jail had been relatively easy; they hadn't even booked him.

Jimmy continually found new ways to prove how unsuited he was to hold his private investigator's license. Sometimes I thought going into business with Jimmy MacKenzie had been a mistake.

Five years ago, I had been sitting at a café, people watching as I drank my coffee, when my attention was caught by a man with a camera. He was only slightly taller than my own five foot three frame and was wearing a very cliché tan trench coat over a dirty pair of jeans and a stained white dress shirt. He had greasy strawberry blond hair that hung in long unkempt tangles framing his weasel-like face and covering his ears. He was a stocky man who had gained far more weight than was healthy and had a very slimy, shifty look to him. In short, he stuck out like a sore thumb.

The man was very obviously doing surveillance on a woman, and he had been pissed when I laughed at him when he blew his cover in a spectacular way. He had been taking pictures of the woman when he got tangled up in a passing dog's leash and ended up sprawled at her feet. The woman turned around at the commotion and saw all the surveillance pictures of her that had fallen out of Jimmy's coat on the sidewalk. I watched as he tried to stammer out a plausible excuse over the barking dog, the frantic owner, and a snot-nosed kid crying over and over, "The bad man hurt Fluffy!"

The woman took one look at the mess and told Jimmy to go back to his client, her husband, and tell him that she had no intention of cheating so he could get her money in a divorce. She broke Jimmy's expensive camera and stormed off as I sat wiping the tears of laughter away. Jimmy had sarcastically asked me if I thought I could do any better. When I told him a blind, deaf dog could have done better, he told me to prove it.

The next day, after I had solved two of his cases, we had come to an agreement. He would remain the owner and manager, but I would work the cases and get forty percent of the profits—in cash. I would get a small paycheck from the company commiserate with what an assistant would normally make, but the rest of the forty percent I would get in cash. All he had to do was meet with the clients and I would pose as his assistant taking notes. Now sixty percent didn't sound like a lot, but with the way he was working before I came along, he was living pretty damn good now that I ran things.

The arrangement worked really well for both of us. He got paid for doing basically nothing, and I stayed off the grid because most of my money came in off the books. Thinking of our first meeting, I should have known better than to let him tail the wife. I just thought that after five years he would have learned *something*. Apparently not.

My messenger bag felt heavier than usual as I trudged along the sidewalk. I kept my head down and decided I was just too tired to take the round-about route I normally took home. It was really late and the streets were deserted. I would have heard something if someone was following me. After almost forty-one hours without sleep, my senses weren't as sharp as they usually were. The events of the night had brought back some very painful memories. Peter had said the streets weren't safe, and I couldn't afford to be careless. Even if I was no longer a child, *they* were still out there.

My thoughts wandered to that night eighteen years ago. I had only been with that foster family for less than six months. They were decent and I really hoped nothing happened that would make them send me back to the group home. It wasn't like I *wanted* things to happen, but they always seemed to. All the therapists had said I was acting out, and they had diagnosed me with all kinds of mental and behavioral disorders to try to justify all the accidents at my previous foster homes.

Fires; things going missing only to turn up later; foster siblings having accidents; food going bad or getting spilled; disappearances; family pets uncharacteristically turning nasty. If something weird happened, they blamed it on me. The thing was most of the time it *had* been me, just not in the way they thought. Eighteen years ago, I found out there were people out there that wanted to kill me for the things I was able to do, and they would kill the people around me to do it.

Two men had broken into the house just after my foster parents sent me to bed, and they were looking for me. I watched from my hiding place in the laundry chute at the top of the stairs where I had hidden when they broke in.

"Where is she?" The man's voice was rough, and I heard a thump and then a groan. He had punched my foster dad in the stomach.

"*She* who? Who do you want?" My foster mom was crying.

"The daughter of Satan you have living with you." The second man's voice was clear and kind, almost patient.

"What are you t—talking about?" Dad coughed out the question, still trying to catch his breath.

"The girl you have. The one you call *Joss*." The nasty man practically spit out my name like it was something sour in his mouth.

"S—she's staying at a f-friend's house tonight." Mom stuttered out the lie, and I knew she was trying to buy me some time to escape.

I crept out of my hiding place silently, trying to sneak into my room.

"You're lying!" the nasty man growled out before I heard a ringing slap when he hit my foster mom. I peered around the wall to see if I could run across the landing without being seen.

Another man came in dragging a kid my age. It was Eddie, my only friend at school. He had defended me against the bullies earlier that day when they were calling me a witch. It wasn't my fault their yogurt was spoiled. They were so mean, they made it go bad. Eddie was crying and the man holding him shoved him so hard that he fell.

My foster mom hugged him to her as the man screamed stuff about God and the Devil. Eddie was ripped out of my foster mom's grip and hurled against the wall, knocking him out. I remember rocking myself, praying that they would forget he was there, that he wouldn't get hurt anymore.

Amazingly, my prayers seemed to have been answered, although he wasn't any kind of threat lying there unconscious on the floor.

While they were distracted, I ran to my room and quickly gathered some clothes into a duffel bag as I listened to them try to convince my parents to tell them where I was. The last thing I did before slipping out the window was silently dial 911 and leave the phone off the hook.

I heard many things that night I would never forget, but the worst thing was that these people believed I was a black witch, a child of the Devil, and that it was their mission from God to send me back to Hell. Now I may have been only ten, but even I knew that meant they wanted to kill me. Eddie had been the only survivor that night, and I was labeled a runaway for the first time.

The police ruled it a home invasion, and I made sure I never stayed in another foster home for longer than eight months again, and I even switched states twice. I wouldn't risk another family's safety for me.

I came back to my surroundings with a jolt when a cat jumped on my shoulder, scaring the crap out of me. I spun into a defensive crouch with my hand over my hammering heart to see the cat land on the sidewalk behind me. My heart was beating a mile a minute somewhere in the vicinity of my throat. Both hot and cold at the same time, I felt almost nauseous from the adrenaline rush.

The cat looked me right in the eyes and time seemed to stop. The breeze that had been gently blowing through the trees, the loose tendrils of my hair laying across my face from the momentum of my panicked movement, everything seemed to be frozen or at least moving in slow motion as my eyes met those of the cat in front of me.

It had brilliant green eyes that, even in the dark, seemed to burn with an emerald fire. I could read a multitude of emotions in those eyes: relief, fear, anger, and affection. I felt safe, connected for the first time in my life. I was released from the moment and time sped back up to normal when the cat spoke.

"**RUN!**"

I looked up past the cat and out of the darkness to see two men coming at me fast. I didn't think twice. Taking the cat's whispered shout, I sprang to my feet and ran. I was only five blocks from home, but I knew I couldn't go straight there; they might follow me, so I headed in the opposite direction.

I heard heavy booted feet hitting the ground too close behind me, and suddenly I was tackled hard. My shoulder and arm landed with a painful crunch on the cement of the sidewalk, barely protected by the denim of my jacket. I felt and heard the bones of my shoulder grinding together with the weight of my attacker, forcing them to try to bend in unnatural ways. I narrowly managed to avoid hitting my head by getting my only free hand up to brace for the impact, but the wind was still knocked forcefully from me.

Trying to catch my breath, I thrashed and fought in vain against the two men that had me in their grip and were pulling me roughly to my feet. I saw the flash of a large knife as my braid was used to yank my head back, exposing my throat to the blade.

I watched as a smallish man with another knife moved to stand directly in front of me making the sign of the cross with the hilt. "You will die for your sins against God this night, witch!" snarled the man.

The streetlight behind him only illuminated his below-average size and revealed nothing of his features other than the fact he very nearly had to look up to see my face. I was pulled roughly against the chest of my second, much larger, captor, and my scalp ached where the hair was being used to restrain me.

"Tell us! Where are your sisters, witch? Where are the others in your coven?" The voice from behind me was deadly, and I felt the heat of his rank breath on my neck.

"I don't h-have any sisters. I don't know w-what you're t-talking about," I stammered out. Peter's warnings about religious kidnappers rang in my ears, echoing events from my childhood. They had found me. I was going to die.

There was a sting at my neck as the blade of the knife was pressed against my skin. "Whore! You will tell us what we want to know!"

I felt warmth where my blood welled from the cut and ran down my throat. "Let me go. I don't know what you're talking about. I didn't do anything!" I hated the weak tone in my voice. I wanted to sound stronger, but the ghost of the ten year old girl I used to be was terrified. No matter how hard I struggled, I couldn't loosen the hold of halitosis guy behind me, and struggling would only make the knife bite deeper into my neck. The street was quiet at this time of the morning, and I knew that if I tried to scream they would kill me that much faster and be gone before anyone even woke up.

The wiry guy in front of me put his hand over my forehead and began to speak. "I conjure you by the bitter tears shed on the Cross by our Savior the Lord JESUS Christ for the salvation of the world, and by the burning tears poured in the evening hour over His wounds by the most glorious Virgin MARY, His Mother, and by all the tears which have been shed here in this world by the Saints and Elect of God, from whose eyes He has now wiped away all tears, that if you be innocent you do now shed tears, but if you be guilty that you shall by no means do so. In the name of the Father, and of the Son, and of the Holy Ghost, Amen."

He removed his hand only to grab my jaw and lean in close, examining my face in the dim light from a nearby streetlight. "She pleads for her life and yet she shows no sign of remorse for her sins. She doesn't weep. Our first sign of her association with the Devil," said the one spouting some kind of weird scripture.

Who the hell were these guys?! They wanted me to cry? Had they scared the kids like this? Had they killed them?

"Your very existence is an offence to Almighty God," the man holding me spit out with a putrid exhalation.

Seriously, had he never brushed his teeth? *Great, Joss! Real appropriate line of thought while you have a knife at your throat!* Maybe I was going into shock? Why couldn't I think? My eyes darted around as I looked for something I could use to help me, some way I could get away.

"Shave her head, strip her of her powers so we can get her out of here and question her properly," he ordered the guy with the knife.

Shave my head?! OH HELL NO! I started to kick and twist as hard as I could. I didn't want that knife any closer to me than it already was, and I definitely didn't want to be scalped. It was no use; my captor's hold was too tight.

I watched helplessly as the shadowed figure in front of me raised his arm and moved the knife higher. I closed my eyes, not wanting to see the huge blade getting closer.

'Lord and Lady, please...help me.' My silent prayer was more emotion than clear thought.

Suddenly, the man let out a surprised yelp, and I felt a heavy body slam into mine. I opened my eyes to see a large dog with his mouth wrapped around the arm holding the knife. The dog had knocked the little scripture guy to the ground and was shaking him so savagely the body was being wrenched forcefully from side to side, making him look a bit like a rag doll. I could see the guy's own blood looking black as it splattered across his face in the orange light from the streetlamp, his terrified screams drowned out by the snarling of the dog.

The man holding me was surprised by the attack as well as the hit we had taken and had dropped his own knife. I grabbed the opportunity to reach up and claw at his face. My aim was better than I could have hoped, and I hit him in the eyes. He howled in pain, releasing me. Using the one maneuver I had learned in my years drifting in and out of group homes, I spun around quickly bringing my knee up between his legs and dropped him. I wasted no time and took off in a limping run as fast as my poor legs would carry me, praying the dog would buy me enough time to escape.

Behind me, I heard the sounds of the barking snarling dog and curses with bodies hitting the ground. Suddenly, there was an agonized scream that cut off with a sickeningly final gurgle. Goddess, forgive me. I hoped they were hurt badly enough to give up the chase. I had no idea who owned the dog, but I swore if I got out of this, I would find out and buy it a HUGE steak!

A few seconds later, I saw the cat running alongside me. "Quickly! Evergreen Cemetery!"

Now I had seen some weird, magickal things in my twenty-eight years, but none of them beat a talking cat. However, seeing as that same cat had just tried to save my ass, I was going to listen first and ask questions later. I changed direction, cutting through several backyards, and ended up running through the field at the elementary school. I could see the cat was still with me.

I dove into the bushes when I heard a muffled shout behind me. I was cradling my injured arm to my body and trying to stifle my gasping breaths so I could hear better.

"One of them is dead but the other is still out there." The cat stopped to listen for a minute as I struggled to regain my breath. "He's looking in the wrong direction. Come on, we have to get to that cemetery."

I looked down to see the cat slinking out of our hiding place, and after carefully checking to see for myself that it was right, I followed it. Hey, it was a talking cat! I wasn't entirely sure I wasn't hallucinating from lack of sleep.

We moved slowly, darting from shadow to shadow the best we could, trying to be silent. About ten minutes later, we were crouched down behind a large tombstone in a darker part of the well-maintained cemetery as I quietly tried to catch my breath from our panicked run. We listened for what had to be half an hour to see if we were followed. Finally, when the night settled back into its quiet, sleepy, normal feel, and I felt that I could breathe a bit easier, I looked down at my companion.

The cat was a large, beautifully striped tabby with bright green eyes that seemed to almost glow in the shadows of the moonlight as it filtered through the light clouds. It was sitting quietly beside me and staring quite intently.

I pressed a shaking hand to the cut at my throat and pulled it away to reveal fresh blood. I wondered how bad it was. "I guess I owe you a thank you for helping me out back there?" I felt kind of stupid talking to a cat, but to be fair, it did talk to me first. I think.

"You need to pay better attention to your surroundings. They would've killed you, you know." Its tone was belligerent, and I would have been offended if it hadn't been right.

I rubbed a hand over my face, belatedly realizing I had probably just smeared blood all over myself. "I know, you're right," I sighed. "I should've been paying closer attention. I should've gotten a hotel after work, but I just wanted to go home. It's been close to..." I squinted at my watch, trying to make out the numbers in the moonlight "... forty-two hours since I slept last, and my instincts aren't as sharp as they usually are."

I tilted my head back so the cat could look at my neck. "How bad is it?" I asked it.

"More than a scratch but it won't need stitches. Once we get it cleaned up, you should be fine."

I had a first aid kit in my bag but didn't want to make the noise necessary to retrieve it. My cut would have to wait. I was so tired. The days without sleep, emotional turmoil, physical exertion, and now the fading adrenaline left me shaky and exhausted.

After hearing more of the cat's voice, I decided that my unlikely savior was male. I looked down at the cat, and I swore I saw a small smile tip his lips.

"I expect you have some questions for me. The first of which would probably have something to do with me being a talking cat, I assume," he said wryly, his tail swishing silently.

If I hadn't been sure that we were still being hunted, I would have laughed. I settled for a soft chuckle. "Yeah, that would definitely be up there on the list, but I think we had better save the explanations for when we get back to my place. You're coming, right?"

"Oh, definitely. I've been looking for you for a very long time; I'm not going to lose you now." I could hear the slight humor in his tone.

I looked sideways at him. "You'll have to explain that one later too." I tried to ignore the pain in my arm as I settled myself more comfortably on the ground with my back to the tombstone, my pounding head resting against it. "So why am I sitting in a graveyard in the middle of the night when I'm being hunted by a crazed lunatic?" I had to know why he told me to come here of all places.

"Because thankfully the Inquisitors are still under the archaic misconception that witches can't stand on hallowed ground. This is the last place he'll look for us." His tone was filled with disgust, and he was looking around carefully. "We'll stay here until dawn." He looked over at me as his ears continued to scan for danger. “Why don’t you lie down and get some rest. I’ll wake you up when it’s safe to leave.”

Somehow I wasn’t surprised that he knew I was a witch. I mean, really, he was a talking cat! A witch was nothing compared to that. I hadn’t missed the fact that he’d said “us” when he referred to the situation I was in either. For some reason, this cat had decided to throw his luck in with mine. The irony of the situation wasn’t lost on me, and I laughed at the cliché picture I presented: a witch in a graveyard in the middle of the night with a talking cat. I let out an amused half-laugh, half-snort at the mental image.

Yup, the exhaustion was definitely messing with me. The emotional roller coaster I had been on probably didn’t help either.

I could feel the fatigue dragging at my battered body, so I took his advice and used my large messenger bag as a pillow. I would think about it later when I was more coherent.

I was enjoying the feeling of having my eyes closed when I realized I had no idea who or what this cat was. “I’m Jocelyn by the way. Jocelyn Matthews.”

His voice came out of the darkness, calm and soothing. “My name is Mateo. Sleep, Jocelyn. I’m here and I won’t let them get you.”

I took one last deep breath before allowing my body to fall into the sleep that it needed so badly. My last thought was wondering why I felt such a strong connection to a cat.

What seemed like only minutes later, I felt something soft tapping my cheek. “Jocelyn.”

Tap, tap. “Jocelyn, wake up.”

The strange events of the night came back in a rush, and I jerked painfully upright, confused but awake. Parts of my skin felt tight and dirty with remnants of smeared dried blood, no doubt. I blinked a couple of times, letting my eyes adjust to the rising light of dawn. Crap. I rubbed my eyes with the knuckles of my right hand, my left too painful to use. I couldn’t have been asleep for more than two hours. I looked down to see the cat from last night sitting by my knee. “So all that really happened last night?”

He chuckled a little. “If you’re referring to being saved from religious fanatics by a talking cat and then sleeping in a cemetery, then yes.”

I sighed, still exhausted and very sore from sleeping on the ground. “Is it safe for us to leave?”

“Yes, for the moment. I would recommend we leave quickly,” he said as he stood and stretched, digging his claws into the dirt for traction.

I climbed tiredly to my feet, my body protesting every movement. Mateo looked amused as I looped the strap of my large messenger bag over my shoulder. “What?”

His head tilted to one side as he eyed my bag. "I was just wondering why you didn't pull a sleeping bag and tent out of your..." his lips twitched as if he was holding back from laughing "...*purse* last night. Maybe a couple of pillows? It would have been more comfortable."

I let out a less than ladylike snort and resisted the urge to smack him. "It's not that big."

"Uh huh."

I rolled my eyes at him and headed off towards home. "Do we take the long way or go straight there?"

He seemed to consider this for a minute. "We go straight there."

As we started walking, I carefully took my jacket off and hung it from the strap of my bag, silently bemoaning the loss of my favorite hat before un-braiding my heavy, waist length hair and arranging it to somewhat shield my face. It wouldn't do much to disguise me, but I wouldn't have my usual profile either, and it would help cover the blood that I was sure I had smeared all over my face and neck.

"I wouldn't recommend going to work for a couple of days. You need to disappear for a bit. Do you have somewhere we can hide?" Mateo's voice was low enough that I had to strain to hear him as he trotted at my side, tail in the air. It looked casual but by the motion of his ears, he was keeping a careful eye out for anything suspicious.

I smirked at his question. "Oh, I think I can manage something."

Very quickly, we were at my house. It was an unassuming little white two-story house that was built in the 1940s on a large, well sheltered lot set back from the main road. I had picked it up as a foreclosure and it was perfect. It had three small bedrooms—two upstairs and one downstairs—one bathroom, a small kitchen, a decent sized living room with a fireplace, and a dining room. The large lot backed right onto a huge park, and it even had a small detached garage. It needed a lot of work, but that was what I liked about it. No one would think twice about a single young woman living here; they would assume it was a rental.

I opened the gate into the backyard and led Mateo up the stairs to the back door, which opened into an enclosed porch area that held my washer and dryer. Once I took off my sneakers, I opened the inner door and let us into the kitchen. Relocking the door behind us, I went through the kitchen and turned right, walking down a narrow hall, and led us into the tiny downstairs bedroom I had turned into a reading room.

I stopped and looked down at the cat carefully, wondering if I was making a huge mistake in trusting him. I decided I really didn't have a choice. I needed to be safe while I slept, and he wasn't showing any signs of leaving my side long enough for me to slip away unnoticed. Besides, he was only a cat, and something told me I could trust him with anything.

I reached behind the edge of the large bookcase spanning the one corner and pulled; the whole unit obediently swung away from the wall noiselessly, revealing a hidden, narrow, metal spiral staircase. As I descended into a basement no one knew existed, I heard the quiet click of the bookcase closing behind us.

We stopped at the bottom, and I watched as Mateo took in our *hiding place*. The space was large, square, and took up the entire square footage of the house above. The floor plan was open save for a few strategically placed support posts. The staircase stopped in the very center of the house and opened into a kitchen that fully took up one quarter of the available space. Copper pots hung from a rack above a large hardwood topped island. To the right, against the outer wall, was a waist-high natural gas, open fireplace complete with a large black cauldron and a brick hearth, the chimney connecting it seamlessly with the wood fireplace in the living room above. Large, heavy wood countertops framed the kitchen which had a double sink, a large side by side fridge and freezer, and a five-burner natural gas stove.

To the left was a large living room with bookshelves lining the windowless walls, broken only by a flat screen TV in the corner and a low alter that faced the north wall. The living room had a deeply pillowed chocolate brown couch with comfy red throw pillows and a blanket hanging over the back, perfect for cuddling up in. A wooden chest-type coffee table sat on a large, plush area rug swirled in shades of beige, brown, and red, complementing the dark hardwood floors that went from wall to wall, adding warmth where the few visible concrete walls were cold. Separating the living room from the bedroom was a floor to ceiling, heavy rust-red and brown colored curtain that hung even with the staircase forming a wall and hiding two more support columns for the floor above. I watched as Mateo stepped into the gap in the curtain that made up the doorway to the bedroom.

My queen-sized distressed-wood bed was centered against the right wall and had nightstands on either side. The down duvet continued the earth-toned theme in the living room and had brilliant red flowers embroidered across it that matched more small red accent pillows. I had hung rods on chains from the ceiling against the walls to hold all my clothes with custom-built drawers and shoe cubbies underneath.

The only real walls providing the necessary support for the floor above enclosed a large luxurious bathroom that took up the remaining quarter of the space and was accessed through a door to the left of my bedroom. It had a corner soaker tub, a large steam shower, toilet, linen closet, and vanity complete with sink. The walls were a soft white, and the floor was done in large, natural beige stone. Instead of continuing the color theme of red and brown, I had really given in to my love of bright happy colors, and the towels and bathmats were vibrant shades of turquoise and lime green.

Mateo came back to stand at my feet. "Okay, I'm impressed."

I smirked. "Wait. There's more." I walked over to the last bit of counter space separating the living room from the kitchen. I opened the cupboard and gestured inside, where it was deeper and darker than it should have been for a simple cupboard. "This tunnel leads to the porch at the front door of the house. It's a tight squeeze, but if I have to escape from down here, I can." If he was going to stay here with someone out there still hunting me, he needed to know the escape routes. And if I was being honest with myself, I was excited to have someone to show my house off to.

I got up and led him back into my bedroom. I went to the far right corner to the space between my nightstand and the wall that was covered by hanging clothes. I pushed them back and pulled a drawer all the way out, exposing another tunnel. "This one goes out under the back porch and branches out into three separate possible exits. The right tunnel comes out of the work bench in the garage. The center tunnel leads to a hidden tree-cave in the park behind the house, and the left tunnel leads to a shed in my neighbor's yard." I looked down at him as I replaced the drawer.

Mateo looked as impressed as a cat can look. I limped my way back to the kitchen; I was famished. First-aid could wait a little longer. "Can I get you something to eat or drink?" I looked in the fridge and started to pull out the makings for a sandwich.

"I am rather hungry, and some water if you don't mind." He jumped up to sit on one of the bar stools around the island. "So did you build all this with magick? I'm assuming it wasn't part of the original plans for the house," he remarked dryly.

I made myself a ham sandwich and poured a big glass of milk from the fridge. "Actually, the basement was already here. When I redid the floors upstairs, I lowered everything down through a large hole. It took me months, but I did all the work myself. The hardest part was connecting the two fireplaces and the gas lines for the stove. Of course, plumbing in the bathroom was no piece of cake either." I put a plate of sliced up ham and turkey deli meat in front of him and a bowl of water after questioning him with a lift of my eyebrows.

"I used a bit of magick for the tunnels. It took me a *long* time to work out how to do it, and I was exhausted afterward, but I didn't want to be trapped down here no matter how well hidden it is. That's why I took out most of the walls for support beams and columns," I said, gesturing to the open floor plan. "If I have to run, there isn't too much in my way. As for the plans at City Hall...well, let's just say that now they only show the upper floors and leave it at that." I smirked.

He chuckled and we sat and ate in companionable silence. The events of the last couple of days started to catch up with me. I finished up and put our plates in the sink, resolving to wash them later. I put the bowl of water on the floor under the stairs so Mateo could get some later if he needed it.

I turned to look at him seriously. "So I know we have a lot to talk about, but I really need some sleep. I've trusted you with more of my life than I have *ever* trusted anyone, so I really hope that I haven't made a mistake."

He looked up at me. "Jocelyn, I would sooner hurt myself than betray you. You have my word."

I felt my brows furrow. "Well," I hesitated. I really did trust him, although I had no idea why. "I guess we can talk about everything later. Make yourself at home."

I turned and went to grab some pajamas before making my way to the bathroom. I carefully closed the door and then turned to face the damage in the mirror.

I took in the tired and blood-smeared face in front of me; I looked like hell. As Mateo had said, the cut on my neck wasn't serious and wouldn't need stitches.

I stripped off my dirty shirts and assessed my other injuries. The left side of my body was the worst. My left shoulder and bicep were turning a nasty shade of purple and black, and the back of my hand was scratched up. I painfully pulled off my now torn capris, having to peel the blood-soaked fabric from my left knee which was scraped and covered in crusted blood and dirt. My left wrist hurt the worst, but I didn't think it was broken. The palm of my right hand, which had stopped me from hitting my head, was missing several layers of skin and had gravel embedded in it.

Figuring the shower was the easiest way to clean all my cuts, I slowly re-braided my hair but carefully pinned it on top of my head, my scalp incredibly sore from the hair being pulled so savagely. I was just too tired to deal with washing it right now.

I took the shortest, hottest shower I could stand, needing sleep so badly the blue and green glass tiles on the walls blurred together to look like a hallucination induced caricature of the sea. I worried that I would fall asleep under the streaming water. I washed the blood, sweat, dirt, and the fingerprints of my attackers off me and then turned off the shower, swaying on my feet from fatigue.

I toweled off quickly, put some comfy clean pajamas on, and padded to my bed for some much needed rest when a thought occurred to me. "Mateo?" I called out.

"Yes?" His voice drifted to me from somewhere in the basement.

"Thanks. You know, for trying to warn me," I said sleepily.

His voice was quiet and kind in the dark. "You're welcome. Sleep well, Jocelyn."

I crawled into my bed very grateful to have made it through another day. With a silent prayer for the safe return of the missing children and a sincere expression of thanks to the Goddess, I drifted off to sleep.

Chapter Three

My eyes blinked open slowly to the pain that was radiating through my body. I stretched cautiously, carefully cataloguing the various aches and pains the fight had left behind. I was sure my bruises would be spectacular this morning.

My eyes moved to the alarm clock on my night stand. A little after eight in the evening. Hmmm...not morning. I had slept for a full fourteen hours, which would explain the obscene noises coming from my stomach. Not to mention I had a guest in the house somewhere. My first guest. Ever.

I forced myself to roll out of bed and padded barefoot to the bathroom to take care of some very immediate needs. I looked longingly at the shower, wanting to wash my hair now that I wasn't so tired, but deciding I was too impatient for coffee and food, I went out into the kitchen.

Mateo jumped off the couch, stretched, and went to sit on his bar stool from this morning. "Sleep well?"

I smiled and nodded. "Like the dead. Sorry I was out for so long."

"Don't be. You needed it," he said.

"I'm making coffee and an omelet. What can I get you?" I measured out the grounds and turned on the coffee maker before putting the kettle on for some tea. I needed a strong cup of willow bark tea to combat the pain I was feeling after last night's close call.

He seemed surprised I asked. "Uh... I'll have an omelet as well, if it's not too much trouble."

"No trouble." I raised my eyebrows at him and asked, "Do you want it with or without the vegetables?" I couldn't help the teasing tone that entered my voice.

I heard him chuckle behind me as I got the necessary ingredients out of the fridge. "Just some of the ham and turkey sandwich meat from this morning if there's any left."

"You got it." As I set about making breakfast, I glanced over at him. "So, are you going to tell me why a talking cat has been looking for me?"

He looked at me carefully. "I'm a familiar. Specifically...a witch's familiar."

"I thought familiars were all black cats," I teased.

He rolled his eyes at me. "Please. Black is so passé."

I laughed and he went on to explain. "The proper term is Danaan—a Goddess-gifted natural witch. You are a descendent from an ancient tribe known as the *Tuatha dé Danann*. When a Danaan is born, a familiar feels an instinctual pull and immediately goes looking for them."

Danaan. I rolled the foreign term around my brain trying to figure out what it all meant. "And you felt a pull towards me?"

"Yes, although you were really hard to find. Normally, a familiar will find their Danaan by the time they're about seven years old. That way they're there to help them when their powers start to manifest."

I thought about my childhood. I could have definitely used the help. "Mine started when I was nine. That's when I started to bounce from foster home to foster home. Too many *incidents*."

He looked at me, curiosity bright in his eyes. "If you don't mind me asking, why were you in the foster system? Where are your parents?"

I made my tea as I thought about the past. "My mom died when I was seven, and my stepfather only stuck around long enough to find out if he could get at my new trust fund. When he figured out it was iron clad, he took me to social services and dropped me off. He signed the necessary paperwork and never looked back," I explained.

The memory didn't have the power to hurt me anymore. My stepfather was a selfish man that I was probably better off without. Even when I lived with him, I was alone. I was ignored most of the time and passed from neighbor to neighbor to be looked after.

"I'm sorry, Jocelyn. I tried to find you sooner. You *needed* me to find you sooner." His voice was full of remorse, his ears drooping slightly.

"Hey," I said softly and waited until he looked at me. "Don't beat yourself up. I moved so often that most of the time I never even bothered to unpack. I'm surprised you were able to find me at all." Surprised and a bit worried. If he could find me, then so could anyone else, as evidenced by the thugs that had grabbed me last night.

I plated our food and made sure to cut up Mateo's into manageable pieces for him. After pouring myself a coffee and grabbing my cup of tea, I sat down and started to eat.

"So the guys from last night—these Inquisitors—are they the ones that have been hunting me most of my life?" I watched as his head snapped up to look at me.

"They've come after you before?" His gaze was intense.

I took a large sip of the tea, making a face at the bitter taste but craving the pain relief it would bring. I nodded in response to Mateo's question, taking a breath before explaining. "When I was ten, they broke into the foster home where I was living and killed my foster parents while looking for me. I called the police and snuck out an upstairs window. The police called it a home invasion, and I was relocated out of state." I took a steadying sip of my sweetened coffee and washed the taste of the tea from my mouth. "That's when I started to make sure I never stayed in one place for too long. I heard enough that night to know it was me they were after. I've caught glimpses of them from time to time over the years." I got lost in the memories for a minute. "They called me a black witch, a daughter of Satan. But I'm not a black witch. I use my powers to help people." I looked at him, almost daring him to contradict me.

"I know you're not," he soothed. "Actually, from what I can see, you barely use your powers at all." He looked around. "Well, except for this place, that is." His tone was wry, and I could almost see a smirk on his kitty face.

I laughed. "No. This is the only time that I've used my powers selfishly. I would never disrespect the

Goddess ordinarily, but I felt she would understand my need to protect myself." I wanted him to understand that I took my strange gift seriously. "It took a long time for me to figure out what I was and even longer to learn to control what powers I have. I searched online, read books, and even contacted local covens to try to understand." Shooting back the last of the tea with a sour face, I got up to pour myself another cup of coffee, noticing the effects of the willow bark immediately when I was able to move a bit easier.

"What I learned was that I'm not like anyone else. The other witches that I've met are all basically powerless and follow Wicca as a religion. But while I follow the ways of the Lord and Lady, I don't do some of the...*stuff* they insist is necessary. They grow gardens and recycle faithfully, track the phases of the moon and the seasons like their life depends on it. Oh, they try to perform spells and chants, and they worship the Goddess, but more often than not, the spells don't work. And when they do, it's more luck than actual magick." I remembered the frustration I had felt when I realized I was alone. When I laughed, he looked at me wondering what I found so amusing.

"Sorry." I smothered a snort. "It's just that they were so...weird! They kept talking about energies and chanting. It sounded like a bunch of new-age hippy crap. One of them told me I shouldn't drink coffee because it filled my body with negative fluids that worked against my body's chakras. I'm sorry but *no way* am I giving up my coffee! They wanted me to dance naked under the full moon and participate in their '*rights*' to be closer to the Goddess. When a bunch of them started having sex in a field, I was outta there!"

I had never seen a cat laugh before, but I saw it now.

"That's because you were talking with witches," he said with an amused smirk, "not an actual Witch—a *Danaan*." I could actually hear him capitalize the second one by the drawn out emphasis in his tone. "Danaan like you aren't human. Gifted by the Goddess herself, they're born with real power. And because of that power, they're naturally very secretive, leading solitary lives, and are very hard to find. If they weren't, then the Inquisitors and others seeking power would find them and kill them," he explained, no longer laughing.

"You talked about these Inquisitors before, and they've been hunting me all my life, not to mention the very close call last night. Who *are* these people?" I got up off my stool and led the way to the couch, thinking I would need to be comfortable for his explanation. I sat sideways, cuddled into the corner of the couch with my coffee mug, and watched as he jumped up to sit across from me.

"You know about the Spanish Inquisition from the 1400s?" At my nod he continued. "How much do you know?"

I shrugged. "About as much as the average person, I guess. Maybe give me a lesson," I suggested. I needed to know as much about them as I could.

"While the Spanish Inquisition was primarily about converting Jews, around the same time the Church was hunting witches in Northern Europe and England. And while tens, perhaps hundreds, of thousands of people have been hunted and killed for centuries, accused of heresy and witchcraft, and have died in various ways and in dozens of countries, long before the birth of Christ and long before the Christian Church got involved, for the purposes of explaining the group that is after you, I'll have to focus on the latter centuries, the ones that targeted witches."

I nodded, horrified so many had been killed for simply believing in something different.

Mateo settled himself as he gathered his thoughts. "Witch hunting was already popular in 1484 when Pope Innocent VIII issued a Papal decree to two men, Kramer and Sprenger, to systematize the persecution of witches. Three years later, the Malleus Maleficarum, or Witches Hammer, was published. The book outlined how to identify, interrogate, prosecute, and execute people who were suspected of performing witchcraft. In reality, it was an excellent way to further crush what they considered pagan religions and line the coffers of the Christian Church. All property of a convicted witch was immediately confiscated and divided equally between the state treasury, church officials, and the Inquisitors themselves. The added benefit was to do away with 'wise women' and help promote and reinforce the male-dominated religion they had created, encouraging the subjugation of women." He looked at me to make sure I was understanding everything.

My hand went to my mouth in horror, the cold, calculated extermination of innocent people for political and monetary gain turning my stomach. I swallowed and waved at him to continue.

"By the late 1600s the church was no longer actively seeking out and killing suspected witches, and had in fact denounced the men and their book, but the damage had already been done. The old traditions and magicks were all but lost. They had created a group of men who were fanatical in their beliefs and their search for the 'daughters of Satan.'" His tail began to flick back and forth in the manner typical of an annoyed cat.

"These men branched off and continued their work, believing that the church had strayed from the true and righteous path of God. Some of them left the old world and traveled here to seek out new followers, which led to the Salem witch trials. These people the magical community now calls the Inquisitors are the direct descendants of Kramer and Sprenger," he finished. His tail was now thrashing back and forth and his ears were lower on his head, clearly showing his anger.

Mateo watched as I tried to assimilate all the information he had just given me. Finally, someone was able to tell me why a group of people I didn't know were trying to kill me. I probably should have figured it out on my own. I mean I had kind of always known it was some kind of religious group, but they had never bothered any of the witches in any of the covens I had briefly interacted with. Now I knew it was because none of those witches had been real.

It was more than likely that they were the ones responsible for the missing kids as well. Peter had talked about the kidnappers spouting religious crap.

But if that was the case, why take them at all? They were just...normal kids.

"Wait...you said that the witches that I talked to were human, not real...umm...Danaan..." I tested out the unfamiliar word. "...so you're saying that I'm not human?" I couldn't believe it had taken me this long to grasp this important fact.

He blinked at me and nodded. "Natural Witches–Danaan, like you–are gifted by the Goddess, and along with many other races and creatures, inhabit this world and live in secret among the unsuspecting humans."

"So what does that make me? How am I different?" I had so many questions that my head was spinning.

"You're Danaan. Your powers would have been passed down to you through your mother. And although she may not have been Danaan herself, both of you are direct descendants of the *Tuatha dé Danann*. According to legend, they were a tribe of demigods who inhabited Ireland one thousand years before the birth of Christ. They appeared out of the mists—Children of the Light—advanced in magick and weaponry, they ruled Ireland peacefully for over two hundred years. When they were invaded by the Milesians, they were offered shelter by the Sidhe, the fairy folk.

"No one knows why a Danaan is suddenly born of a seemingly human mother. Some argue that they are born of the Lord and Lady, making them demigods. Recently, it is believed that the powers lay dormant, rather like a recessive gene. Once the appropriate genetic cross is made, a Danaan is born." He rolled his eyes at this idea. "What I can tell you is that Danaan are very long lived and have powers that were passed to them by the Goddess herself. They're *extremely* rare."

"Long lived." That seemed to be rather ominous somehow. "How long lived exactly?"

"The other Danaan I shared my life with each lived to be over five hundred years old," he said matter-of-factly.

I froze, my breath catching in my throat. Five hundred years? Crap, this was a lot to process. I was going to live for at least five hundred years? I shook my head, taking a deep breath. "I'm sorry. This is a lot to take in. I'm...I'm going to go and take a shower. I need...I just need to think about all this for a few minutes, okay?"

"Take all the time you need, Jocelyn. You will have many questions, and I promise, I'm not going anywhere. We'll talk more when you're ready," he said with complete understanding.

I got up and made my way to the bathroom. I turned on the shower with shaking hands and watched as the steam filled the room. The hot water felt nice but did little to release the tension in my shoulders. I felt fragile, like my whole world was shattered, and I was only a breath away from breaking into a million pieces. As I lathered my long hair, I thought about everything that Mateo had told me.

I was possibly a descendant of demigods being hunted by a religiously fanatical group of misogynistic men that had been systematically slaughtering witches, attempting to eradicate the Wiccan faith and Goddess worship for the past seven hundred years. And it was quite possible that I would spend the next five hundred years or so hiding from them.

I was going to live for *centuries*.

I felt myself slide down the wall to sit on the floor of the shower. I heard an insane giggle and realized that it came from me, and conversely I felt tears welling up. Get a Grip, Jocelyn! One day at a time. When today is done, you can think about tomorrow.

'For behold, She has been with thee from the beginning'

The familiar line from *The Charge of the Goddess* comforted me and reminded me that the Lord and Lady had protected me last night and would until it was my time to go to the Summerlands.

There were several things I needed to know, and Mateo seemed to be the only one who could give me the answers. Pulling myself together, I wiped away my tears, got out, and toweled off. Wrapping myself in my comfy terry towel robe, I went to get dressed. Glancing at the clock and seeing it was after ten o'clock, I decided that it was too late for jeans and put on my favorite pair of flannel pajama pants instead, pairing them with a black tank top. I grabbed my hair brush and headed back out to the living room and Mateo.

Aware of his eyes following me, I grabbed an apple from the kitchen and cut it in half width-wise, exposing the star shaped core—a natural pentagram. I knelt at the altar. It was time to give some long overdue thanks.

There were two candles on the low table. Striking a match, I first lit the green one on the left and then the red on the right. I placed the apple on the offering plate and ignited the small cone of incense resting on a large seashell in the center of the table. I bowed my head and prayed to the Lord and Lady, thanking them for my safety and continued good health, for sending me a guide and mentor to show me the Path, begging for patience as I tried to come to grips with all the new information I had been given. I prayed for the lost children and for Peter. I prayed not for vengeance, but for closure. That I would gain the knowledge to find out what happened to them at least.

Finishing, I whispered, “Blessed be,” and pinched out the candles, leaving the incense to burn itself out.

I sat back down in my spot on the couch and looked at the cat in front of me as I worked the tangles out of my long hair. “First things first. Not to be rude, but why should I trust you? I mean, I know you tried to warn me last night, and a lot of what you’ve told me is believable, but so much of it’s too fantastical to possibly be true. Why should I trust you? What’s in it for you?” In my experience people didn’t do something for someone else unless they were getting something out of it.

“Jocelyn, I have been looking for you for twenty-eight years. It’s my job to train and protect you. Familiars are tasked by the Horned God to be a protector and guardian and chosen by the Goddess for their Danaan to be a companion, teacher, and friend. I’ve been pretty much alone for much longer than you’ve been alive, and I’m looking for a friend and a home. If you let me, I can make your life safer and teach you to use your powers to their full potential. I don’t want anything but to be a part of your life, and for you to accept me as I am." His words were honest and held a bit of hurt.

"I'm sorry. It's just...no one has ever tried to help me for the sake of helping before. I help people, people don't help me." It was true. Growing up, I would protect the younger kids in the foster homes until it was time for me to move on. Once I had learned some control over my powers, I helped my many foster parents by scrying for lost items or even casting the occasional luck spell. All in secret of course, but it made me feel better to know that I had tried to make their lives better in some way. And now there were my clients, and Peter, and the lost tribe.

"How long are you staying before you move on to your next Danaan?" I stumbled over the still strange term and how it applied to me, but I needed to know. If he was so willing to teach me about my powers, I wanted to know how long I had him as a teacher.

"Jocelyn, I'm with you till the day one of us dies. You're stuck with me for life," he said with a trace of humor.

Huh. "Well, how long do familiars live? Because if you've been looking for me for twenty-eight years, then you're really old for a cat." I knew he said that he'd lived with two other...Danaan, but there was no way he was with them for their entire lives.

He chuckled. "Well I'm almost two thousand years old, so I don't think I'm in danger of dying any time soon. Familiars are basically immortal as far as I know."

Holy crap! Well, there went my theories! "Oh! Well, then I guess...I guess you have a lot you can teach me," I stammered. I felt really stupid now.

I had another question. I didn't want to offend this ancient being who was to be my teacher any further, but I really didn't have another choice. I needed to know. "So you said you were here to teach and protect me. And while I appreciate the warning last night, how is a house cat supposed to help protect me?" I mentally cringed, hating how cynical that sounded.

He looked at me carefully and apparently came to some kind of conclusion. "I'm more than just a house cat. This was just the most inconspicuous and nonthreatening form I could take. I'm a shape shifter."

I wondered if the expression "blow your mind" was actually possible. "So you are what normally, a human?"

"No." He tensed and shook his head. "I can't take human form." His answer was final, and he didn't offer any additional information.

His abrupt answer set off a cascade of questions he obviously wouldn't want to answer. I wanted to know if he was born a shifter. How had he become a familiar? Why could he shift from animal to animal but not into human form? He obviously didn't want to discuss it. I thought of a safer question.

"So what form do you take normally? Do you have a favorite?"

The tension in his small body relaxed when he realized I wasn't going to pry. "Yes, but I didn't want to scare you as I'm usually much larger. I prefer to take the form of a Clouded Leopard. I usually shift into some kind of cat: cougar, tiger, lion, house cat. But I can take the shape of pretty much any animal. I'm most comfortable as a leopard."

I smiled. I loved cats and the thought of having a large one living with me was a dream I had had since I was little. Thinking of that, maybe there was more to our connection than I knew. "Well, if we're going to be roomies, then I think you should be comfortable in your own home. Do you..." I wasn't sure how this changing thing worked. Would he want privacy? "Um, you can use the bathroom to change if you want?"

He chuckled. "I think you're going to become fairly used to me changing form, so I have no problem showing you now."

I had to admit I was more than curious. He jumped off the couch and moved to the open area between the living room and kitchen to accommodate what would be his larger size. I watched in fascination as his outline began to blur and stretch.

Suddenly, I was looking at a beautiful, exotic looking cat whose shoulder was about even with my mid-thigh. Mateo was now about three and a half feet long with huge paws and a long, thick tail that was almost as long as his whole body. His coat was a beautiful mix of browns and greys with clearly defined black rectangle-like shapes covering his body. They reminded me of the markings on a Burmese Python. He was beautiful.

His familiar brilliant green eyes remained the same and were fixed on me warily, waiting for some kind of reaction.

My less than eloquent response was, "Holy Crap! You're beautiful!"

His chuckle came out much deeper now that he was so much larger. "Thank you. Changing shape is how familiars are able to protect their companions."

I remembered the dog that had attacked the man with the knife. I remembered hearing the barking, snarling, and pained shouts of the Inquisitors as I ran. The sickening final gurgle as a man choked on his own blood. The cat telling me one of the men was dead.

Mateo had been the dog that had stopped them. Mateo had killed one of them. He had killed one of them to save *me*. I wasn't happy the man had died, but I was very, very glad to be alive. The memories from last night were racing through my mind, and I was very aware of how close to death I had come. My hand drifted up to the scabbed-over cut on my neck. I felt tears gathering in my eyes, and my vision blurred as I looked at my fiercely beautiful new friend.

"Thank you, Mateo. I know I said it last night, but really, they would have killed me if it hadn't been for you. Last night I was too tired to be on my guard properly, and it would have cost me my life if you hadn't found me," I said, my voice shaking and tears pouring down my cheeks.

He looked steadily back at me. "It was my honor, Jocelyn."

All the stress from the attack, on top of the revelations Mateo had given me, it was just too much. I slid off the couch and onto the floor, hugging my knees with my arms, and started crying.

I felt Mateo's warm body come up beside me and a loud comforting rumble in my ear as he nudged me with his head trying to soothe me. I took the comfort he offered and wrapped my arms around his neck, burying my face in his fur. He was warm and reassuring and he had saved my life.

"Easy, little one. It'll be okay," he murmured into my hair. Laying one of his huge paws across my lap, he used my hip to gently pull me closer in a large feline hug. He continued to purr loudly, the rumbling resonating deep in my chest and doing much to calm me. "They will never get that close again, *paulo dea*. I'll protect you; I'll teach you to protect yourself."

I wondered what he said, but it wasn't important right now. I had too many questions and too much information thrown at me. I knew he couldn't protect me from everything, but for now it was nice not to be alone anymore.

I pulled back and wiped the tears from my face. "I'm sorry. I must still be tired or something. I never cry."

"You've had a very rough couple of days and then given a lot of very disturbing information. I think you have every right to break down. Don't worry, Jocelyn, I won't tell anyone." Then he winked at me.

I smiled weakly and wiped the tears from my face. "You can call me Joss."

I pushed myself up to sit on the couch, trying to compose myself. "So what's the plan then? How do I protect myself from these maniacs?"

"First up is teaching you a few very basic defensive spells, like a repulsion blast, shield wall, and cloaking spell. In fact, I would be willing to bet that you've done the cloaking spell on your own without knowing it a few times." He cocked his head and gave me an assessing gaze. "Let me guess, you always won whenever you played *Hide and Seek* as a child."

I hadn't had many occasions to play games as a kid, but now that I thought about it, I had been very good at that game. "So let me get this straight, you think I won those games because the other kids literally couldn't see me?" It sounded a bit farfetched. "I was what...invisible or something?"

"I wouldn't say that. Had anyone you weren't concerned about looked at you, they would have seen you. But the kids you were playing with couldn't see you because you didn't want them to. It's as simple as that. They could have looked right at you but would have seen nothing that they didn't expect. If you were hiding behind the drapes, they would have seen the drapes but not the bulge hiding your body or your feet underneath them. It's a type of glamour, similar to what the supernatural world uses to hide from humanity."

It sounded way too simple, but at the same time it made sense. "So, I have to...what? Think about not being seen?"

"In essence, yes, but what we'll work on is channeling that desire into a single compartmentalized thought. That thought will trigger the concentration required to enable you to remain unseen for as long as you choose without having to consciously think about it," he explained, seemingly happy that I had grasped the concept so quickly. “It’s the first spell that I’ve taught all my Danaan.”

“Great. I’m learning the spells for kindergarteners,” I deadpanned.

He chuckled. “Everyone starts somewhere, Joss.”

For the next few hours, he schooled me on the mental exercises that became my cloaking spell.

“Try not to think too hard. Relax, quiet your mind,” he murmured. “There is nothing to see.”

I giggled. “These aren’t the droids you’re looking for.”

I opened my eyes to see Mateo rolling his.

I started laughing, not able to hold it in. “I’m sorry, but I was waiting for you to tell me to use the force or something.”

I looked up to see it was almost one-thirty in the morning, and I was exhausted all over again, making me a bit loopy.

“We’ll stop here for the night. Using magick like this with such a single-minded purpose can be draining when you’re not used to it.” Mateo praised me despite my strange sense of humor. “You’ve done very well.”

I did feel pretty good about the progress I had made. I could successfully cloak myself and hold it in place with very little effort for about thirty minutes before my attention started to wander and the spell would start to fade.

Mateo watched with a smile as I slumped on the couch. “Danaan are sometimes mistaken for ghosts by humans as their cloaking spells weaken from lack of concentration. As the spell weakens, the Danaan appears as a sort of transparent, blurry figure that the human can see through until they either regain their concentration and become unseen again or drop the spell entirely."

I thought of something I hadn't before. "So does the cloaking spell only work on humans?"

He looked thoughtful for a minute. "No, it works on most of the Sidhe as well, but not all of them. If you start to get tired and become transparent they will easily recognize the spell for what it is."

"Shee?" I asked, puzzled over the unfamiliar term.

Mateo growled in the affirmative. "Remember I mentioned there were others, the supernatural world? Non-humans are known as Sidhe."

I rubbed my forehead and then my eyes. My whole head felt fuzzy. "I can't take any more information tonight. I'm tired." I looked up at him. "Are you comfortable enough out here? If you're going to be living here, we should get you some kind of bed or something. No offense, but I really don't want cat hair all over my couch," I teased. Kind of.

He chuckled. "I've never needed anything but the floor. Unless you're offering to share your bed, Joss?" he asked with a wicked purr and a spark in his green eyes.

I laughed. "Yeah, 'cause cat hair on my bed would be *so* much better than cat hair on my couch. Forget it." I playfully bumped his shoulder with mine. "Besides, you're huge and I'm not getting shoved out of my own bed by a cat. Friend or not."

We laughed together and I decided that having him live here was going to be nice. I had never really had a real friend before, especially not one I could share everything with.

Rising from the couch and stretching, I headed for my bedroom. "We'll go to the store tomorrow. I have to pick up some more groceries, and we will have to get you some food as well," I said. "Goodnight, Mateo."

"Goodnight, Joss."

Chapter Four

Waking up the next morning, I felt refreshed but still stiff and sore. I looked at my clock and saw it was almost eight. Perfect. I knew I had to spend the day upstairs so my neighbours wouldn't think that the house was deserted. I very rarely slept up there but needed to keep up the illusion that someone lived in the house above me. Otherwise, my few neighbors would get suspicious about my life.

After spending some time in the bathroom getting ready, I went out in search of my new roommate.

"Mateo?"

I looked around but the place seemed to be empty. The cupboard that led to the tunnel at the front of the house was open, and I assumed he had gone outside. I mentally smacked myself; it wasn't like there was a leopard-sized litter box anywhere.

I grabbed the milk out of the fridge and headed upstairs to start my day, listening carefully at the top of the stairs to ensure the house was empty before using the latch to open the bookcase. I wandered into the kitchen and started some badly needed coffee and more willow bark tea before turning to start the stove. Just as I was getting ready to pour the eggs in the pan for my scrambled eggs, a meowing at the back door made me smile. On the other side of the door, a green-eyed tabby cat waited impatiently.

"Morning, Mateo," I said as I let him in the back door.

"We need to install a cat door or something up here. That was humiliating," he grumbled as his tail thrashed around showing his irritation.

I tried to smother my giggle. "Someone's grouchy this morning," I teased and added more eggs to the pan.

We sat down at the kitchen table to eat. "So what's the plan today?" he asked.

I thought for a minute. "Well, it's Saturday so Jimmy won't expect to see me until Monday." I was filled with dread and sadness at the conversation we were going to have over the lost little girl. It killed me that I wasn't able to find her. And now there was Ray-Ray and little 'Shell to think about as well. "I thought we would go and do some shopping for part of the day at least. We need groceries."

Mateo blinked, clearly thinking. "Hmmm...okay. While we're out shopping this afternoon, we'll need to go to a garden center and then make a quick stop in Chinatown for supplies. We need to make a few changes in your yard to help you protect yourself; the garden center should have everything we need."

"And what's in Chinatown?" I asked, dishing up our breakfast.

"We have to buy some supplies so you can do some spell work. You need to be able to see through the glamour the supernatural world hides behind. Tonight we're going to the Troll Market, and you need to *see* to get in," he said.

I choked on my eggs. "Troll Market?!"

As I coughed out the egg and took a drink of my coffee to clear my throat, I struggled with the idea of a Troll Market. There were trolls? They were real? What, in the name of the Goddess, would trolls need a market for? *Deep breath, Joss, you're not a stupid human anymore. Time to learn your place in the world.*

"We need to get you a few more things for your kitchen downstairs, and I need to talk to a guy about the missing Inquisitor from the other night." His voice had hardened when he talked about the Inquisitor. I got the feeling he wasn't going to let my attack go.

"Okay, so I get that it's not your regular grocery store, but what should I expect when we get there?" My fork was frozen halfway to my mouth, still loaded with eggs, as I stared at him. I was beyond curious.

"It's not really a Troll Market; everyone just calls it that because of the Trolls guarding the entrance. It's a hidden market where the Sidhe go to buy, sell, or trade for things they need," he explained in between bites of egg. "And it's a place where we're free to be ourselves without the worry of humans around."

"Yeah, and what kinds of creatures are we talking about here?" Goddess save me, it was like trying to pull teeth.

"Oh, sorry," he apologized, chuckling. "Well, obviously there will be the Trolls at the entrance. You'll almost always see fairies, Dwarves, Gnomes, were-animals, Centaurs, Vampires, Merfolk, and the occasional elf."

"So you're telling me all the fairy tales are essentially true, that all the creatures in them actually exist?" A loud clang rang out. I had dropped my fork, the sound of it hitting the plate startling me. I was excited and horrified at the same time.

Mateo laughed. "Well, not *all* of them. I mean, I've been around a long time, and I have never heard of anything more ridiculous than a zombie, and yet humans make movies about them every year." He shook his head looking bewildered. "Humans are so weird."

I laughed but I was secretly relieved I didn't have to worry about rotting animated corpses along with everything else.

He started to wash his face in the regular manner of a cat. "But as for the rest, you shouldn't be all that surprised. The humans had to get their myths and legends from somewhere."

"Well, let's get going then; it sounds like we have a very full day," I said with false bravado. I put our dishes in the sink for later and, taking my tea and a fresh cup of coffee with me, went to get ready.

An hour later found us arguing in the garage beside my Jeep.

"Dog, Mateo," I said with my hands on my hips.

"You can take me to the store as a cat," he replied stubbornly as he sat at my feet.

"I could, but it's not common enough and would draw attention to me. No one thinks anything of a woman with a dog." If he thought that a woman riding around with a cat was keeping a low profile, he was living in the wrong century.

"I hate being a dog. It's so undignified." His tone was filled with disgust, and then he proceeded to clean his face again as if the very idea made him feel dirty.

"Hey, that *dog* saved my butt two nights ago. I like him," I pointed out.

He stopped washing his whiskers to glare at me. "The only reason a *dog* protected you at all was because it would have been really strange for a *tiger* to attack two muggers on a street in suburban Seattle," he challenged.

"Suck it up, Teo. You can come with me as a dog and help pick out your new bed or you can stay home." There was no way I would be running errands with a cat at my heels. That would be too weird.

"Fine! But I get to pick the dog," he relented with an agitated tail swish.

"Can you be a Poodle? Oh! Or a Yorkshire Terrier. I've always wanted one of those." I bounced excitedly before holding up my messenger bag. "And just think, you can ride in my bag."

Served him right for calling it Paul Bunyan's Backpack.

"And get lost in that thing?" He let out an angry hiss. "Belgian Shepherd or I come as a cat and embarrass you. Take it or leave it, Joss. And NO leash!" Mateo gave me his ultimatum, totally falling for my joke about the poodle.

I couldn't help but laugh. I hated those useless little lap dogs. Nothing but dressed up rats as far as I was concerned. Why anyone would want to humiliate their pet by putting it in a dress was beyond me.

"Whatever you want, Teo. I hate lap dogs."

"Then why did you...?" He snorted as he began to change, catching on to my teasing. "See what happens next time you need help with a spell, funny girl," he threatened, his voice deepening to a dog growl as he completed his shift. "You'll be lucky if I don't give you one to turn you into a toad."

I opened up the tailgate of the Jeep as the agile brown dog leaped in the back. "You know, you really do make a beautiful dog."

"Whatever," was his clever response.

I was still snickering as I climbed up into the driver's seat and ran my hands over the steering wheel affectionately. I loved my Jeep. It was a deep forest green TJ with a black soft top and big tires. I needed the 4x4 to get out into the surrounding mountains to collect some of the plants and other ingredients I used for my spells, and the Jeep was perfect. And it was cool.

Our first stop was the pet supply store. Mateo freaked out and refused to get out of the Jeep when he read the sign on the doors that read: *All Pets On A Leash Are Welcome!*

I managed to find a huge comfy bed designed for giant breed dogs. I won't tell you the complaining I had to endure over that! They just didn't sell leopard-sized cat beds at the local pet supply store. Imagine that.

The massive bed measured four feet by six feet, and I had to fold it to get it into the back of the Jeep. Good thing I had taken out the back seat before we left the house.

Our next stop was the grocery store where I picked up the necessary groceries and arranged for a meat order to be delivered to the house later in the day. Mateo grudgingly told me he preferred to eat mainly meat. He insisted he was fully capable of finding his own food, but no friend of mine would be forced to "find his own food." I mean I had never had a friend before, so there was no way I was going to let him forage for his dinner.

By the time we finished all my errands, it was after one in the afternoon and I was hungry. We went through a drive-thru, and after buying several burgers for the two of us, we headed north to downtown Seattle.

Mateo had me stop at a large nursery to buy several shrubs and trees. We were going to plant a protective circle of birch, cedar, and oak trees around the house. Between the trees we would plant gardens of roses and clover. It kind of bothered me that my nice lawn would have clover running through it because previously I had called it a weed. Mateo explained it was an inconspicuous way to close the botanical circle without making it *look* like there was a huge circle around the house. I had to admit it was clever.

We arranged for the trees and shrubs to be delivered first thing Monday morning, and then we climbed in the Jeep and headed off to our final stop in Chinatown.

"Where are we going again?" I asked Mateo, who was now sitting in the front seat looking carefully at the passing traffic.

"There's a metaphysical bookstore and herbalist two blocks away from Chinatown. We're headed there," he replied as he finished off his fourth burger patty.

"Okay, and what are we doing there?" Getting information out of him was like trying to get ketchup out of those stupid glass bottles. Impossible and frustrating.

"Picking up some supplies for tonight."

I breathed out an irritated sigh. Maybe if I squeezed him... I saw his lips twitch into what I could have sworn was a doggy smirk.

"Cut the crap, Teo. Seriously, what are we doing?"

He chuckled. "We have to pick up some Clary Sage oil made from a plant that was picked in the first hour after moonrise of a full moon." He looked over at me with a cocked eyebrow. "I didn't think you would have any on hand."

I humphed out a breath and switched my gaze back to the road as he laughed at me. As irritating as he could be, I was finding him fun to be around. I liked having a friend.

Soon I was parking the Jeep in front of a dingy little shop with a faded and cracked sign written in a language I couldn't speak. Honestly, the place looked abandoned.

"Are you sure this is it?" I asked doubtfully as Mateo jumped out of the Jeep behind me.

The windows were so dirty I could barely see inside, and what I could see didn't inspire a lot of confidence.

"Yeah, we'll find everything we need here. Come on." He led the way to the door and waited for me to open it.

As I opened the door, I heard the sound of chiming bells and looked up to see a string of four, surprisingly shiny, silver bells over the door. On either side of the frame were two very lifelike statues of sitting foxes with bright red bibs around their necks. Strange.

The interior of the shop was dark, cluttered, and very dusty. Dried plants hung upside down from the low ceiling, their tips brushing the contents of the rows of shelving that created narrow aisle ways throughout the shop. My nose was overwhelmed by the multitude of scents wafting through the air, not all of them pleasant. Holding my hand to my face, I tried to stave off the urge to sneeze.

"How can I help you, young woman?" A scratchy broken voice with a heavy Asian accent carried over the shelves, and I struggled to see where it came from.

I shifted to the side to see an ancient looking little old man standing behind a dirty glass display case at the back of the store. He couldn't have been more than four and a half feet tall with long, stringy, salt and pepper hair falling around his face and down over his stooped shoulders. He was wearing a wooden hat on his head that was carved strangely like a large leaf.

The little man was wearing a stained linen outfit that looked like a cross between hospital scrubs and a pair of pajamas. His face was deeply wrinkled, and he had the cliché long Fu Manchu moustache. But what caught me were his eyes; they were deeply sunken in his face but were a brilliant sapphire blue and sparkled with wisdom and humour.

"Ummm... we need essential oil of Clary Sage...if you have some, please?" I answered, unsure of myself and hoping he spoke decent English.

He chuckled at my stammered out question. "You will find what you seek on the shelf to your left."

Mateo startled me as he appeared at my side and spoke to the man. "We need the good stuff, Shido."

The man seemed unsurprised at a talking dog as his eyes narrowed and his gaze shifted between me and Mateo and then back again, his expression widening in understanding. "Ah, so you have found her at last, have you, Mateo?"

Mateo nodded. "Yes, she managed to keep herself well hidden all on her own," he said with a trace of pride.

I had never had anyone proud of me before and that small trace warmed me.

"She has much power and intelligence then. She will do well," the old man said with a smile.

"*She* is standing right here, if you don't mind," I muttered, a bit irritated as they talked about me like I wasn't there.

The two of them chuckled.

"My apologies, young woman. I will fetch your oil from the back." The old man offered me a deep nod and a warm smile before shuffling towards a dingy curtain leading to what I imagined was a storage area.

I was startled to see animal tails peeking out from underneath the back of his long tunic top.

"What is he?" I whispered to Mateo, getting the feeling that I had just met my first member of the supernatural community.

Mateo's eyes sparkled with approval. "He's an Obake, specifically a Kitsune. A type of shape shifter."

I blinked, confused. "But he looks human. You said shape shifters couldn't become human."

"I said he's a Kitsune, not a familiar. He's a different kind of shape shifter. He can only shift between his human form and that of a kind of fox," Mateo explained.

"But I saw a tail..."

"Actually, I have four of them," the old man said, shuffling slowly back through the curtain.

I blushed, embarrassed he had caught us talking behind his back. "I'm sorry, I just—"

He held up a long-fingered hand with wicked-looking, long, yellow nails as he chuckled. "Do not apologize." He held out a palm with three small seeds in it. "Please, put these under your tongue and see for yourself."

I tentatively took the seeds from his hand and looked down at Mateo with a raised eyebrow. At his nod, I put them under my tongue. I blinked at the faintly bitter taste and opened my eyes, about to ask why I had gritty, bitter tasting seeds under my tongue but was stopped by the things my eyes were seeing.

The nasty, dirty, little shop was now sparkling clean with spotless shelves filled with neat rows of candles, bottles of oils, jars with all types of herbs, books, and strange instruments that I had no idea what they were used for. I turned to the old man to comment on the change but was further struck speechless when I saw him.

Where before I had seen a little old Asian man, I now saw a tall humanoid figure with the head of a snow white fox. The stained linen pajamas had been replaced with silk kimono type robes in white and blue. He had beautifully pointed ears accented with a soft grey fur, a long pointed face with long whiskers, and a delicate black nose. His eyes, though, remained the same brilliant blue.

"Jocelyn Matthews, may I introduce you to Mr. Inari Shido. Mr. Shido, this is my Danaan, Jocelyn Matthews." Mateo introduced us with a hint of laughter in his voice.

The blue eyes narrowed slightly as the fox-like creature held out a softly furred hand that had long, sharp nails and a thumb that was placed too high on his hand. "Jocelyn Matthews. It is my great honour to meet you. I have heard many good things about you."

He had heard of me? I put my hand in his and found his palm and the pads of his fingers to be rough, much like the animal pads on the bottom of Mateo's feet. "It's nice to meet you, Mr. Shido." I was happy to hear that my voice stayed steady and betrayed none of the shock I was feeling as he bowed low over my hand. "If I may, how have you heard of me?"

"I hear many things, young woman," he answered, still holding my hand. "You are the Jocelyn Matthews that works *unofficially* as a private detective, are you not?"

"I am, but how...?"

He looked down at my hand and gently touched the ring I wore. "This is a very beautiful ring. Very unique."

I blinked at the change of subject. "Thank you. It was my mother's. I wouldn't call it unique. I've seen them often."

It really wasn't anything special. I had seen several of them over the years. Three intertwined silver bands that, when worn properly, rolled on and off the finger. Most of the ones I had seen seemed to be souvenirs from Mexico. Mine was slightly different in that one of the three bands was gold and the silver ones had Celtic knots engraved on them. It was beautiful.

"Your mother's?" He looked up at me and his eyes softened. "Then it is very unique as it is a piece of her you carry with you."

I smiled at the memory. "She loved it. She never took it off."

The moment was broken as two beautiful white foxes ran up to sniff me curiously. Mateo growled and snapped at them—a warning to keep away from me.

They yipped and ran behind Mr. Shido, who laughed. "They are only curious, Mateo."

"Maybe, but I don't need them taking the ring off her hand or the money from her purse either," Mateo replied with a sharp look.

Mr. Shido chuckled. "You are still angry about that? It was almost three hundred years ago. Holding a grudge is bad for your heart, I hear."

Mateo snorted. "We had to walk ten leagues to the next town."

"Medea forgave me."

"No, she didn't. You just never saw her again to reap the revenge she had planned." From his tone, it was obvious that Mr. Shido wouldn't have liked the revenge at all.

Mr. Shido shuddered slightly at the thought.

I looked down at the small cute faces looking back at me and realized they were the statues that had been on either side of the door when we had come in.

Mateo turned to me to explain. "The foxes are Mr. Shido's messengers, but they're very mischievous and clever and are very attracted to shiny things. Like *money*." He shot Mr. Shido another sharp look that caused a clearly unrepentant smile to pull at Mr. Shido's mouth.

Good to know. "So this is all real? The dirty, little shop..."

"Is all a glamour to discourage humans from entering. Although, I have been raided several times by the local police. They seem to think that I am selling marijuana." Mr. Shido laughed.

I laughed. "No pot selling for you, huh?"

He got a new twinkle in his eye. "Oh, I am selling it, just not to humans, and not for the reasons they think I am."

Huh?

Mateo laughed. "Leave her alone, Shido. She's already dealing with a lot." He sobered. "She was attacked by Inquisitors two nights ago. I barely got there in time."

The smile melted off Mr. Shido's face, and his blue eyes hardened visibly. The two foxes at his heels gave out low growls. "Do they live?"

"I killed one of them. The other's in the wind. That's one of the reasons we came here today. We have to go to the market tonight and she needs to be able to see the world without the glamour," Mateo said seriously.

I leaned on the counter tiredly. I didn't like thinking about the other night or how things could have gone.

"When you go to the market, be sure she is hooded. I do not need to remind you, one such as she is very rare," Mr. Shido advised Mateo with a serious and knowing look.

I got the feeling there was more going on than I knew about. I sighed. I knew I was in danger before, but now it felt like the whole world was against me instead of just some delusional religious zealots.

Mr. Shido patted one of my hands gently in reassurance. "Do not worry so, young one. Your Mateo is very powerful and very wise. He will protect you." He squeezed my hand and looked into my eyes steadily when I looked up at him. "And should you get separated from him and find yourself in danger with no one to turn to, you will come here. I will shelter you until your Mateo can come for you."

I heard Mateo draw in a surprised breath, and I looked at Mr. Shido in confusion. "Why would you help me? Why would you put yourself at risk like that?" I really wasn't used to people doing things for me.

He pulled a strange looking necklace from inside his robes. "Because you are worth protecting. You will be very important in times to come."

I looked down at the offered necklace. It was a natural rock, like you would find along any river, but it looked somewhat like a small frog in profile with its mouth open. It had a perfect hole naturally worn through it where the eye should be, and it hung from a red leather cord. I could tell right away that it was very special, as it seemed to be warm in my palm and had a very faint vibration coming from it.

"A witch stone. This is very generous of you, Inari," Mateo said softly.

"Guard her well, Mateo. She is more precious than you know."

I looked up from the necklace in my hand to ask why I was special, but Mr. Shido and the foxes had disappeared. The store had returned to its ugly, dirty, and abandoned look.

I looked down at Mateo in confusion. "Where did..."

"The seeds are only temporary. Come on, it's time to go," he said as he turned and headed for the door.

I looped the leather around my neck to join the silver chain I usually wore and watched as the rock glowed briefly before it quieted and looked just like a strange rock on a leather cord around my neck. I couldn't even feel the vibration anymore.

I grabbed the bottle of essential oil off the counter. "Wait, shouldn't we pay for this?"

"Trust me, after the necklace, the bottle of oil is nothing. Come on."

I followed him to the front of the store and out to the Jeep. Once we were both in and were on our way back to our house, I looked at him. "Mind telling me what that was all about?"

I watched as a frown crossed his dog face and could see he was deep in thought. "I'm not sure. According to myth, Kitsune are creatures from Japan and are quite revered for their abilities in agriculture and fertility. In reality, they're very wise, and in the case of Mr. Shido, very benevolent. The more tails they have, the older and wiser they are. They can get up to nine tails by the time they are 1000 years old. I would guess that Inari is over five hundred years old as he has four. Kitsune don't give their personal protection often. That necklace is a very powerful protection charm and is more valuable than diamonds to those of the Sidhe community and twice as rare. Inari is one of the few creatures I call friend and the only one besides me you can trust with the knowledge of who and what you are. For him to give it to you as a gift is very important."

I turned my attention back to the road, scared of what this could mean. "I'm in danger aren't I, Teo?" I asked him softly.

"No more than you were yesterday. Only now you have me, and apparently a powerful Kitsune, to protect you. I'll be able to get more information from the market tonight," he said softly.

Chapter Five

We got home just as the delivery truck arrived with the meat order. I'd have to wait to close the protection circle around the house because the trees I ordered couldn't be delivered until Monday morning. I loaded as much of the meat as I could into my small kitchen freezer and then took the rest downstairs to our hidden house. It took me a while to load all of it into the larger freezer, but now Mateo had a variety of chicken, beef, and pork to eat for the next month or two.

"So what do we do first?" I asked, putting away the last of the groceries.

Mateo was back in his leopard form and checking out his new bed in the living room. "It smells like cedar." His nose wrinkled as he looked at me. "Why does it smell like cedar?"

I sighed and walked over to it. "Apparently, it discourages fleas and..." I looked sideways at him, a smirk pulling at my lips "...covers that doggy smell."

He hissed at me. "Well, we don't have that problem since I'm a leopard when we're at home."

"Seriously? You just made me buy a dozen cedar trees for their protective qualities. Why are you complaining?" My hands went to my hips. "For someone over two thousand years old, you're sounding awfully juvenile."

"It's a *dog* bed." He gave it a disgusted look.

I threw up my hands and walked into the kitchen. "I am not having this conversation with you again. Use it. Don't use it. I don't care."

Hearing his footfalls as he followed behind me, I ignored his tantrum and asked, "What do I need to do for the spell first?"

"We need to lift the mortal veil on your sight. You'll need your smallest spell pot and a good hot fire in the hearth. We need to get the brew to a boil," he said, the argument over the dog bed forgotten.

As I set up everything we needed, Mateo watched me intently. I carefully rinsed out the copper spell pot with salt water and set it on the fireplace. Putting my hand on the cauldron, I reached for the knob that turned on the gas flames. I bowed my head and closed my eyes.

"Herbal potion, cauldron brew,
now be charged with magick true.
With intent, I speak this charm,
that all be blessed and none be harmed.
Ever minding the law of three,
this is my will, so it will be."

I opened my eyes and lit the fire.

Mateo was looking at me with a strange look on his face.

"What?"

"That is a very ancient spell of preparation. I don't know of one Danaan who still uses it. Where did you learn it?"

I shrugged. "I don't remember..." I had a faint memory of someone singing it, but I couldn't focus on who or when. "I like to start my potions this way. I find it helps me to focus on the task and reminds me to cast my spells without hurting anyone." I looked at him, uncertain. "It's not bad, is it?"

He shook his head quickly. "No. No, it's very good. I'm just surprised, that's all."

"So what do I do?" I asked.

"Put a quarter cup of spring water into the pot to boil," he said.

As I did that he told me to put a pinch of anise seed, lavender, thyme, and dandelion on a glass plate and told me the verbal part of the spell.

"While you're waiting for the water to boil, use the index finger of your right hand to trace a counter clockwise spiral from the inside out. It mixes the herbs and uncovers the clouded sight of a mortal," he explained.

Once the water was boiling, I added the dried herbs and then nine drops of the Clary Sage oil. I repeated the incantation Mateo made me memorize while concentrating on my goal.

"Lord and Lady reveal to me,
vision that was hidden by thee.
Grant to me your sacred sight,
that I may see the world aright.
Place in me your sacred trust,
let all be seen without fear or lust.
I am yours as you are mine,
clear thought and vision intertwined."

Once the potion cooled enough, I used a dropper and, following Mateo's direction, squeezed three drops in each of my eyes. Once they stopped watering from the stinging, I looked around. "I don't feel any different."

Mateo chuckled. "You won't because there isn't any real difference. When we get outside you'll see some things you haven't ever seen before, but other than that, the only thing that's changed is your ability to see and sense magick."

"I want to see." I went upstairs and through the bookcase to look out the living room windows on the main floor. I stood staring at the street in front of the house, and at first I didn't see anything out of the ordinary. Then I started to see small differences. Birds with three legs sat in the tree across the street. Large bumblebees with human looking heads and feminine upper bodies flitted around Mrs. Jamison's daisies next door.

I moved to the kitchen window and looked out over the backyard and into the dense forest of the park behind it. I was struck by some of the large trees in the park. Some of the trunks seemed to move unnaturally and looked like they were alive with faces in the bark.

"I never would have guessed," I murmured to the grey tabby cat at my heel.

"It's not something that can be explained. You have to see it for yourself," Mateo said softly.

I nodded. "The trees?" I half asked.

"Wood nymphs for the most part. Sometimes they look like young women sitting in the tree, but most of the time they're a part of the tree itself. If the tree is cut down, then the nymph can sometimes find a new tree to inhabit, but usually they die with it. They're too tied to the nature of the tree to adapt."

I could hear the sadness in his voice and understood it. How many trees had humans cut down in the name of progress and expansion with no regard to the creatures who depended on it? The senseless clear cutting in Brazil immediately came to mind. Acres lost every day, species wiped out before they were even discovered, and those were the inhabitants humans *expected* to find. Knowing there were beings linked directly to the trees themselves literally losing their lives was tragic. And that was just the rainforests. The pollution of the oceans, strip mining, air pollution – the implications of the wider picture were too much to think about.

"I want to go for a walk." I looked down at him and watched a frown form on his face. "I need to see as much as I can so I'm not so shocked when we go to the Troll Market tonight."

Mateo thought for a moment but then nodded. "Alright." He went into the hall, so someone passing by outside wouldn't be able to see him, and returned a minute later in his dog form.

We went out into the warm summer day and strolled down the sidewalk. I was just a young woman out enjoying the sunshine with her dog.

There really wasn't all that much to see. More of the occasional wood nymphs and the three-legged crows seemed to be keeping an eye on us but otherwise left us alone.

"What are the bee women?" I asked in a low voice as they buzzed through the daisies.

"They're known in Greek mythology as Thriae, but in actuality they're just a type of insect-like fairy. They don't interact with real fairies much and behave more like bees. They tend gardens and make honey, but not like any honey you have ever seen or tasted. They are rumoured to have the gift of prophesy, but if they do, they don't tell anyone. In ancient times, there were actually some colonies that lived among humans, and they would sometimes gift some of their honey to special humans. It has healing properties and was highly prized. The humans became angry at the small quantities that were given out and tried to force the Thriae to give them more. The Thriae disappeared into myth, never to be seen by humans again," he explained.

I thought they must have re-cloaked themselves in glamour. Why subject themselves to a type of slavery?

Something that was given as a gift suddenly turned into an expectation. The humans' self-entitlement was disgusting. I would have walked away too.

A whole new history was becoming available to me, new explanations for past events, new ways to look at interactions and politics. The world was a new and fascinating place.

We walked a few more blocks towards the school, and we came across a large dilapidated property. The house was obviously condemned and sagged on its foundation in the center of, what was probably, two acres of badly overgrown land. The windows were broken and cracked, and the roof was missing in several places. It was quite an eyesore in an otherwise nice neighbourhood. It had a realty sign on the curb with a sold sticker. I overheard a man in a truck idling at the curb talking about the demolition crew showing up Monday morning.

"That's a shame," Mateo said when we were far enough away that the man wouldn't hear a talking dog.

"What is?"

"The house they're tearing down has a fairy tribe living in it. If they tear it down during the day, all the fairies will be killed," he explained.

I stopped in my tracks. "What?!"

"There's a fairy tribe—" he started to repeat himself.

"I heard you the first time. Why wouldn't they just move?"

"They probably don't know it's going to happen. It's an Unseelie tribe and they're only active at night."

"We have to do something." I couldn't let them be killed, not when I knew what was going to happen and had the power to stop it.

"Joss, they're Unseelie. They hate humans and do nothing but cause problems. They aren't going to listen to you. Hell, they'll probably attack you! There's nothing we can do. Besides, we don't need every Sidhe, Inquisitor, and Creature in the state knowing you're Danaan," Mateo said.

"What do you mean *Unseelie*? What is that?" I asked, ignoring his reasons for the moment.

He looked around and saw a deserted children's playground at the school. He started to walk towards it, and I sat down on some benches so he could explain.

"The fairies are split up into two groups: the Seelie and the Unseelie. The Seelie Fairies are active during the day. They have colourful wings like butterflies or dragonflies and like wide open sunny places like fields and large open forests. They are generally pretty friendly and can be quite helpful. The Unseelie are their complete opposite. They like dark, damp places and dense forests. They have beetle or moth wings and are only active at night. They are secretive and generally bad-tempered towards humans and other Sidhe alike. They cause mischief as often as they can and reserve kindness for members of their tribe. They won't listen to you." Mateo looked at me like that should convince me to abandon my thoughts of helping the tribe.

"I don't care, Mateo. I'm going to help them if I can. They deserve to be warned at least."

"By the Goddess! You are so much trouble, you know that?" he spat at me. "They are not going to listen to you. They will attack you before you even get the chance to explain. And how are you going to keep the fact that you're Danaan a secret?"

I thought about it. He knew so much more about this world than I did. I wondered if I would be able to ignore my conscience and let it happen without interfering. I shook my head. "I'm sorry, Mateo, I can't. I can't let them get killed. There has to be something we can do, some way for me to get a chance to talk to them before they decide to attack me."

Mateo huffed out an exasperated breath.

I pressed my advantage. "I live by the tenets of the Goddess, dictating that I do no harm. By doing nothing I feel like I'm doing harm because I didn't intervene when I could. I can't just sit back and watch this happen, Teo." I looked at my new friend, pleading for his understanding.

"Fine." He looked up at me. "If we do this, we do it my way. I tell you what to do and you do it. No arguing. Got it?"

I nodded quickly, surprised he was willing to help me.

"Fairies may be small, but they're fierce fighters and have no problem dying to defend their homes. The Unseelie are more likely to attack first and ask questions later." He was still not happy but was going to help me.

"What do we do?"

"We go home and start gathering things to bribe them with to hopefully hold off an attack long enough to request a meeting," he stated, and we headed back home quickly.

I found an old basket I had bought at the supermarket last Easter; it had had some flowers in it I had re-potted, and I never got around to throwing the basket out. I gathered some sunflower seeds and dehydrated cranberries I usually put in my salads. We went into the park, and I picked several types of mushrooms and rock moss Mateo said would be a good gift for an Unseelie tribe. I ripped apart an old feather pillow and put a large handful of the downy feathers into a sandwich bag and added a small shot glass of some honey I had in the cupboard.

Mateo still wasn't happy but thought we might have a shot at getting them to at least listen to me.

It was just after dark when we started walking back to the condemned house. Despite the warmth of the evening, Mateo had me wear a hoodie with the hood pulled up and then *cloak* myself like we had practiced before we left the house so no one would see me going for a walk at dark. He was just a stray dog. Mateo was very worried about the Inquisitors that were still in the city, no doubt looking for me in the same area where I'd escaped them. My neighborhood. He was right. This was probably a bad idea.

It was weird walking down the street and knowing no one could see me. A man walking his poodle looked right through me, and I had to move quickly to avoid bumping into him. It was habit to think someone would move over on the sidewalk, but the man wasn't going to move over if there was nothing to walk around.

It wasn't long before we got to the property that housed the fairy tribe. We approached the opening in the fence where a beautifully paved walkway to the front door used to be. Now it was a badly overgrown path, littered with broken stones and exposed tree roots. Mateo gave me some instructions while we stood in the shadow of a tree.

"Keep your hood up but drop your cloaking spell and walk to the front door. Stop when you get halfway there. Set the basket down and slowly back away. We wait on the sidewalk until the guard comes to speak with us. When he does, you're going to respectfully request to speak to the Chief. If we're lucky, they'll agree. If we're not, be prepared to run. Fairies are suspicious of creatures bearing gifts."

"Then why did we bring the basket full of stuff?" I asked with wide eyes.

Mateo ignored me. "Take the amulet Inari gave you out of your shirt. I'm hoping they'll recognize you as someone who has protection. It *may* make things easier."

"May?" I asked nervously.

"Most fairies hate humans," he deadpanned.

I sighed and rolled my eyes. "I'm not human according to you."

He let out a low growl. "I'm *very* aware of that. I'm hoping they'll think you're an elf hybrid or something. Keep your hood up. If they figure out what you really are, we're screwed."

Well, wasn't this fabulous? I took a deep breath, reminding myself I was the one that wanted to do this.

I dropped my spell and slowly picked my way through the broken paving stones towards the house. I heard some rustling in the dead bushes that served as a hedge. It sounded like a squirrel, but I knew better. I was being watched. The air around me was like an oppressive weight, the atmosphere the epitome of every scary movie I had ever seen, complete with the idiot girl walking to her doom. I was sure this was the house the neighborhood kids called haunted. My heart felt like it was in my throat. I knew a regular human would be scared and would likely not have gotten this far, and they would have no idea what they were walking towards. I knew what I was walking into, and the prickle of danger over my skin had raised the hair on the back of my neck.

When I got halfway to the house, I carefully placed the basket on the ground and slowly backed away. I really hoped none of the neighbours were looking out their windows because I must have looked like a nut case.

When I got back to Mateo, he pressed himself close in front of me. I took comfort in his protection but wasn't sure how effective a dog would be against attacking fairies. Lord and Lady, I hoped it didn't come to that.

I watched carefully and saw two shadows dart out from under the house to inspect the basket. There was a shrill sound like that of a bat and a third shadow joined the first two briefly before zipping back under the house.

"The Chief will have been alerted to our presence. Don't make any sudden moves. They'll be watching," Mateo said quietly.

I held my breath as one of the small shadows came closer. The amulet on my chest began to vibrate softly, barely more than a hint of a humming—something to ask Mateo about if we lived through this.

It wasn't long before I could make out a small man with the wings of a beetle. He was only about five inches tall with black hair, and he had gray skin that seemed to be stretched too tight over his small bones. His clothes looked like they were made out of dead leaves, cobwebs, and scraps of dark coloured fabric.

Hostile black eyes narrowly appraised me, and I thought I saw him eye my amulet. "What do you want, *human*?" he snapped out in a harsh, grating voice.

"I respectfully request the honour of speaking with your Chief. I have some information I feel may be vital to the well-being of your tribe," I stated with a respectful nod, happy to hear none of the nervousness I was feeling showed in my voice.

"And what do you want in exchange for this *information*," he sneered, his voice clearly stating he didn't believe I had any information the Chief would find valuable.

"I want nothing more than to pass it along and depart in peace."

The guard snorted in disbelief. "I will pass along your information, should I think it worthy."

"With respect, I would prefer to offer the information directly to your Chief."

"Fine," he spat and flew back to the house.

Several minutes later he came back, a small bow and arrow drawn and pointed at me. "You will be permitted to speak with the Baron. Walk to the steps. Any farther and we kill you where you stand."

Mateo growled softly at the threat, and I put my hand on his head to quiet him. "We thank you for the opportunity and promise not to take any more of his valuable time than necessary."

Mateo and I slowly retraced my steps back up the broken pathway, past the spot where I had stopped previously, to the ruined steps of the house, and stopped as instructed. A taller fairy flew forward out of the shadows of the dilapidated porch. He was maybe six inches tall and was wearing a suit made out of old black velvet. His shoulders were draped in spider webs, and his long silver hair was brushed back into a tidy ponytail at the base of his neck. His skin was olive toned but looked chalky, as if he were dead. With large, elaborately decorated, dusty gray moth wings and a small but wicked looking sword strapped to his hip, four other fairies flanked him, their large black beetle wings humming. Dressed in uniform, they were clearly his guards. Another small group of moth-winged fairies flew forward and seemed to hold some kind of status by the way the others deferred to them.

I heard rustling overhead and glanced up to see several bats grasping onto the porch roof with small fairies perched on their backs. The fierce glittering of their small black eyes matched those of the bats. This was the aerial protection, I assumed with a faint shudder. My attention was brought back to the Chief when he spoke.

"My sentry tells me you have information for me, madam." His voice was deeper than I would have expected for someone of his size, and I was impressed with the level of respect he showed me.

I was at a bit of a loss as to how I was supposed to address him but figured *sir* was safe enough. "I do, sir. I hope I do not offend you by presuming you don't know what happens in your territory, but—"

The nasty little guard who'd escorted us here took offense anyway and erupted in fury, flying up into my face and threatening me with his own small sword. "That is Baron Blackthorn, leader of the coastal tribes, you are addressing, you worthless human! Watch your tongue before I cut it out of your useless head!"

Mateo snarled fiercely, his hackles rising as he tensed.

The Baron held up a hand to silence the guard. "Quiet, Nettle. While she has the *sight*, she has no knowledge of our ways. You will show her the respect she has shown us thus far or you will find yourself cleaning mole holes for the next moon."

The guard fell silent at the admonishment, drifting slowly back to the porch and bowing low. "Excuse me, my Lord."

The Baron turned back to a still tense but calmer Mateo and me. "Please excuse the rudeness of my sentry, madam. I would hear your information and then decide if it is a presumption or not."

Goddess, the guy wasn't just a chief, he was a Lord. The many ways I could screw this up were staggering. I remembered playing *tea party* with my mom as a child and the way we would pretend we were royalty, greeting others to our table. I had nothing to lose by being excessively formal. As my last foster mom liked to say, "Good manners never offended anyone."

"My Lord Blackthorn, my friend Mateo and I were out walking this afternoon and overheard a human planning the destruction of this house and property two days hence to make way for a new block of human houses. I feared your tribe would be killed and decided to offer the warning."

His guards grew restless at my words, the advisors to the side murmuring quietly amongst themselves, and the Baron was silent for a long moment. I started to get nervous.

"Why would you trouble yourself to warn us? What is it that you want in return?" he asked.

"The doctrines of the Lord and Lady require their followers do no harm, and I felt if I kept my counsel, then my inaction may cause your tribe harm. I want nothing in return for the information except that you do not reveal my existence to others. I have my own enemies and am taking a great risk to give you this warning," I told him truthfully.

"What is your name, madam?" he asked.

"Jocelyn Matthews, my Lord."

The Baron looked at me for a long moment and then switched his gaze to Mateo. “Have you nothing to say?” Obviously, he recognized Mateo as something other than a dog.

“No, Baron Blackthorn. She interferes against my advice. I am here only to ensure she comes to no harm,” Mateo said shortly.

I rolled my eyes. I couldn’t help it.

The Baron must have caught my expression because he smothered a smile, composing himself quickly. “I have several large tribes living in the area, Lady Matthews. The Chiefs and I are responsible for many.” He waved a hand towards the advisors, who I now knew to be the leaders of the tribes under Baron Blackthorn’s domain. “Where would you have us go? Especially if time is as short as you claim.”

I thought for a long moment. What did I know about fairies? I replayed the little bit of information that Mateo had given me earlier. “I admit, my Lord, I know little of fairies. However, there is a large park located behind my house only a few blocks from here. There is a series of hollow tree caves scattered in the darkest part of the park. Most are well hidden from the humans. I only know of them because I dug a tunnel out of my house as an escape route in case I am attacked by my enemies. The caves may be a safe place for your people to shelter until you can find a more suitable home.” It was the only suggestion I could offer, and I hoped he wouldn’t be offended.

I could feel Mateo stiffen in anger when I mentioned my escape tunnel, but I figured the show of trust might convince the Baron to believe in my good intentions.

"You surprise me, Lady Matthews. Not many would go out of their way to warn an Unseelie fairy tribe of impending danger or expose themselves in such a way; you are unique. I find your information to be vitally important. As you have said, you risk much to bring me this information and even more by revealing such information about yourself. These are perilous times, and I suspect we have a shared enemy." He raised his voice so everyone could hear him. "Your identity will be kept within the tribes. None shall speak of you by name or describe you in any way." His words held a command and all the fairies present nodded in response. He gestured behind him and a younger male fairy dressed in a similar fashion stepped forward. "I would ask that you take my son, Bracken, with you and show him the caves."

He spoke to his chiefs. "Alert the tribes. Tell them to gather their belongings quickly. We begin leaving two hours before sunrise."

The Baron turned back to me. "We are in your debt, Lady Matthews, for your timely warning. I always pay my debts."

"No thanks are needed, Lord Blackthorn. I have done only what was right. We will leave you now to return home. Your son, Bracken, will be shown the caves so you may relocate your people as quickly as possible. I'm sure you have much to carry, so with your consent, I will take the gifts I brought and leave them in the caves for your arrival," I offered.

"That would be appreciated, Lady Matthews. I will think on a way to repay your unexpected kindness." He bowed slightly and turned to issue orders to an ever growing group of fairies.

I pulled my hood farther up, making sure my face was hidden, as I turned to follow Mateo. We left quickly with the small fairy, Bracken, following silently behind us.

"We will talk about this, Jocelyn," was all that Mateo said to me.

Cutting through the school, it wasn't long before we were in the darkest part of Carkeek Park behind my house. I pulled a small flashlight from my messenger bag and led Bracken to the caves. It was actually a rather pretty piece of the park in the daytime, if a little gloomy. At night it was creepy and dark, the moss-covered trees seeming sinister in the shadows. We followed a small stream as it wound its way through the length of the park. The headwaters sprung out of the rocks in a small waterfall and were well hidden. The hollow remains of huge old growth cedar trees were scattered in a secluded grove. I crawled forward under the largest one, the overgrown branches making it awkward because of the basket. Mateo took pity on me and took the handle in his mouth to carry it easily into the surprisingly large damp cave.

My flashlight illuminated a cavern that was about nine feet high in the middle and eight feet deep before it narrowed into the depths of the roots that led to my escape tunnel. The cavern had several small crevices and tunnels branching off it where roots had rotted away. I hoped it would be large enough for the fairy tribes.

I hadn't been in here since I created the tunnel that led to my basement home, but I was pleased to see that the wards were still strong.

I turned to the young fairy that had followed us. "I can remove the wards around my tunnel if you like?"

The small man eyed me carefully. "Thank you, my Lady, but I don't think that will be necessary. I appreciate you guiding me here and allowing us the option of taking refuge." He paused as if unsure of his next words. "These trees are large and the caves seem extensive. Would you be opposed to us finding a permanent home here?"

I was surprised. "Not at all. However, I would speak with Lord Blackthorn about it before a final decision is made. I rely on this tunnel as an escape. As I said, I have my own threats and must be prepared for my own protection. Living so near to me on a permanent basis may in fact put your people at risk."

He nodded. "I understand completely, my Lady. By your leave, I will return to my father so I may guide the tribe to safety." He bowed gracefully.

I nodded and he was gone. “Well, while I’m here we might as well take the short cut home. I can check to make sure that the tunnel is still sound.”

Mateo was silent but went into the tunnel that led to the house quickly.

I mentally sighed, knowing that he was angry.

We got back to the house without any problem, and by the time Mateo stalked out of my bedroom, he was already back in his leopard form. I went into the bathroom to wash away the dirt and to put off the inevitable confrontation.

I had no sooner walked into the living room when I was confronted by a very angry leopard.

With every step he took toward me, he increased in size, his voice growing deeper and more menacing. “What were you thinking telling them about your escape tunnel?! You do realize that they can come in here and kill you as you sleep any time they want, right? They have all but guessed you’re some kind of Sidhe! If they realize you’re Danaan, we’re going to have to run. How am I supposed to help you when you won’t help yourself?!” He was so angry. He morphed from a Clouded Leopard into a massive Bengal Tiger, and by the end of his rant he was snarling.

Growling, he stalked towards me. I was scared of his intentions and backed into the counter in the kitchen, wondering if he would attack. He was almost on top of me. I could feel his breath on my face, every angry word blowing my hair around. I was leaning back over the sink, cringing away from his anger. I felt so small. In his tiger form, he dwarfed the large island and made the ceilings feel impossibly low. I felt a tear leak out of one of my eyes and stream down my face.

He must have seen my fear and visibly calmed down, flowing back into his leopard form as he backed away. "I'm sorry, Jocelyn. Please don't be afraid. I would never hurt you."

My heart raced and I could barely catch my breath. I sank down to the floor with shaking legs, trying to calm my nerves, more tears in my eyes. Being stalked and roared at by a very angry Bengal Tiger was enough to make even the strongest person wet their pants. Thankfully, I hadn't done that.

I looked up and Mateo had changed into a very contrite Belgian Shepherd and was lying on the floor in front of me with his head on his paws, his ears back. His eyes were full of remorse. "I'm so sorry, Joss. I lost my temper. I just can't stand the thought of you getting hurt."

I looked at him and understood. I remembered the feeling of helplessness as my foster family was beaten and killed. "Teo, all my life I've followed my instincts. Every time I got the feeling I should run, I did. Every time I had a hunch about a case, it paid off. Not once have they let me down. I can trust Baron Blackthorn. *We* can trust him."

Mateo huffed and I watched as he shifted back into a leopard. I reached out and he crawled towards me. He pushed his head under my hand, and I put my arms around him.

He started to purr and the sound rumbled through my chest, calming me. "I'm sorry for scaring you,

Joss..." he raised his head to look at me "...but I stand by what I said. With all due respect to your instincts, it's my job to keep you safe, and I can't do that if you expose our home."

I nodded, knowing I couldn't just make decisions on my own anymore. For the first time in my life, I had someone else to take into consideration. Mateo lived here too, and I had to realize my actions affected him as well.

"It won't happen again. I promise." I hugged him and then pushed up off the floor. "Are we still going to the Troll Market?"

He nodded. "I really need to talk to someone there, and we need some more spelling supplies."

"So what does one wear to the Troll Market?" I could hear him laughing as I went to change out of my dirty clothes.

Chapter Six

By eleven o'clock we were out the door and headed towards Seattle. I had taken the soft top off of the Jeep, and Mateo was enjoying the ride as he took in all the scents on the night air.

"So, where is the Troll Market?" I asked, looking at him sideways as I drove. "Do I head for the Aurora Bridge at Troll Avenue?" I asked casually, trying not to snicker over the thought of the colossal statue of a troll being the actual entrance to the Troll Market. In 1990 the Fremont Arts Council hosted a contest to rehabilitate the area, and the winners built a massive statue of a Troll under the Aurora Street Bridge.

"No," Mateo growled under his breath, sounding disgusted. "Shido was on the Arts Council at the time and suggested it; he thought it was hilarious. Sometimes that Shifter has the most warped sense of humour."

I tried to stifle my laugh. I thought it was pretty funny given everything I had learned in the last twenty-four hours.

"You know the Old Seattle?" Mateo asked, bringing the conversation back to the actual entrance of the Troll Market.

My head whipped around to look at him. "The part underground that they run tours for the tourists?" Surely not there.

"That's the one. The tunnel system is much more extensive than the humans know about. There's no football or baseball game tonight, so head towards the Triangle Pub at 1st Avenue and Railroad Way by Century Link Field. Park anywhere nearby. We can walk to the main gate from there," he said.

"Okay," I drawled out, unable to believe it. "Are you sure? I thought Trolls only lived under bridges?" My lips twitched and I looked sideways at him, waiting for the inevitable reaction.

Mateo only snorted at me and mumbled something like, "Stupid humans," and "Grimm brothers," under his breath.

A short time later we parked in a rather seedy area behind the pub, surrounded by the columns supporting the Alaskan Way Viaduct above us.

"Aren't we going to be kind of obvious?" I asked doubtfully as I climbed out of the Jeep. "I mean a dog can't exactly walk into a pub."

When my feet hit the ground, the streetlight on Railroad Way went out, plunging the already dim area into virtual darkness. The only light was from the neon beer signs in the pub windows across the street and a lone dim light bulb above a door surrounded by graffiti.

My steps were cautious, and my eyes kept darting from shadow to shadow.

"Relax, Joss," Mateo said softly as he led me across the street. At the very back corner of the historic building was a green door that served as the back entrance of the Triangle Pub. The Pub was over a hundred years old and used to be a brothel once upon a time. Now it was a popular place to get a drink while watching sports on one of the many televisions inside.

As we approached, the light over the green door went out, making me jump slightly. Shrouded in almost complete darkness, I reached out for Mateo, needing the feel of his fur under my hand to reassure me that this was okay.

His soft ears brushed my fingers as he ducked under my hand. "It's alright, this is completely normal. Watch." The cobblestone sidewalk in front of us started to disappear, and I looked on in amazement as a steep narrow stairway appeared where broken and cracked paving stones had been only moments before.

"Jeez, Teo, it's a good thing I'm short," I said, eyeing the black hole in front of me.

He chuckled and led me forward. "This entrance expands and contracts depending on the size of the being entering it. It can be as big as a house or as small as a fairy. Although, it doesn't get much traffic from the larger Sidhe these days because of the increase in human activity around the entrance."

"Cool." I hoped my voice wasn't giving away my tension as we walked into the bowels of the earth. "How did the stairs appear? How did it know that we weren't just regular humans? Was someone watching us?" I couldn't see the hand in front of my face. My tone may have been even but the rambling questions showed my nervousness. So much for sounding brave.

"The entrance was charmed to detect Sidhe and other creatures when it was built. Even if you hadn't known what you are, if you had walked back there last week, the same thing would have happened because the magick would have recognized you for whom and what you are," Mateo explained.

I could only imagine how much that would have freaked me out. Scenes from a dozen horror movies flashed through my mind, each one ending in me running away screaming, a masked man in a still bloody skin suit with a chainsaw in hand hot on my heels.

Stairs gave way to a sloping floor that made me stumble a bit at the change in terrain. As we made our way farther underground, the air became chilled. I was suddenly very glad that Mateo had insisted on my moss green, heavy wool, hooded cloak to go over my T-shirt and jeans, despite the heat of summer. I usually only used it when I was gathering plants in the mountains, but now I was grateful for its warmth. It was freezing in here. As we walked further into the darkness, I could feel the hair on the back of my neck stand up, my feet numb in my Converse. I stopped, shivering in the inky blackness, frozen and afraid to take another step for fear of tripping, or falling, or running into a wall, or getting eaten by something. I could feel my fear rising and my breath getting shorter. I did *not* want to be in here.

I flinched back as something brushed my hand.

"Easy, Joss, it's just me," Mateo said softly. "I should have warned you about the entrance. You're passing through the wards. A human would have been too scared to make it this far. Hang on to me. I won't let you fall. Everything will be fine." His voice caused an echo, and I realized we were now in a much larger space.

I felt him push his head under my hand and his back bump into my leg. He was taller than he was as a dog, and his hair was softer. He had changed back into his leopard form. I was still nervous but knowing he was with me, I was no longer scared. There had never been anyone I could completely rely on before, but after everything we had been through together over the last few nights, I knew he wouldn't let anything happen to me.

We had walked about thirty steps forward when the tunnel started to feel a bit warmer and brighter. Suddenly, I could see a faint dim glow in the distance.

"Pull your hood up. We're almost there." When I had done it, he chuckled. "Hang on to your broomstick, little witch, you're about to get your first look at real Trolls," Mateo said in a low voice, a hint of teasing in his tone.

Sure enough, as we got closer to the light, I could see two large, shifting shapes in the flickering light from the torches hanging in brackets along the wall. My amulet began its subtle vibration under my shirt as I blinked, my eyesight adjusting from the darkness behind us. The tunnel was wider here than it had been when we left the street above. It was about eight feet wide and fourteen feet tall with a domed ceiling fashioned out of old red bricks.

At the end of the tunnel was a large rusted iron door with large signs on it that stated, "TUNNEL SEALED BY ORDER OF THE CITY OF SEATTLE" and "DANGER—TUNNEL CONDEMNED"

Flanking the very solid looking door were two huge, brutish Trolls. Each one was easily seven feet tall with arms that were too long for their bodies and almost reaching their knees. The one on the left had a huge nose with a wart on the side of it. It had black, beady eyes with huge, bushy eyebrows and long, dirty brown hair that looked more like tree moss than hair. The one on the right was almost a twin of the first but was humpbacked with oversized ears that were pierced with bits of bone and wood decorated with bird feathers.

Both of them were in dire need of a dentist with black and yellow teeth that showed easily in their gaping mouths. They each carried huge gnarled clubs with metal spikes running through them and wore the remnants of, what used to be, grey cotton tunics over too small leather trousers. The pants were ragged and fell in tattered lengths at their knees, exposing huge, calloused, and moldy looking feet with long, broken, yellow toenails. The two of them were the embodiment of every child's nightmare. Shrinking further into the privacy of my hood, I clutched at Mateo's fur, nervous to be this close.

The two of them moved to block the closed door. I was confused as to how to even open the door, so blocking it was really unnecessary.

"No human." The mountain on the right grunted, making me cringe involuntarily.

Mateo snorted. "If you think she's a human, then why are you talking to her?"

"No human," insisted the pierced Troll.

I could practically feel Mateo's frustration. "Would I bring a human here? No. Now open the door."

I almost giggled. They were thinking really hard, and I could almost hear the gears grinding in their brains. They really didn't look very bright. I mean, they were arguing with a talking leopard in front of someone they thought was human!

The one on the left grunted. "Cat talk."

That must have settled something in their minds because they moved, and the one with the wart opened the huge rusty door with ridiculous ease.

"Thank you," I offered as we walked past them. I got a grunt for my trouble.

When I looked around I was stunned by what I saw. The ceiling was at least thirty feet high and was as wide as the two-lane human street somewhere above us. In some spots, glass blocks acted as skylights to the world above and would allow natural sunlight in during the day. "Can't the humans see though the blocks?" I asked.

"They work like a one way mirror. From above they look like pavement, but from below they're transparent blocks. The humans have no idea this place exists," he explained in a low voice.

Red brick-walled shops with ornate arched doorways lined the cobblestone street, but it wasn't like any street I had ever been on before. Trees were growing in two even rows down either side and had flowers that glowed brightly, which cast enough light it was like the street lights on the human streets above. How they grew in the subterranean environment was surely magick. There were no cars, only the occasional rickshaw that seemed to move around on its own; the whole place was a hive of activity.

A low hum of noise rose around me from the multitude of *beings* walking the street. The Market was as busy as any human mall. Fairies flitted about from tree to tree, going in and out of what looked like large bird houses. I realized that the fairies had a market of their own in the tree tops. Colorful birds perched in the trees; short, stocky men that looked like Dwarves wandered by, crossing paths with a Centaur; and a couple of little men that looked just like the gnome in Mrs. Jamison's garden bickered while eating some kind of black bread.

There were others that looked human except for the beaks they had in place of their nose and mouth. Some were cloaked and deeply hooded like me, while others were dressed in fine silks and brightly colored linens. Some beings were beautiful and graceful; others were the stuff horror movies were made of, with leathery wings and twisted forms; others still, looked completely human like me. All were welcome here and seemed to co-exist peacefully.

A tall, unnaturally pale guy gave me a long appraising look and inhaled deeply before flashing me a fangy smile. As I shrank away from him, I realized he had to be a Vampire. The inhumanly beautiful woman at his side frowned and ran her tongue across her own razor sharp fangs, clearly threatening me. Mateo let out a low feline growl, and she sniffed at him in dismissal, brushing past us and dragging her reluctant companion with her.

"Come on, I'll give you a tour before we go meet my friend. Keep your hood up, your head down, and stay close to me. Don't talk to anyone unless you have to," Mateo told me softly.

I flexed my hands in his fur to let him know I heard him. Another girl might have thought he was being overbearing and rude, but I knew I was way out of my depth here. I would be listening to my two thousand year old friend, thank you very much.

We carefully made our way down the left side of the street, and I looked around trying not to gawk. There was so much to see, but I didn't want to get caught staring. The center of the main street had a courtyard with a large fountain that was fed by a real river carefully shaped with stone to make it into a natural canal. As we crossed the bridge over the river-like canal, I looked to my left, following the deep water with my eyes as it wound down a smaller side street with narrow sidewalks. I could see people both swimming in the water and walking on the sidewalks along the banks, both entering and leaving several shops lining the street.

"The Market has almost a dozen streets and is divided up by purpose, each side-street being reserved for a specific species or category. The shops on the main street are ones that are all-purpose, catering to multiple races and species. That's Pisces Place. It's where the Merfolk, Naiad, and Selkie have shops," Mateo explained, seeing where I was looking. "Across the main street on your right is Bootes Road, the livery and stables where you can buy, rent, or board your mount."

Sure enough, when I looked to the right, I could see several paddocks off of a large barn. It looked like something out of an old western movie except the animals in the paddocks were creatures right out of myth. Large, horse-sized goats with two sets of spiralling horns; eight-legged horses; large deer-like creatures with the hind legs and wings of an eagle; huge oxen; and even a hippogriff. Honestly, I was going to have to brush up on my mythology if I was going to be able to function in this world.

Mateo led me up the left side of the main street. The next street we came across on the left looked decidedly high end.

"That's one of the only two, all Sidhe, hotels in the city. Obviously, it's for a more upscale crowd," Mateo explained.

I'll say. It looked like a supernatural version of the Waldorf Astoria. There was an expensive restaurant, a couple of clothing stores, as well as several posh looking cafés surrounding it. Some kind of winged monkey stood at the entrance, opening and closing the doors as patrons came and went. I paused to have a very *Wizard of Oz* moment before Mateo nudged my hand.

The next street we came to looked more like a forest lane. It had several smaller versions of the luminescent trees, a well-maintained dirt path, and radiant flowers growing outside every storefront.

"Sagittarius Road. The elves are pretty diverse in their wares. They sell everything from plants, to saddles and tack, to art and weapons. Although, the weapons they do sell are nowhere near the quality they use themselves. You'll only find apprentice made weapons and armour here." Mateo stuck close to my side, ready to nudge me forward when I lingered too long.

I looked and saw tall, fair-haired people moving from store to store. They looked completely human except for their serene grace and delicately pointed ears. They were beautiful.

I lingered in front of a store that had candles burning in the window, the smoke from the flames forming into shifting shapes of flowers, birds, and elegant animals. They were astounding. Mateo nudged me forward again, eager to continue.

The next street had several human looking ethnic restaurants, coffee houses, bookstores, a Best Buy, and an honest-to-Goddess Super 8 hotel. I giggled at seeing something so human amongst all the magick.

Mateo chuckled at my reaction. "Too normal for you?"

"Shut up! I just wasn't expecting to see a Super 8. I mean, really, we just passed a barbershop where I saw a Dwarf getting his beard braided and a sign in the window advertising a special on talon trimming. The Super 8 and the Best Buy don't exactly fit in," I whispered to him, embarrassed that he had caught me having a human moment.

"True." He smirked.

The main street narrowed and turned into what was obviously a vegetable and meat market. When I went to walk down it, Mateo bumped me to the right and we crossed the main street. "Nothing special to see down there. We'll walk back on the other side of the street."

I stopped to look in the window of an Apothecary, the scales and ceremonial knives in the window drawing my eye. It looked like a reputable place, and the drying plants were hung correctly in orderly rows inside. For someone like me it was a veritable toy store.

Mateo herded me away from the window, probably guessing I would stand there all night if he let me. We made our way back towards the entrance of the Market, and Mateo continued my tour after promising to come back to the Apothecary before we left.

The next side street we came to had several burly, heavily bearded men coming and going from it. They were short and stern looking with heavy leather tunics and pants that were decoratively studded here and there with metals and stones. Not one of them was taller than my shoulder, putting them well below my own five foot two and making me feel unusually tall.

"Dwarfs," Mateo offered, answering my unasked question. "They sell the heavier weapons. Swords, armour, helmets, hammers, shields, chainmail—that sort of thing. Dwarfs are master metal workers and miners. They live deep in the mountains, choosing to build their cities underground to be closer to the raw ore they use for crafting their weapons. The whole street is devoted to multiple shops for the sale and repair of weaponry." He looked up at me and smiled slightly. "Needless to say, angering a Dwarf really isn't the best idea. They tend to be rather grouchy."

We continued walking, but I got hung up looking in the window of the most amazing shoe store, like a typical woman. It was huge and had shoes of every color, size, and shape—everything from stiletto heels to brilliantly decorated sandals, heavy combat boots to fairy shoes. I was sure I glimpsed gold and diamond studded horse shoes before Mateo pushed me forward.

"Oh, we are *so* coming back here, mister!" I said sternly to Mateo.

He laughed. "Then we'll be steering clear of the next street as well. It's where the Gnomes have their jewellery stores. They make Harry Winston and Tiffany's look like flea market junk. Stones the size of the Hope diamond are more their forte. *That* pretty piece was lost in a card game. The loser was convinced the winner had cheated somehow. So before he turned it over, he put a curse on it. No one ever expected it would ever make it into human hands, and once it did, no one really cared enough to worry about the curse and its effect on humans. Like the Dwarfs, Gnomes like to work with metal, but they prefer precious metals and jewels. Even the elves come to buy from the Gnomes when it comes to jewellery."

True to his word, Mateo hustled me past Lapis Lane so I only caught a glimpse of brilliant flashes of color and sparkling points of light, small men and women no taller than three feet bustling around the obvious shoppers.

"Mateo," I whined, and he chuckled lowly.

"Another time, Joss, we're running late. Come on." He pushed me from behind, forcing me to keep walking. We passed a small office space that had a single long counter with several people seemingly signing items in and out. I paused trying to figure out what was going on. "What's that?"

"A charging station. Cell phones, laptops, and the like are really popular, but not every species has access to electrical outlets and the internet. The whole market is a Wi-Fi hotspot, and you can take your devices there to be charged. You fill out a form when you drop it off and when you're finished shopping you can pick it up fully charged," Mateo explained.

The whole thing made perfect sense, but it still amazed me that some of those creatures would need a cell phone. Mateo gave me a small push again as I watched a couple of fairies with dragonfly wings fly in carrying a cell phone between them.

"But cell phones?"

We walked as he explained. "Well, we used to use birds to communicate, but not only are they messy, your letters can be lost when something bigger eats the bird. Plus, birds are easily bribed and can be captured. When humans came up with phones, and then later cell phones, it made much more sense. And now fairies can communicate like everyone else. Birds were a big problem for them because to most birds big enough to carry a letter, fairies are food."

The next street was much wider and it was obvious why when I watched Centaurs making their way in and out of the various stores amongst all the other, more humanoid, shoppers.

"The Centaurs are master leather workers and archers. Anything and everything that can be made out of leather, the best comes from the Centaurs. Their bows and arrows are comparable to the ones the Dark Elves make but are readily obtainable," Mateo explained.

"Dark Elves?"

"Like there are dark and light fairies, there are dark and light elves. The elves you've seen around the market are all Light Elves. They interact with others the most. Dark Elves, on the other hand, are secretive, aggressive, ruthless in battle, have a well-documented disdain for other races, and will fight without provocation. In a secretive world, they are a mystery. Not much is known about them for sure other than their weapons are of the highest grade and they live in the deepest, darkest forests in the world. Anywhere that is virtually inaccessible is generally the domain of the Dark Elves. They're vicious fighters, relentless trackers, and their *only* loyalty is to themselves." He looked up at me in time to see a shiver run down my spine.

"We should go to meet my friend now." Mateo's face shifted from severe to one of concern. "Maybe this was a bad idea," he mumbled half to himself. "I should have left you at home and come alone."

I was filled with conflicting emotions: anger at his assumption that he could leave me anywhere or tell me to stay like a naughty child and worried he was concerned about me being here. "It's too late now. I'm already here. Why are you so worried? We've been here for over an hour and nothing bad has happened."

He studied me carefully and his worry was almost palpable. "We're going to a bar in the seediest part of the Market. A bar where things regularly turn nasty. You could get hurt, Joss."

I reached out and put my hand on his shoulder. "Nothing's going to happen. We're going to go in there, and you're going to talk to whomever while I sit with my back to the wall and a drink in my hand. I won't take my hood down, and I won't talk to strangers."

He looked skeptical but nodded. He turned down Centaurus Street, and weaving carefully around the shoppers, headed for the end. Slipping through a narrow break in the wall at the end of the street, we walked down a tight alleyway that seemed more like a sewer tunnel without the water. The brick ceiling was only a few feet above me now. Without enough room to walk side-by-side, I tried to stay on Mateo's heels as he made his way through the clutter and garbage. It was dark, dirty, and creepy. There were things scurrying around in the darkness that had me flinching and feeling distinctly claustrophobic.

The passageway opened up into a seedy looking back alley that was more suited to a cliché horror movie set than the beauty and bustle of the main street of the Troll Market only a few yards behind us. Torches hung here and there, dimly lighting the dark and garbage strewn alley. The walls were tall blackened brick and looked like they had never been cleaned after the fire that had caused Seattle to be rebuilt on top of the old one. The air was oppressive and rank with the smell of unwashed bodies and filth. There were shops and kiosks here as well, but where the ones in the main street were bright and had friendly owners hawking their wares, these ones were dark and sinister. The windows were cloudy with a dirty film and displayed sinister looking wares. I could feel the malevolent atmosphere pushing on my skin and making me nervous.

A boney hand with talon-like nails snaked out and grasped my forearm, scaring me. “Have a drink, little pretty pretty. One sip and you’ll forget all your troubles.” Noxious smelling breath drifted over me making me stagger slightly, the voice a cackling whine. The scary woman breathed on me again from behind black, cracked, and broken teeth set inside a too wide mouth, and I tried to hold my breath. She looked like every horrible description of a witch I had ever heard. She had large black eyes, sallow sickly looking skin, and her hair was long, greasy, and heavily tangled. Her nose was oversized, hooked, and had an honest-to-Goddess wart on the side of it with whiskers sprouting from the center. Her black robes were tattered and dirty and emanated their own special brand of stench as she pulled me closer to her, offering a foul smelling cup that had a purple tinted fog spilling from it.

I tried to pull away from the crone-like woman gripping my arm, her strong fingers like a manacle that refused to budge. The stench of her breath made me dizzy. "No, thank you." I pulled harder but couldn't get my arm back. "Let me go."

"Don't be like that, pretty pretty. Such lovely skin you have. For a few drops of your blood, I'll—" Her wheedling cackle cut off with a screech as Mateo struck out and raked her arm with his sharp claws, leaving four ragged gashes oozing something black and instantly releasing me from her grasp.

He snarled loudly and took another swipe at her as I clutched my arm to my body, rubbing away the sting and filth as I tried not to cower behind him. "Keep your filthy hands off, hag! You won't be getting one drop of her blood, and if I catch you here again, I'll make sure you won't need anyone's blood ever again!"

The hag dodged his second swipe and wore a fearful expression on her face. "Wasn't doing nothing wrong, Shifter. Didn't know the pretty pretty was spoken for. No harm done."

Mateo snarled, exposing his wickedly sharp, dagger-like canines, and she backed away. "Leave, hag, before I change my mind about killing you."

By the time she scurried away and Mateo had turned back to me, I was shaking.

"Are you alright? Did she hurt you?" he asked quietly.

I shook my head. "No, not really. Just scared me a little."

He looked around and I got the feeling he wanted to comfort me but felt like he couldn't here. There were several menacing characters watching from the deepest shadows, and showing weakness would have been a huge mistake.

Chapter Seven

I pulled my cloak closer around me as we made our way towards a dark and sinister looking bar with Mateo pressed closely to my side.

"Come, we'll get you a drink while I talk to Anansi," he said, nudging me towards the doorway with his head.

The wooden sign over the entrance showed the gory severed head of Medusa with *The Gorgon's Head* carved below it in block letters.

Mateo saw me read the sign and explained. "Anansi named the bar after his ex-wife. He said, like Medusa, she was once beautiful and sweet until after they got married when she turned into a deadly monster who could freeze him with a look. After their divorce things got *really* ugly. When word got around he had named his bar after her, she tried to press charges against him for death threats and libel."

I stifled a giggle, the stress from the confrontation with the hag gone in the wake of the revelation that even among the Sidhe, things as normal as a nasty divorce still happened.

"Don't talk to anyone and stay as deep in that cloak as you can so it's not easy to see your face. We don't want anyone finding out about you. In fact, it would be best if you remained *unnoticed,*" Mateo said as we passed through the entrance.

I knew by the way that he stressed unnoticed he was asking me to invoke my cloaking spell so I would be all but invisible. I nodded minutely as I adjusted my hood, wordlessly letting him know I understood.

We went inside and I was assaulted by thick smoke, unfamiliar smells, and a cacophony of sound. Some kind of music that reminded me a bit of Indian sitars was playing loudly from behind a speaker in the corner. There was a typical round bar in the middle surrounded by mismatched barstools occupied by a mix of drinking patrons, all talking loudly in a variety of languages—some seemingly in squeals and grunts. Bartenders stood in the middle backed by hundreds of bottles and flasks made out of a variety of materials: glass, leather pouches, baskets, and even some potted flowers.

Mateo didn't waste any time, and he immediately led me to a quieter back corner. My nose wrinkled when I felt my feet sticking to the floor with every step. The table he led me to was set up in the deepest shadows and would allow me to sit with my back to the wall. It was already occupied but a fearsome snarl from Mateo had the person–or was it a creature–vacating it quickly. I got a quick glimpse of tentacles before the figure was absorbed into the crowd. The area around me looked like it was set up with a variety of gaming tables.

I sat down and gathered my cloak around me while Mateo went to order me a drink. "After the waitress brings it to you, disappear. I'll be back soon." I nodded and he was gone.

A minute later I saw him head to the back of the bar and watched as he was greeted by a terrifying creature. It was a tall, thin, wiry, bare-chested man with skin as black as the fur covering the rest of his body, which was unmistakably a giant tarantula complete with eight furry legs. He was horrifically unsettling with long, ebony hair. Huge, black, wickedly sharp fangs that reached his chin were slick with venom. Eight onyx eyes seemed to take in everything around him, including me. What kind of creature had married *that*? Maybe she had turned him into that? Mateo had said the divorce was nasty.

I shivered and tried in vain to shrink further into my hood when those fathomless black eyes briefly paused on me as he surveyed the bar. His movements were as calculating and sure as any tarantula I had seen in a pet store. His body may have been thin and spidery, but he was obviously strong, and I knew nothing went unobserved around him. Despite his fearsome appearance, he seemed genuinely happy to see Mateo, and the two of them went into a back room and out of my sight.

Quickly, a waitress approached the table with my drink. She looked like a lioness walking upright but with a slightly human cast to her feline features. Her eyes glowed a brilliant gold, and she was human from the waist down. She wore a skirt that appeared to be nothing more than two panels of fabric that attached at the hips, leaving her long, shapely legs exposed with every step. She had large naked breasts barely covered by her long tawny blonde hair. Her forearms were furred and her hands looked like long-fingered cats' paws with claws rather than human hands.

"Elven wine, from your-r-r companion," she said with a purr, setting a chalice on the table in front of me.

"Thank you," I said, taking a small sip. It was amazing, sweet tasting like ripe summer berries but with the slight burn of the finest whiskey.

I must have made a moan of appreciation because the waitress gave me an appraising look and appeared to be trying to see past the privacy of my hood. "You'r-r-re too pur-r-re to be in here; you should be car-r-reful or someone will notice," she said in a low voice.

I looked up into her slightly worried eyes. "I will. Thank you for the warning."

She walked off with a swish of her long fur-tufted tail, swatting at the wandering hands of some of the other patrons, and I quickly invoked my cloaking spell. As I sat there, I watched the happenings of the bar warily. I was able to use the hood to my advantage, not relying entirely on the spell, remembering Mateo had said it wouldn't work on everyone. I was quickly learning about the many types of creatures that previously I had thought existed only in legends and scary stories. I had to admit, in this bar, it was filled with more of the scary story type of people, and I really didn't want to draw their notice.

Mateo was right. I shouldn't be here. But I knew that had I stayed in the main square, I wouldn't have felt safe either. Knowing he wasn't far away and could get to me quickly gave me a peace of mind I hadn't ever felt before. And strangely enough, I knew he felt the same way.

There was some kind of card game not too far away that captured my attention. There were five players: a Dwarf, who was dirtier and more threatening than any I had seen on the main street; a massively muscled black Minotaur with impressive curving horns; a slimy guy who looked like some kind of frogman; a man, who appeared to be a Vampire by the look of his fangs and pale skin; and another man who was cloaked and hooded like myself.

The man captured my attention with his dark allure. Not only did the cloak hide him, but he sat with his back to a brick column that cast a deep shadow. From what little I could see, his features were rugged and strong, and he had the dusty look of someone who had been travelling for some time. When he reached forward to place a bet, the hood shifted a bit and revealed close cropped hair that was little more than a shadow over his head. Dark coffee-colored skin with the scruff of several days' growth graced a strong jaw and chin that still showed the barest hint of a cleft. His cheek bones were high and angled perfectly towards his hidden ears. But his eyes were what caught me; they were the near black of the finest dark chocolate. He looked to be much taller than the other occupants of the table with the exception of the Minotaur, and he was wearing a sleeveless leather tunic of the deepest black that laced up in the front over a forest green linen shirt. He was altogether gorgeous.

As I studied him, I was startled when his eyes met mine, penetrating my cloaking spell and the deep folds of my hooded cloak. Embarrassed to be caught staring, I quickly averted my eyes to the frogman just in time to see him palm a card and switch it with one in his hand. It was deftly done, and had I not looked at that exact moment, I knew I would never have caught it. The frogman exchanged a speaking glance with the Vampire, and I knew they were in it together.

Dirty cheaters!

When I looked back at the man, his attention was back on the game, having missed the whole thing. After watching a few more hands, I realized the Dwarf was in on the cheat as well. The man casually glanced at my corner a couple more times as I silently watched the game but did nothing to call attention to me.

What in the name of the Goddess was taking Matco so long? I could feel pressure building behind my eyes. I was getting tired from trying to hold my cloaking spell for so long, and the drink I had carefully been nursing was now empty.

The crowd around the bar parted with jeers and raucous laughter, and everyone's attention was drawn to a heftily built woman who looked like a Centaur but with the body of a red spotted cow as she awkwardly made the rounds through the bar. She desperately flashed a picture that held the image of a very young Centaur. "Please? Have you seen m-m-my calf? He's only two years old. Please, som-m-meone took him-m-m."

For the most part she was being ignored or laughed at, and my heart went out to her. Unfortunately, in a place like this, she wasn't getting any kind of sympathy and absolutely no help.

My view was rudely interrupted by a body. The chest was clearly male, bare and well-muscled but with an obvious beer gut. The torso became furred at the bottom of his rib cage and got thicker over the muscles of his goat legs and cloven feet, allowing me to identify him as a Satyr. I flushed ten shades of red when I realized that Satyrs apparently didn't wear pants, and he was *very* happy to see me. I quickly looked up to avoid the sight of his very erect penis and overlarge balls; he was taller than me by a few inches, and when I looked up into his face, he was wearing a goatee and a distinctly lecherous smile just for me.

Lucky, lucky me. So much for trying to stay unnoticed.

He took another step forward and took a long, slow sniff and then licked his lips. Was this normal behaviour? Was he hitting on me or sizing me up as a meal? I had encountered predatory guys in human bars before, but *nothing* had prepared me for an experience quite like this one. My eyes nervously flickered back to the now twitching penis. I wasn't used to creatures like him being so close to me and was terrified he might try to brush that *thing* against me.

Seeing my glance, he chuckled. "Yeah, it's big. If you pet it, it spits." He winked at me.

I jerked back, trying to distance myself from him and his sexually aggressive behaviour, half afraid of his threat becoming a reality.

"Mmmm...aren't you a breath of spring air. Tell me, sweetness, are you a thief? Because you sure have stolen my heart." His tone was oily with practiced seduction, deep and absolutely serious.

When I sat there stunned at the sight, never mind the truly terrible pick-up line, he decided to try his luck again.

"My name's Silvani. I'm a little...*horny*." He ran his tongue over his thin lips and touched the horns growing out of his forehead above his long goat-like ears. "How about I buy you another drink and we get to know each other? Intimately..."

He gestured to an unseen waitress for a drink before turning back to me. "You have a beautiful mouth. Do you like kids? I ask because I'd like to turn your mouth into a daycare."

I gagged and almost threw up in my mouth. He saw me swallowing my revulsion and smiled lecherously. "Good, you swallow. I like that in a woman."

I didn't know what to say. Was this guy for real? "Do those lines ever *actually* work for you? I mean...you're kidding, right?"

"Awww...come on, sweetness, you know you like it." He eased closer to me and punctuated his statement with a thrust of his hips, bringing me way too close to his bits and pieces. He sat down at the only other stool at my small table. "Why don't you come and sit on my lap and we can talk about the first thing that *pops* up?"

He patted his lap in invitation, and the obscene thing he called a cock twitched as if in agreement.

I looked past Silvani, trying to spot Mateo; my eyes went to the card table and locked with the amused gaze of the hooded man. I was glad someone found this funny.

The man gestured to the waitress who had brought me my wine and whispered in her ear.

My unwelcome table companion trailed a presumptuous finger up my arm and reached for my hood, refocusing my attention to the problem at hand. I jerked away so violently I almost tipped off my chair. Righting myself quickly, I shifted my gaze back to the annoyance in front of me. "Look, I'm not interested. I'm waiting for someone. Someone who *isn't* you. I suggest you leave before he gets here." I really didn't want to have to do something drastic to get rid of this creep.

"Pssh!" He waved off my suggestion arrogantly. "I've been watching you for half an hour; he's not coming. Lucky for you I showed up." He tried to put his hand on my thigh.

I pulled out of his grasp and subtly reached down to pull up my pant leg, reaching for the knife I had sheathed there. "Last warning. Touch me again and I'll geld you!" I warned him. I didn't care if I started a fight or if this was the way all Satyr greeted people in this community. I was having none of it.

Suddenly, sitting in the corner didn't seem to be such a great idea. He had me trapped. How had this clown even seen me back here between the gloom of the place, my spell, and my cloak? Obviously, I had been too tired to hold onto the spell.

"Awww...don't be like that. We're having a nice conversation. Unless you just want to skip it and get to the good part? I'll show you where the phrase 'randy as a goat' came from." He closed his eyes and leaned forward as if to kiss me.

Just as I pulled my knife, there was a snarl behind him, and he was knocked from his stool to the floor.

An enraged Mateo stood over Silvani. He had shifted to a Bengal Tiger and his razor sharp teeth were inches from Silvani's throat, saliva dripping from the five-inch canines.

I stood, fully revealing my hooded presence. Making sure my knife was highly visible, I warily looked around to make sure Mateo wasn't about to be jumped from behind.

As my eyes passed over the card table, the man smirked and winked at me from the darkness of his own hood. Realization hit me like a bat to the head; he had told the waitress to find Mateo and warn him I was in trouble. He somehow read the shock on my face through the shadows of my hood and nodded once, acknowledging my thought.

Silvani was pale and sweating under Mateo's angry growls. His erection had deflated like a popped balloon, and I was willing to bet his balls were trying to crawl their way back under the shelter of the beer gut. "I didn't mean any harm. I was just keeping her company for you is all!"

"The lady told you she wasn't interested. You should have listened," Mateo snarled.

As I stepped back, I stumbled over someone's foot. I would have been sent tumbling but sure hands caught me. When I gasped in fear, the support fell away as the hands released me. Looking down, I saw long, thin hands with eight nimble, grey and black fuzz covered fingers. I looked up to see eight fathomless black orbs staring at me over long venomous fangs.

Little house spiders scare me—falling into the grasp of a six foot tall arachnid? I did what any normal spastic girl would do. I screamed.

I violently jerked back, causing me to stumble yet again, and this time there wasn't anyone hurrying to catch me. Just as I imagined I was about to hit the ground, I landed in someone's lap. Bracing myself for more horrors, I cracked open an eyelid.

I met the amused gaze of the hooded card player. "Well, hello there."

Hurrying to right myself, I stammered out an apology. "I'm so sorry...I was...it's just...ummm..."

"My pleasure," he offered with a twitch of his lips that told me he was holding back a laugh. His voice was low and smooth, confident. "Don't worry, Anansi is basically harmless," he whispered.

His words reminded me of the reason I had landed in his lap. Clutching my cloak around me and making sure my hood still shrouded my face, I turned to see Mateo still snarling over the Satyr who had nearly molested me. As I stood there shaking, my eyes shifted to see the terrifying Anansi standing with his arms crossed over his chest as he watched the scuffle. One of those black eyes must have caught me staring, and he turned to me.

"My apol-ogies for fright-ening you." His voice was reedy and low, a strange over enunciated accent edging his drawn-out speech. Each syllable almost sounded like a separate word. I realized the large fangs made speaking tricky.

"N-no, I'm s-sorry I reacted t-that way. It...it w-was rude." Every second word seemed to stutter as it left my mouth. All I could think was, "*Holy fuck! It's a freaking six foot spider! There is no table high enough to get away from that! Raid! I need Raid! Why don't I have Raid in my bag?*"

I took a small step back and felt my butt hit something. My head spun to see the card player. For the moment he wasn't a threat. My head darted back to keep a watch on the embodiment of every arachnophobe's worst nightmare. My breath was coming in gasps, and I flinched when I felt a hand at the small of my back. When it pressed a bit harder, a thumb casually caressing me, I realized that for some reason the man was supporting me in my mini freak out.

Anansi smiled around his fangs, and the sight wasn't as friendly as I think he intended. Another row of smaller razor sharp teeth were exposed, these ones somehow looking even more menacing than the large fangs on display. As black as the rest of him, they looked more like protruding sharpened extensions of his jaw than teeth and caused me to shudder in fear.

How the hell did the man call this thing *basically harmless*?

"No of-fence ta-ken. I know I am not everyone's idea of...cud-dly." All but two of his eyes were trained on me now, and I couldn't control my shaking. "Al-though I would be wil-ling to offer you a demon-stration."

My heart was hammering at the speed of a hummingbird's wings as I gasped for air, and all I could think of was the child's nursery rhyme. *Come into my parlor, said the spider to the fly...*

A roar pulled my attention to the ongoing confrontation between Mateo and my would-be molester. I shrunk back further into the supporting palm of the man behind me.

Everyone in the bar seemed to be highly entertained by the show in front of them, but we were drawing far too much attention. People were starting to take notice of me, wondering what all the fuss was about, and we didn't want that.

"Mateo, I'd l-like t-to leave. The d-desperate little man is b-beneath our notice," I said, wishing for a steady voice, hoping to portray an aura of bored authority, but my stuttering made it a spectacular failure.

Mateo backed up and off the humiliated Satyr so he was standing with his back to my legs. I clutched at his fur, terrified of the entertained giant tarantula-man still staring at me. Mateo's tail wrapped around my leg and seemed to somehow help me to breathe, but I wanted nothing more than to leave.

"Anansi, your bar needs a better class of clientele," Mateo said, still glaring at the cowering Silvani.

"Ah, but then where would I find my enter-tainment?" He chuckled.

We turned to leave but a noise behind me had me whirling back to see Silvani on the ground clutching his chest in pain.

He had pulled a knife.

Mateo's claws had left four long, deep, bleeding gashes that went from his shoulder to the opposite hip. Any deeper and he might have been disemboweled.

"Last warning, Satyr. Next time I eat goat for dinner," Mateo spat, and he turned to look at me. Fury warred with concern before he flicked his eyes to the door, indicating that we were leaving.

As we made our way to the door, I touched the arm of my lioness-like waitress to get her attention. She fell into step beside me as I whispered in her ear.

"Please take the hooded man at the poker table a cup of your best wine." I nodded in the direction of the card table and my unlikely saviour. "Tell him it's from me and that he has my thanks for the help. Also, please tell him the game is fixed," I whispered and pressed a fifty dollar bill into her hand, hoping it was enough and they took human money here.

Her feral eyes gave me an assessing look; she nodded and gave me a small smile, exposing her own wickedly sharp teeth. "Come back and see us again. Honour-r-rable customers like you ar-r-re always welcome her-r-re."

I nodded and squeezed her arm slightly before making for the door on unsteady legs. Yeah, not likely.

Mateo and I quickly made our way back to the center square of Main Street, and I shakily lowered myself to sit on a partially secluded bench that had a wonderful view of the large fountain. It was a few minutes before I caught my breath and the adrenaline faded from my body. As Mateo paced in front of me, he very slowly morphed from the huge Bengal Tiger to the smaller Clouded Leopard that was his regular form as his anger faded to irritation.

"I should have had you wait here," he grumbled to himself. Some of it was hard for me to make out.

"It's done. We're both alright."

He stopped pacing to sit beside me. "You could have been hurt. The Satyr was the least of our worries in that place. I should never have taken you there."

"I wasn't hurt. It was actually pretty entertaining before goat-boy got pushy." I bumped his shoulder with my knee, trying to make light of everything. Now that I wasn't in the thick of things, it was actually pretty funny.

"Entertaining? I take you to a bar that has some of the most vicious beings in our world and you call it *entertaining*?" He shook his head in wonderment. "I saw some of the species in there, and I wouldn't call them entertaining. How is it that in forty-eight hours you find out almost every mythical creature you have ever heard of is real and yet you're not scared out of your mind when you come face to face with them?"

"Trust me, your spider friend? Scared the daylights out of me! I *hate* spiders." I shuddered at the memory of his long furry fingers on me. Shaking off the urge to do a girly shrieking freak-out dance worthy of Goldie Hawn in *Bird on a Wire* when she takes a shower with a cockroach, I merely shrugged. "But I figure, just like in the human world, there are good people and bad people. So to speak," I said with a smile.

"Yes, but any one of those creatures could have killed you," he stated.

"A human with a knife or a gun could kill me just as easily, as we found out two nights ago," I said, reminding him of the very human Inquisitors who had very nearly succeeded. "Just because someone looks scary doesn't mean they're going kill you. I've met and seen many people who looked nice and who were beautiful but who were nasty to the core." Too many foster homes, cheating spouses, and missing person's cases would do that to you. I let the view of a happy family of Merpeople relaxing in the fountain wash away the unpleasant memories of my youth.

"Were you able to get all the information you needed?" I asked, hoping to distract him.

He let out a huff. "Yes, and more. There's been an increase in Inquisitor activity lately. More and more of them seem to be in and around Seattle. It seems there have been quite a few children disappearing over the last month. Three to be exact, with rumors of a fourth. It's not normal for Sidhe children to go missing," Mateo said. "Anansi seems to think the same Inquisitors that attacked you could be responsible. He was very happy to hear that at least one of them won't be bothering anyone again."

"I saw a—I think it was a Centaur? She had the body of a cow though. She was asking if anyone had seen her calf in the bar." I felt a clenching in my chest as I thought of the desperate face of the mother, the tears running down her cheeks as she begged for any scrap of information.

"Bucentaur—half man, half bull. Or in her case, cow. She won't give up. Apparently, her calf was one of the first to go missing. There is also a Dwarf and a Kirata child missing."

"Kirata?" I was distracted from the thought of the anguish the parents must be going through by the unfamiliar term.

"Your waitress was a Kirata. The males are tigers from the waist up and human from the waist down. Females more closely resemble lions," he explained absently. "Fucking Inquisitors need to be stopped!"

The unexpected curse had me looking sharply at Mateo. It was the first time I had heard him curse, and while I had no real problem with it, it caught me off guard. "It's not just Sidhe children that are missing. I can think of three human kids in the last month as well."

He looked up at me. "Let's go back to the Apothecary and get your things. Anansi is combing his web of informants for more information; he's going to let me know if he hears anything. We can think about this tomorrow."

After a very fun trip to the Apothecary, where I found out the Market did indeed take human money, we left the store with a new mortar and pestle; sea salt; a new set of scales; a lockable iron box; and measuring spoons with odd measurements on them like thumb drop, pinch, and palmful; as well as various hard to find herbs, plants, and other spelling ingredients. It was close to two in the morning when we finally made our way back to the human streets above the Market.

We were just as careful as when we went in, and the streets were eerily quiet, which was probably why I heard the sounds of a fight so easily in the alley just ahead of us. Both Mateo and I froze when we heard the thuds and grunting as someone took some heavy blows. Mateo let out a chilling growl when we caught the words that were being said.

"Minion of Satan, repent your sins and offer your life to the glory of God!"

Inquisitors.

Chapter Eight

"Stay here!" Mateo growled at me and took off in the direction of the fight.

"Oh, fat chance of that!" I mumbled to myself and took off after him.

When I rounded the corner into the alleyway, I saw three men kicking and punching a body on the ground while a fourth read from a bible. Mateo had shifted into a huge wolfhound and turned to give me a dirty look for following him.

"Don't look at me like that. I can help!" I snapped.

Mateo jumped into the fray, scattering the Inquisitors beating the downed man. Dropping my bags, I swirled my cloak over an arm so I wouldn't trip and ran in with my knife drawn. I went straight for the unconscious guy and rolled him over to see it was the same man who had helped me in the Gorgon's Head. Only now, without the hood, I could clearly see that his ears were delicately pointed like the ones I had seen on the elves in the Market.

"Lord and Lady!" The exclamation came out unbidden, almost a prayer. The elf's face looked like raw, bloody hamburger.

My attention was drawn back to the ongoing fight. Mateo was a blur, leaping and savagely biting before spinning to take on another. The guy with the bible was running down the street the best he could with a limp, and something told me he was one of the guys from the other night.

While Mateo was bravely fighting two of the attackers, the third one was advancing on me and the elf lying beside me. I raised my knife, angry that these men were so bigoted as to needlessly hate something just because it was different than them. They had attacked me, attacked the elf that had helped me for no reason, and may be involved in kidnapping innocent children. I was furious.

That self-righteous cockroach of a man rushed us, and all I could think was "Stop!" as I threw up my hand.

To my surprise he seemed to slam into an invisible wall, falling back and hitting his head hard on the pavement.

Mateo, meanwhile, had one of the others on the ground and the man wasn't moving. The last two helped each other to their feet and ran into the darkness.

"Mateo." He didn't seem to hear me as he viciously shook the lifeless body of the downed Inquisitor.

"MATEO!" He turned around with a snarl, and his green eyes seemed to be glowing. Blood was dripping from his razor sharp teeth and muzzle.

When he realized it was me, his fury faded into irritated anger. "We have to get you out of here. They'll be back with reinforcements." He shook his head and shaggy coat, and in typical dog fashion, sprayed me with drool and blood.

I gave him a dirty look as I tried to brush the nastiness off my cloak. My dry cleaner was going to have a fit. "What about *him*?" I asked, gesturing to the elf as I wiped some kind of wetness off my cheek. *Yuck*!

"What about him? We're leaving," he snarled before turning as if to lead me away.

"We can't just leave him here! He's hurt and when they come back they'll kill him!" I protested, not believing he had even suggested it.

"Jocelyn, that's a Dark Elf; he can take care of himself!" Mateo roared, shifting into his usual shepherd form.

"For Goddess' sake, Teo, he's unconscious! We can't leave him here to be found by humans! And I *won't* leave him here to be killed by Inquisitors! Now either help me or go home!" I yelled, trying to pull the large body into a sitting position. The elf moaned and my attention was drawn back to him as I assessed his injuries.

His face was awash with blood making it hard to do an accurate assessment. One of his eyes was completely swollen shut with a cut on his eyebrow. His nose was obviously broken, his cheek had a huge gash in it, there was a two-inch cut near his hairline, and his mouth was split in more than one place. I felt around the back of his head, and he groaned as my hand brushed a lump from a blow to the head. When I pulled my fingers away, they too were red.

I heard Mateo sigh and move closer. "Lift him up a bit and get him on my back." I struggled a bit as Mateo nosed his way under the unconscious elf. "Straddle me and keep him steady. I'm going to shift."

I attempted to balance the unconscious elf and hold on tight as Mateo began to shift upwards, fawn and black fur melting into black satin, lifting me and the elf on my lap higher and higher as he changed from a shepherd into a massive black Andalusian stallion. We were a long way off the ground, and I grabbed on to Mateo's long, thick, silky mane to keep the two of us from toppling off. I could feel Mateo's massive muscles shifting under me as he tossed his head in irritation, his long forelock covering most of his face and making me wonder how he was able to see. My breath caught at how beautiful he looked and how much I appreciated him doing this for me.

"Let's get a move on; I'm not in the right form to defend you when they come back," Mateo grumbled and then loudly snorted all over the dead Inquisitor still lying where Mateo had dropped him. It was more than a little disturbing to see such a beautiful horse with a muzzle dripping with blood. It made me think of the horses of the Wild Hunt from Celtic legend that chased down the wicked and carried mortals off to the land of the dead or a demon horse from the land of Mordor. I *really* needed to read up on so-called mythical beasts and have Mateo tell me if they exist or not. I did find it interesting to learn that Mateo may shift from form to form, but the gore on him stayed the same. Good to know.

I gripped hard with my legs and held on to the elf draped across my lap as Mateo slowly started walking.

It didn't take us long to make our way back to the Jeep. With a little maneuvering, a lot of pulling, shoving, and more than a few moans and groans from the elf, I managed to get him into the front seat. I buckled him in and was just finishing putting the convertible top back up as Mateo dogtrotted back with the bags I had dropped. We were quickly on our way. I put the Jeep in gear and drove away from the waterfront. Mateo was in his usual public form as a Belgian Shepherd, sitting in the back as we argued.

"No, Joss, we are NOT taking him home! You promised to talk to me about these things, and I am telling you as your roommate, your friend, and your protector—I don't want this!" Mateo growled.

"Well, where do you suggest I take him? He needs medical care and we can't exactly dump him at a hospital. I can help him, but I can't do it in the back of my Jeep!" There was no way I was abandoning him somewhere without at least seeing to his injuries.

The silence in the Jeep was deafening as the two of us refused to give ground.

"We'll take him to a motel or something. You can do the healing there and then set wards on the room to keep him safe," Mateo grudgingly offered.

"Thank you." My voice was quiet, but I hated the thought that he was mad at me for something I knew was right.

It was a good compromise, and as I turned into the first motel I could find, some of Mateo's tension faded from his body. We weren't in the best part of town, and the place was a dump, but it was somewhere no one would ask too many questions.

I asked for the largest room they had, and at this time of the morning, I'm sure the desk clerk thought I was either a housewife arranging her affair or a hooker renting a room for her trick.

Whatever. He would never guess the truth, and he didn't ask any questions as I expected.

The horse would have been too conspicuous, so Mateo went with some sort of huge dog that looked like a Mastiff, but it was still a struggle to get the injured elf to the room. I unlocked the door and was momentarily struck dumb, my mouth falling open in a mix of horrified and amused shock.

The room I was given turned out to be their *Honeymoon Suite* and was the picture of every tacky cliché B-movie I had ever seen. It was indeed a large suite, complete with peeling gold leaf wallpaper; tattered red lace curtains; red velvet lamp shades with gold tassels from the '70s; a large, gold, shell shaped tub sat in the corner with cracked and peeling cherub faucets. The highlight of the suite was an honest-to-Goddess heart shaped bed set in the middle of the room, complete with a padded heart-shaped headboard, garish red velvet coverlet, and a coin operated vibration option.

I stumbled as Mateo bumped me from behind, breaking my momentary stupor. "Joss, move; this guy weighs a ton!" he complained.

I couldn't help my giggles as we struggled to get the dead weight of the elf in the room.

Once we had him on the bed, we both breathed a sigh of relief. *By the Goddess, he was heavy.*

He was also very tall. Seeing him laid out on the bed made me realize it as we had to bend his knees to get him to fit, making him well over six feet tall had he been standing.

I looked over at Mateo, back in his leopard form, to see him staring around the room with wide eyes. He chuckled. "Okay, I see why you were stunned for a second. This place is hideous!"

We shared a good laugh at the ridiculousness of the situation but agreed that as horrible as the room was, it was perfect for what we needed. Not being able to keep straight faces, we decided to strip the velvet coverlet off the bed and were relieved to find the plain white sheets underneath were clean.

While Mateo dragged the horrid bedspread away, the first thing I did was look to our protection. I warded the door and single window by tracing a rune of protection on the door in chalk and one on the window with a grease pen before closing the tacky, heavy, red curtains against prying eyes. By sheer luck the bed ran east to west. Although the elf's feet had to be at the head of the bed to ensure that his head was pointed east to help with his healing, which was why we had needed to bend his knees to make him fit. The headboard was in the way.

I moved everything I would need to the nightstand beside the bed. I didn't want to know why there were power outlets wired into the floor beside the bed, but it was convenient for our purposes. The room came with a coffee maker and microwave, and while not ideal, it would do to help me blend the healing herbs and make the necessary poultices. I always carried a small supply of plants and herbs in my messenger bag, along with a first aid kit, and I was grateful I had formed the habit when I was occasionally living on the streets. Homeless kids couldn't afford doctor's bills.

Using the coffee maker, I filled the water reservoir and added some marigold petals to the carafe before turning it on to make a steaming hot infusion, rather like a tea.

"Have you done a healing like this before?" Mateo asked as he came back to sit beside me.

"Healing a Dark Elf in a seedy motel's Honeymoon Suite?" I joked.

Mateo rolled his eyes. "No, smartass, used magick to heal such serious injuries."

Using the salt we had just bought, I drew a huge salt circle around the bed that extended almost to the edges of the room. At Mateo's instruction I added a second layer of protection inside the first. Starting facing north, I pulled out seven of the quartz crystals we had bought, and with their points facing outwards, I moved clockwise creating a second slightly smaller circle inside the first. According to Mateo, the circle would serve a dual purpose in protecting us as well as the elf and promote his healing.

"Nothing as formal as this, ritual wise, and never for something as serious as this. I used to patch up some of the other kids at some of the group homes I spent time in. I wouldn't do the circles or the candles, mostly just muttered the spell under my breath. Little kids generally don't ask as many questions as adults will, and they aren't suspicious of things they don't recognize. You can make it a game, sing the spell like a nursery rhyme, or pick flowers from the garden to 'make it all better,'" I explained.

"No one thought it was strange the kids healed so quickly?"

I laughed. "When a little kid goes running up to an overworked and disinterested foster parent excited about their boo boo going away like 'magic,' they generally get patted on the head and told to go play." I smirked down at him. "Sometimes the truth is so fantastic it can't be anything other than a lie." I shrugged. "Besides, I was never in any one place long enough for anyone to catch on."

After placing a couple of pillows under the elf's knees to take the strain off his back (not to mention help him fit on the bed), I began carefully stripping his black suede tunic off. He had the physique of an Olympic swimmer. I couldn't help but admire the wiry strength of his body and the perfectly defined muscles of his abdomen, despite the ugliness of the purple blooming over his dark skin. The bruises on his left side made me pale, and I suspected several of his ribs were broken. I was glad I had propped up his knees; it would make it easier for him to breathe. There wasn't too much skin that wasn't covered in bruises, but by the number of old scars scattered over his body, this wasn't his first fight.

As I was taking various herbs and roots from my bag, Mateo asked, "You're not using human medications?"

Looking at him, I got the feeling he knew the answer to his question already, but I answered him anyway. "My spells don't work unless I use raw ingredients. I'm not sure why. Bandages and gauzes are fine, but man-made pills and salves just don't respond to my spells. I found out as a kid that they give me a rash." I shrugged. "I use what works."

After washing my hands in a Rosemary mixture I had in a flask in my bag, I used my new mortar and pestle and mashed up the little comfrey root I had on hand and then scraped it out and put it to the side for later. The coffee maker finished brewing, and I poured some of the hot infusion into my now empty pestle, using it as a makeshift bowl. Using one of the hotel facecloths, I dipped it into the marigold tea to wash his wounds. The astringent and antiseptic properties of the marigold would help stop the bleeding and make sure the cuts were properly cleaned. It wasn't too long before the antiseptic liquid was tinged a healthy red with all the blood I had cleaned off my unlikely patient. After two more fresh pots of marigold infusion, he was finally clean.

When I was done, I sprinkled powdered geranium root on the deepest of the cuts on his forehead along his hairline, cheek, and eyebrow and immediately noticed the coagulating effect. Looking at his face, I was worried that both his orbital bone and cheek bone might be cracked or broken, but there wasn't much I could do about it if they were.

Once everything was clean and the bleeding stopped, I mixed the ground comfrey root with the remainder of the marigold infusion and made three poultices out of the gauze from my kit so I could put them over the battered side of his face, his ribs, and the lump on the back of his head. It would bring down the swelling and promote healing, but first I would have to set his nose. I took a deep breath and with a sickening crunch, realigned it. It looked straighter but started to bleed again. I put some gauze in his nostrils and pinched the bridge until it stopped again.

I took butterfly bandages out of my bag and closed the cuts near his hairline, cheek, and eyebrow. Realistically, the cuts probably needed several stitches each, but I didn't have the materials on hand to tackle that. I mentally added Crazy Glue to my list of supplies to replenish my first aid kit; I knew it could be used to close wounds in a pinch. The butterfly bandages would have to do this time.

Sitting back, I breathed easy for the first time. I had done everything medically that I could. Now I would do what I could magickally to help things along. I had already placed the crystals on the circle, and I had the poultices ready. Reaching into my bag, I pulled out four small white tea light candles and some matches. "Do you think these will work?" I asked, holding up the tea lights. Tapers or pillars were more traditional.

He eyed my bag with a raised eyebrow. "You going to pull out a kitchen sink next? Maybe an x-ray machine?"

I rolled my eyes at his continued abuse over the size of my messenger bag and shook the candles, reminding him of my question.

"They'll work fine. The important part is the candle itself, not the size of it. Remind me to teach you how to light candles with magick when we get home," Mateo said, watching me intently. Now and then his ears would flick to the door to assess any noises he heard, but from the lack of tension in his body, I assumed we were fairly safe for the moment.

I nodded, a part of me eager to learn anything he could teach me, but the bulk of my attention was on the magick needed to heal the elf.

I set the four small white candles at intervals just inside the crystals on the compass points. Making sure the necessary elements to the spell were at hand, I began.

While lighting the candles I spoke one line for each candle.

"Lord and Lady hear my plea,
the strength to heal I ask of thee.
Magick mend and candle burn,
injuries heal, good health return."

I blew out the match and picked up the waiting poultices. As I applied them, I continued the incantation, focusing all my energies on the purpose and meaning behind the words.

"Stem the blood flowing through,
seal the wounds with skin anew.
I charge these herbs to aid my spell,
that this hurt elf be made well.
Dispel the pain, let these wounds heal,
banish the suffering, no pain to feel."

Stepping back, I felt the slight drain on my energies telling me the magick was working. I had done everything within my knowledge to help him. I looked down at Mateo to see if he had any suggestions.

He purred his approval. "You did well. You know more about healing magick than some twice your age."

I smiled a little at the compliment. "I spent so many years hiding, I was too scared to go to a hospital when I got hurt or sick for fear of the Inquisitors finding me. And then I found out that most medicines actually made me sicker; I got pretty good at healing spells."

"You might want to leave him some willow bark tea if you have some. He'll need it for the pain when he wakes up," he suggested.

"We're leaving him?!" I asked, my eyebrows shooting up in wide-eyed surprise.

"You can't stay here, Joss. Danaan are rare and valuable. You're safest if we keep your identity a secret. If he wakes up and sees you after everything you've done, your cover will be blown," he said firmly. He took a long assessing look at me. "And you're exhausted. That was a lot of magick. You need to rest."

I nodded, knowing he was right, and prepared the willow bark tea using the coffee maker yet again. Leaving it on the night stand for when he woke up, I gathered everything up and repacked my bag. I took the now half-full bag of garbage, knotting and dropping it at my feet, ready to go. I wasn't leaving anything behind that could be used to trace me later.

I didn't have my athame with me so I would be breaking the salt circle with my hand. Kneeling at the edge of the circle facing east, I let my hand hover over the salt.

"Lord and Lady, my thanks to thee,
your help and guidance a gift to me.
I leave the circle in perfect love and perfect trust,
leaving one of your children in need of
your guard as you must."

I brushed a small gap in the salt and stepped through it, taking my bag and the garbage with me, Mateo following quickly. I replaced the salt, completing the circle once more, and looked around to ensure nothing had been forgotten. The elf let out a groan on the bed.

"We have to go," Mateo said, his tone sounding urgent as he shifted back into his public form as a shepherd.

"Do you think he'll be alright?" I asked quietly as I looked back at my patient, knowing we had to leave but worried about his health.

Mateo wound in front of me, urging me towards the door. "Did you see all his scars? He'll be fine, Joss. Now hurry, we need to get home."

Putting on my cloak and pulling up the hood, I took a last look at the unconscious man on the bed and thought I saw a flash of his eyes. "Thank you for helping me. May the Goddess protect you. Blessed be," I whispered before slipping out the door behind Mateo.

By the time we made it to the Jeep, my strength was seriously flagging. The late night, the emotions of experiencing the Troll Market, the multiple skirmishes, and then the energy it took to perform the magick necessary to help the elf had all taken their toll on me.

Mateo jumped in and settled himself in the passenger seat; I climbed in behind him and sat behind the wheel trying to gather myself for the ride home when Mateo spoke.

"Are you alright?"

"Just tired. You'll have to talk to me on the way home so I don't fall asleep at the wheel," I replied as I turned the key and the engine rumbled to life. My dashboard clock read four-thirty in the morning.

Mateo let out a low growl. "How about we talk about you running into a fight with four Inquisitors when I specifically told you to stay behind?"

I let out my own growl. "Seriously? You really expected me to let you run into a fight against four men all by yourself? And since when do I have to 'do as I'm told?'"

"How am I supposed to keep you safe if you keep getting yourself into trouble?! I found you two days ago and already you've been attacked by Inquisitors, confronted a tribe of Unseelie Fairies and invited them to practically live with you, been accosted by a hag, hit on by a Satyr, gotten in another skirmish with Inquisitors, and involved yourself in the affairs of a Dark Elf! How am I supposed to protect you?! You're a walking, talking beacon for trouble!" He barked out the rant in a furious stream of frustrated anger.

Now I was pissed. "I did just fine protecting myself all these years! If you don't like how I live my life, you're free to leave any time!" The thought of him walking out of my life hit me hard in the chest, and I struggled not to cry. I had been alone for far longer than the few days he had been in my life, but those few days had become precious. I couldn't imagine going back to my empty house now.

"Don't be ridiculous. What is it with you always pushing me away? Every time things get difficult, you think I'm leaving," he said exasperatedly.

"Because *everyone* leaves!" I blurted out before I could stop myself.

I could feel him staring at me from the passenger seat, but I refused to look at him. I was too close to my breaking point, and if he left it might actually shatter me. Losing my mother had been hard, but I had only been a child when she died. While I mourned her passing, I knew she hadn't made the choice to walk away. My stepfather, on the other hand, had walked away without a backward glance. The many foster homes over the years hadn't cared if I stayed or left, only missing the extra income I brought in rather than my actual company. Only my last foster parent seemed to care about me as a person, but because of who I was, I couldn't allow myself to get too close to her. Even the relationships I had with my lost tribe were superficial at best.

It was a long silent ride back to the house. The sun was starting to lighten the sky as I parked the Jeep in the garage and locked the door behind me. I hurried into the house and down into the hidden basement, wanting nothing more than a hot bath and some sleep. I hadn't seen Mateo since he jumped out of the Jeep behind me, and I wondered if he had left already. He was right; I was a lot of trouble. But to be fair, none of these things had happened until he arrived.

No, that wasn't true. The Inquisitors had always been there. They had gotten too close on several occasions over the years, but I had always managed to disappear before they found me. No one had had to pay the price my foster parents paid so many years ago. Now, I had run into them twice in less than a week. I didn't want to move. I had a great life. I had an actual home, a job that I loved and was good at.

Seattle was my home now. This was the most settled I had *ever* been. I had lived here for over ten years, and my little house was the first thing I could call my own. For the past three years, I had been all but invisible, able to come home to my hidden home and know I was completely safe. I didn't want to have to run again.

As I sunk into the steaming hot water of my tub, the tears started to flow. *Lord and Lady, when had I become such a cry baby?* I had cried more in the last three days than I had in the last decade. The water did a lot to soothe the aches in my body but did little for the one in my heart. I got out and changed into my pajamas and crawled into bed feeling more alone than I ever had before, the silence of my empty house echoing the loneliness in my heart. I curled around my pillow, but as new tears welled in my eyes, I heard a deep rumbling purr approaching. The bed dipped under the weight of the leopard crawling onto it.

As he lay down full length against my back, a heavy head rested on my side. "Nothing can prove to you that I'm not leaving, nothing but time. If you need me to say it every day for the rest of your life, I will. I'm not ever leaving you, Joss. I will always be here for you no matter how difficult you are or how dangerous your life gets. It's you and me now, and I wouldn't have it any other way."

His words broke the dam inside, and I rolled to face him, burying my face in his fur. For the second time in as many nights, my new friend held me while I cried.

"Sleep now, *paulo dea.* I'll be here in the morning," was the last thing I heard before sleep took me.

Chapter Nine

I woke the next morning to the sound of my cell phone vibrating. A glance at my clock told me it was way too early to be awake considering I had seen the sun rise. I looked at the call display: Jimmy. Perfect.

Mateo climbed off the bed with a disgusted growl and went off in search of somewhere quieter to sleep as I answered the phone.

"Jimmy, it's seven on a Sunday morning. Why are you calling me? You're not in jail again, are you?" My voice was rough with sleep, and I hoped he knew he'd woken me up.

"No, I'm not in jail. Jesus, Joss, you'd think I get thrown in jail all the time the way you talk." Jimmy's voice was grouchy and insulted.

"Twice in six months, Jimmy," I pointed out. "The last time was only three days ago, so I don't think I'm out of line in asking the question."

"That wasn't my fault! I was—"

I rubbed a hand over my tired face and interrupted. I didn't need to hear his excuses again. "Why are you calling me, Jimmy?"

"I got a message this morning from Mrs. Binkley. Another missing kid case. She said the clients are anxious."

Mrs. Vera Binkley was an elderly widow with a fondness for stray dogs and cats, who took in foster kids. She had been my last foster mom when I turned eighteen and got out of the system. Never one to turn away anyone or anything, she was one of the good ones who took in kids because she loved them and wanted to help them, rather than for the money like most of the places I had lived.

I asked her to be our permanent answering service/receptionist when I got "hired" by Jimmy, her paycheck coming out of my cut. Even though I hadn't seen or spoken to her in almost a year, she had instantly recognized my voice over the phone when I called her. Like I said, one of the good ones. Even though she was more the age of a grandmother, if anyone had been my *mom* over the years, it had been her. She was the only foster parent I had ever called *Mom*. To every child that crossed her doorstep, she was *Momma B*.

Now all our business calls were to a number at her house. The arrangement worked out perfectly: she could stay at home with kids who really needed her and still get a paycheck *and* we had someone professional answering our phone, leaving us (meaning me) free to be out on the streets actually working. Mrs. Binkley would take the calls, gather the initial information chart over the phone, and then contact us based on priority. Had this been a cheating spouse call it would have waited until Monday. A missing kid warranted a Sunday morning wake-up.

"Of course the parents are anxious. Their kid is missing." Goddess, did this guy not come with any emotions at all?

"No, I mean, apparently they asked for you directly. They only want to talk to *you*." His tone was accusatory.

"Me? But I'm only your *assistant*." Two hours of sleep wasn't enough to prepare me for the crappy day it looked like I was going to have.

"I called them and told them that, but they told me they were referred to you by a Mr. Shido? What's this about, Joss? I thought you didn't want to be recognized. You always said you liked our arrangement," Jimmy said, starting to sound a bit bitter.

I sighed loudly. *Mr. Shido*. Suddenly things started to make a bit of sense. Mateo was going to have a canary. "I do like our arrangement. Nothing's changed. Give me their number and I'll deal with it. Mr. Shido is an acquaintance of mine and probably thought he was doing a good thing."

"You're not going out on your own, are you? 'Cause you need a license to be a private investigator in the state of Washington, and we have a verbal contract. You can't just quit without—" Jimmy was starting to babble.

I got out of bed and went to the kitchen to get a pad and paper. "JIMMY! I'm not going out on my own! I'll call these people and Mr. Shido and explain. You'll still get your cut, don't worry. Now give me the damn number!" Freaky little slime ball was only worried about losing his cash cow.

There was silence for a minute then, "206-555..."

I wrote down the number he rattled off, wondering how I was going to explain this to Mateo. "'Kay, thanks, Jimmy. I'll stop in the office in a couple days after I run down this case. Call me if something else comes up."

"Keep me posted. I wanna know your progress. Speaking of cases, what's happening with the Johnson—"

"Uh-huh...I'll call you later," I said absently as I hung up the phone, not listening to whatever it was he had to say. He was about to ask about Tonesha Johnson. I did not want to kick over that hornet's nest. He was going to have kittens when I got around to telling him I couldn't solve the case. The weasel still tried to play the boss every now and then, and this personal request would be working every single insecurity he had.

He's going to be fun to deal with for a while. I rolled my eyes at the thought.

I rubbed my hands over my face trying to wake up. I put on a pot of coffee, intentionally making it extra strong knowing there was no way I would be going back to sleep.

"Who was that? And why did you mention Inari?" Mateo mumbled from his spot on his new bed in the corner of the living room. Apparently, the dog bed had become acceptable.

I thought over our conversations of the last couple of days. "Have I told you what I do for a living yet?"

I heard a loud yawn and he came around the back of the couch with a stretch. "No, actually you haven't. No details anyway."

"I work as a silent partner in a private detective firm—Mackenzie Investigations. That was my idiotic and incompetent *boss* Jimmy. Apparently, Mr. Shido recommended someone call us and ask for me specifically to help them find their missing child." I turned away quickly, not wanting to witness the coming explosion.

Mateo didn't disappoint as he let out what I assumed was a string of curses in what sounded like several languages.

One thing made me stop and think now that I was more awake. "Mr. Shido said he had heard of me when you introduced us yesterday. How? And how does he know where I work?" I wondered aloud.

"I would guess one or more of the people you helped in the past were Sidhe. Inari may have heard of you that way and now he knows you as Danaan. He probably felt you would be a good option for helping these people." Mateo practically snarled when he said Inari Shido's name. "Over five hundred years old, you would think he would know better than to expose you this way..." The grumbles were under his breath, but I still heard them pretty clearly.

"This is about the missing kids we heard about at the Market last night, isn't it?" I asked quietly as I poured myself a cup of much needed coffee.

"Oh, I would bet money on it." Mateo shook his head. "Which means we need to go back and talk to the nosy Shifter. We need to find out who the client is and what he told them about you exactly." He looked up at me with a resigned look. "I don't suppose there is any way I can convince you not to get involved, is there?"

I hung my head slightly. "They're only kids, Mateo."

"You already made the decision to look into this before the phone call this morning, didn't you." It was a statement rather than a question.

"When I saw the look on the face of the Bucentaur mother at the bar last night," I confirmed, looking at him solemnly. "This is what I do, Teo. I help find lost and kidnapped kids, sometimes elderly people or precious items, but the missing kids are what I'm passionate about. I didn't have parents. These kids do. Parents who love them, and they're lost and scared somewhere. And who knows what the Inquisitors are doing to them right now. We need to find them, Teo, before it's too late." I pled my case, praying to the Goddess he would support and help me with this because my usual methods wouldn't work among the Sidhe. And I would need him to back me up against the Inquisitors.

He nodded and I could see him thinking things through. "I get it, Joss. I do. I had already decided to look into things as well. Not to rescue kids, but because the Inquisitor activity in the area was hitting too close to you. I need to eliminate this threat to keep you safe. If finding the kids is a step towards finding these zealots, then so be it."

I sipped my coffee as I waited, knowing he had some kind of plan.

"We're going to have to handle this carefully. I still don't want your identity compromised, and if the parents haven't been able to find the kids on their own, then the Inquisitors are getting smarter. And we still don't know these kids are even alive. If they are, why were they captured in the first place? How?" He was thinking out loud.

I could see a highly tactical mind working behind Mateo's eyes and respected him all the more for it. Not for the first time, I wondered what his story was. What had his life been like? What kinds of things had he seen over the past two thousand years?

"Why don't I call Mrs. Binkley and get some more information? It's too early to go and see Mr. Shido anyway," I offered.

Mateo nodded. "It's somewhere to start. Will she be up?"

I put down my cup to reach for the cordless phone. "If I know her, she was already up baking bread when the call came in." Seconds later, a sweet but professional voice answered.

"MacKenzie Investigations. How may I help you?'

"Hi, Momma B, it's Jocelyn."

I smiled as I heard the familiar sound of her dusting the flour off her hands. "Of course it is, dear. So *good* to hear your voice. How are you? You don't come home near often enough. Are you eating? You always look so thin."

It was her typical greeting, and I loved her for it, especially her reference to *home*. I had only lived there for four months before I turned eighteen and the state quit providing foster homes for me. Mrs. Binkley had offered to let me stay longer, free of charge or obligation.

"I was there just a couple of days ago, Momma," I reminded her.

"Yes, but that was the middle of the night, and we didn't get a proper visit."

I had taken Peter to Momma B's after finding him beaten on the street. "How's Peter? Or did he leave already?" Even though he had agreed to go, you couldn't count on a street kid with the trust issues Peter had to stick around for long.

"Oh, that boy is a godsend! He's been doing some repairs around the house, small things, mind you. He's still pretty banged up. And the little ones have really taken to him. He's so sweet and patient with them. He taught Gidget a new trick! That old dog now sits up and begs for cookies. It makes the kids laugh and keeps them occupied while I do my ironing. I hope you don't mind, but I have him staying in your room while he visits." Her voice was warm and full of affection for her newest son.

I knew he was likely within hearing distance when she mentioned my room. I hadn't had a room there in years, although she always kept a guest room free just in case one of my lost tribe needed a place to stay. I kept a change of clothes there in case of emergency, and we had found that any of the street kids I brought her were more willing to stay if they thought they were using my room. "Of course I don't mind. I'm glad to hear he's still there. He's a really great kid."

"Yes, he is a sweet boy. So helpful. Thank you for bringing him by to help out an old lady," she said sincerely.

Now I knew he had to be listening because she made a point of sounding like he was doing her a favor by staying. The old dear never missed a trick. "Tell him I said hello."

"I will. Now, you didn't answer my question, sweetheart. How are you doing?" Her tone was firm and demanded a truthful answer.

"I'm doing really well, Momma B. Yes, I'm eating, I promise. I even made a new friend."

"Oh, honey! That's so great. You always work too much; you should be out having fun. Now, about this friend... Is it a boy? You need a nice boy to settle down with. I worry about you in that big house all by yourself." She was too cute for words, and her concern touched me.

"My house is tiny, Momma. And you don't have to worry. I got a dog. He's sweet and protective—sometimes overprotective—but he's great," I said, sending Mateo a teasing look and sticking out my tongue when he rolled his eyes at me.

"That's great, dear, but please tell me the dog isn't your new friend. A dog can't replace the companionship of a nice boy."

"If I found a nice *boy* I might get arrested. I'm twenty-eight years old; I would think you would be pushing me to find a nice *man*."

"Horse Pucky! When you get to my age, you'll realize that twenty-eight is still young. And don't change the subject, young lady. I worry about you!" she scolded.

I couldn't help but laugh at my new reality. By the time I got to her age, I wouldn't even be one fifth of the way through my life. "I'm sorry, Momma. I promise when things slow down, I'll try to find a nice young man to spend time with."

"Pish tosh! Things never slow down around you. While it's admirable that you are so devoted to helping others, you aren't going to be any good to them if you work yourself into an early grave." Her voice was softly stern.

"I know. But kids have been disappearing more often lately, and I can't just sit and do nothing. You know that." My thoughts turned to Peter, and then to Tonesha and the two other kids that were still missing. I would try again after the crap with the Inquisitors was over. Maybe Mateo would be able to help.

"I know, dear. And I'm so proud of you. I just want you to be happy."

I swallowed past the lump in my throat when she said that. I loved Mrs. Binkley and hearing that she was proud of me choked me up. "I am happy. And I'm getting out more, honest." The Troll Market counted, right? I had even been to a bar and been hit on.

"I'm guessing you're calling about the new case? Did Jimmy call and wake you up?" she asked.

"Yes, ma'am. But it's important. I understand they asked for me personally. Something about a referral?"

Papers shuffled in the background. "The referral was from a...Mr. Shido? The client's name is Mr. Nandi; he and his wife lost their two year old son thirty-two days ago. Mr. Nandi was reluctant to offer details to anyone but you. Apparently, their son was taken from them while they were on a family trip to the Olympic National Forest. The poor man sounded desperate on the phone. I tried to tell him Jimmy was the head of the firm, because I know you like to be unrecognized as a part of the company, but he was set on speaking with you. I called Jimmy though; I thought he would be able to convince them. You need the time off and Lord knows that man needs to start doing more work in his own darn company."

"It's fine, Momma B. Mr. Shido is a new acquaintance of mine and may have been a bit confused when he made the referral. He's quite old and very eccentric. I'll call the client and get some more information. These people need our help, and this kind of thing isn't really something Jimmy is any good at."

"Alright, dear. Now you be careful on this one, okay? I worry about you."

"I know you do, Momma, and I love you for it. I'll be careful, I promise."

Mrs. Binkley rattled off the contact information, and with more promises to be careful and to call more often, I hung up.

"From the name you were given, I would venture to guess the new client is the Bucentaur mother you saw at the bar last night," Mateo offered.

"It's a man who called us. The time frame for the disappearance fits, but why do you think it's her?" I asked, wondering how the name led him to believe it was the woman from last night.

"Nandi is a common surname among the Bucentaur community," he explained.

"So now we go and see Mr. Shido?" I guessed.

"Yes. The sooner we get some answers out of that Shifter, the sooner I can make some solid plans," Mateo growled out.

I headed off to the bathroom to get ready. I needed a hot shower and another cup of coffee before I could function well enough to face the outside world on only a couple of hours sleep. A world that was getting more and more dangerous with every passing day.

Chapter Ten

Pulling up to Inari Shido's shop was a much different experience than last time. Before, the place seemed to be a dingy, nasty, run-down, abandoned, little store to steer clear of. Now, with my Sidhe sight, it was clean, professional, and inviting. It was even more impressive than the Apothecary at the Troll Market. Where the Apothecary catered to clients wanting strictly medicinal and herbal supplies, as well as the accompanying equipment, Mr. Shido's was also filled with untold oddities and antiques.

Brilliantly coloured kites hung from the ceiling, suits of armour stood silent sentinel along the walls, and skeletons of unknown animals both big and small were placed in various places around the shop while elaborately painted Russian nesting dolls decorated a glass display counter filled with ceremonial pipes and knives. Jewel toned preserve jars caught the morning sun, casting rainbows through the room. The air was rich with the scents of the hanging herbs and spices. Weapons hung in display cases on the wall alongside what looked like different types of wands. An ornately decorated sarcophagus leaned against a wall and had a stuffed bird perched on top of it that looked like a peacock but in vibrant shades of red and orange. Still, other counters had selections of stones, feathers, and furs for sale. Scales, cauldrons, fans, mirrors, hats, cloaks, fabrics—everywhere I looked was a feast for the eyes, and I could appreciate it all the more now I knew everything was real.

I jumped slightly as the two foxes appeared suddenly, yipping softly and practically dancing around my feet, adorable in their gold trimmed red bibs. Mateo growled low as they skipped around us just out of his reach.

“Back so soon?”

Mr. Shido’s voice drifted from the back of the shop, and Mateo’s growls got louder, his shepherd body bristling as his irritation with the Shifter made itself known.

“You can’t be surprised to see us,” I said with tired irritation and crossed my arms over my chest. “My office got a phone call this morning.”

Mateo paced angrily in front of my feet, taking a snap at one of the foxes before interrupting me. “How dare you reveal her! She’s—”

Halting Mateo’s angry tirade, Mr. Shido held up a slender furred hand, although it looked more like a paw. “Calm yourself. I revealed nothing, I assure you. I said nothing to them of what she is or where she could be found. I merely told them her name and that she is someone who is aware of our community, someone who may be able to help, as she lives among the humans and can move about freely.” He whistled softly, calling the foxes to him, more than likely saving them from Mateo. Once they were quiet at his feet, he looked at me. “I have promised you my protection; I would not do so only to place you in danger at the first opportunity. Such a thing would bring dishonor."

"You were the one to warn me I should stay hidden; why would you expose me even a little?" I asked.

His eyes softened and he smiled knowingly. "I knew you would hear of the children while at the Market. Can you tell me you did not intend to look into the situation after you heard about them?" At my resigned sigh, he smiled kindly. "It is in your nature to protect children. You need the information the Nandis possess, and the children of our community need you to help them where we cannot. This is your path; I sought only to ease the way without risking your exposure. The Nandis will not be surprised when you do not wish to meet them face to face, and now you have a way to contact them that does not require it."

"Why didn't you just give us their phone number in the first place?" I asked, confused at the convoluted plan.

Mateo answered me. "Because as members of the Sidhe community, they would have been highly suspicious of a stranger offering their help. Among the Sidhe an introduction is necessary. In fact, outside of certain places, it's mandatory to ensure anonymity. Shido has provided the necessary assurances that safeguard our existence, and they chose to contact you." He looked at Mr. Shido. "My apologies for jumping to conclusions. I should've known you wouldn't go back on your word."

"It is quite alright. You have only just found her after searching for so long. It is natural for you to be so protective, especially considering the trouble she seems to attract." Mr. Shido said the last with an amused twinkle in his eye.

I threw up my hands. "Oh, come on! It's not like I planned this. My life was pretty quiet before I met you guys, you know." At the thought of the chaos my life had become, I remembered the elf. "Speaking of danger, can you check on someone for us? We helped him last night, but if I go back there to check on him myself, he'll know who I am."

"You have gotten in *more* trouble since I saw you yesterday?" Mr. Shido asked with raised eyebrows.

"You have *no* idea," Mateo grumbled.

I flicked one of his pointed ears before telling Mr. Shido about our adventures at the Gorgon's Head, the fight with the Inquisitors, and saving the elf.

Mr. Shido listened intently, his expression growing graver as the story progressed. "A Dark Elf. I had heard there was one in the city. You have, I believe, gotten in deeper than you know. If he is who I think he is, you may have already exposed yourself." Mateo growled at that, but Mr. Shido continued. "It is rumored one of the missing children is an elven child, but what most do not know is the child is a Dark Elf. The best trackers have been scouring the planet to reclaim the child. If a Dark Elf is here, then it would be wise to assume the rumors are true and that the child is in Seattle." His tails began to swish back and forth as he thought. "It is unlikely there would be more than one in the city. It is certain the elf you saved last night is a tracker, in which case he will be the best of his kind and not eager to be indebted to anyone. He will wish to meet with you to acknowledge the debt."

Mateo started swearing under his breath. The hackles on his neck started to rise. "I told you not to mess with the elf! Didn't I tell you not to mess with him!?"

I rounded on him. "How was I supposed to know? We couldn't just leave him there anyway. Any human could have found him, and think of the crap that would have stirred up!"

"I will go to see this elf of yours and try to smooth over the issue. Perhaps he will consider your healing to be payment for his assistance in the bar," Shido offered.

Mateo snorted. "Not likely."

"Nevertheless, I will see where we stand. I will contact you when I know more," Shido assured us.

I thanked him and then followed a very grumpy Mateo back out to the Jeep.

He was growling in the seat next to me as I fastened my seat belt. "Can it, Mateo. There's nothing to be done for it. We'll worry about the elf after we hear back from Shido. For now, we have kids to find," I snapped as I started the engine, feeling my lack of sleep keenly.

He sighed. "What is the human saying about the road to hell?"

"The road to hell is paved with good intentions," I quoted. "Maybe, but I still wouldn't have done anything different. I can't walk away from someone who needs help. You were the first one to jump in. I just cleaned up the mess."

He couldn't argue with that. A few minutes later, I parked in front of one of the local coffee shops. "I'm hungry and I need coffee. We can eat here, and I can call the Nandis while we eat. We can figure out a plan after I talk to them."

The Willing Addict was a favorite haunt of mine, and the baristas all knew me. It was also a favorite of the local police because it stayed open twenty-four hours. Many a long night was made possible for the city's finest due to the quality of the coffee at *The Willing Addict.* Mateo made himself comfortable under a corner table on the patio while I went inside to get our breakfast and a huge cup of coffee for me.

"Morning, Jocelyn!" Kenny, one of the fixtures of the place, was behind the counter.

"Morning, Kenny," I said with a smile.

Kenny was one of those guys that had never realized the age of grunge had passed. He was an older version of Kurt Cobain—if Kurt Cobain had started to lose his hair without recognizing it. Kenny still wore the ripped, baggy jeans, stained T-shirt with the holey sweater on top, and worn-out Doc Martens on his feet that everyone wore through the '90s. His messy stringy hair was always either under a beanie or pulled back into a messy ponytail. I was pretty sure, in Kenny's mind, he thought Kurt Cobain was living the good life with Elvis somewhere.

"Any of the boys been in this morning?" I asked as Kenny started pouring my usual monstrous coffee for me. Sometimes he overheard valuable gossip from the cops who hung out here between calls. Kenny looked like a stoner, and definitely lived the life of one, but he liked his gossip just as much as the weed and coffee he lived on. And the cops always had the best gossip, forgetting Kenny was even there as they discussed their cases. "Can I get three of your sausage breakfast burritos too, please?" I added.

"Sure thing." He nodded. "Some of them tried to come in earlier, but they got a call about an attempted kidnapping before they could do any more than grab their java. They should be back soon; they still gotta pay me for the joe," he said as he put my breakfast in the microwave to warm.

The mention of the attempted kidnapping caught my attention. "Who was it?"

"Umm...Stevens and Vincetti," he said as he handed over my coffee. "$10.45."

I gave him twenty bucks. "Their coffee's on me. If they get here after I leave, tell them to call me."

He grinned. "Will do." As he passed me my plate of burritos, he asked, "You hungry this morning or what? I can never eat more than two of these things and you're half my size."

I nodded to the window. "I got myself a dog. We missed breakfast. If I don't feed him, he might try to eat a pedestrian," I joked, Kenny's laugh following me out the door.

I sat down at the table beside Mateo, who was doing his best sleepy dog impression by basking in the warm morning sunlight. Placing two of the breakfast burritos in front of him, I teased, "Good thing these aren't for dinner; I hear dog farts are deadly."

A low growl came from him, but there were too many people walking by for him to say what I was sure would have been a crushing comeback.

After finding the paper with Mr. Nandi's phone number, I pulled my phone and my notebook out of my bag. Finding my pen, I dialed the number.

"Hello," a very low gravelly voice answered.

"Mr. Nandi? My name is Jocelyn Matthews from McKenzie Investigations; I'm returning your call. Mr. Inari Shido referred you to me."

"Yes, M-m-ms. M-m-matthews. Shido said you m-m-might be able to help us."

His voice was very deep and he seemed to draw out the "M" sounds when he spoke. Knowing what I did about what he was, I couldn't help but think he was holding back a moo. "I understand your two year old calf is missing."

There was a pause. "I didn't tell your receptionist *that* inform-m-mation."

He caught my calculated slip revealing that I knew what he was, and now I had the opportunity to earn a bit of trust. "I had intended to try to find your son and the other missing children when I heard about them. With your help that job will be easier."

"Why would you find children for no reason, M-m-ms. M-m-matthews?" he asked, sounding skeptical.

Thinking back to my own childhood, it was easy to answer. "Because all children should be with loving parents, Mr. Nandi."

"What do you want in exchange for finding m-m-my son?" There was a hint of suspicion in his voice.

This was the part I hated. It seemed so mercenary to ask for money in exchange for finding a child. "Because you contacted me, the usual rates will apply; sixty-five dollars an hour with a four-hour minimum but a five hundred dollar a day cap." I swallowed, feeling a bit sick. A cheating spouse I would and could gladly charge money for, but a missing child was different.

"Because I contacted you?" he questioned.

"As I said, I already intended on finding the children. Had I found them and then demanded payment, not only would it look like I took them and was demanding ransom, but it wouldn't make me a very good person. However, since you contacted me through the agency, I have no choice but to charge you the company rates. Otherwise, my boss would find out and demand why I was working outside of the firm for free. It would raise all kinds of questions that, as I'm sure you can appreciate, would be rather difficult for me to answer." He hummed his agreement. "And as I said, with your help it will make it that much easier to find your son and hopefully the other children as well."

He was eager and hopeful when he answered. "What do you need from-m-m us? I'll pay your fees and m-m-more if you find our son."

"I'll need some of his hair and a favorite item of his, a toy or a blanket; something he has an attachment to and a picture of him if you have one." I put my hand over the phone's mic and whispered to Mateo.

"Can you shift into a bird?"

At his subtle nod, and not so subtle eye roll at my apparently stupid question, I went back to my conversation with Mr. Nandi. “Give me your address and a bird will come and pick up the items.”

I wasn’t surprised to find out he lived in the small isolated farming community of Guemes Island where human contact would be restricted to the few full-time residents and people who visited the island in the summer. It was pretty far north, but Mateo subtly nodded as I repeated the address back to Mr. Nandi so I knew he would be able to fly there and back. As I was finishing the phone call, I saw two uniformed cops pull up to the curb in their cruiser.

“Well, if it isn’t Nancy Drew!” a young guy in his early twenties said as he got out of the passenger side of the police car.

“Shut up, Vincetti. I’m just an assistant. Go find Jimmy if you want someone to hassle. He’s the investigator, not me.” I smirked.

“Investigator,” an older balding man with a grey ‘70s style porn-stache snorted in derision as he hiked his pants up his expanding waistline. “That man couldn’t *investigate* his way out of a wet paper bag, and you know it.”

“Hey, Stevens.” I smiled. “You still not letting the kid drive?” I nodded towards Vincetti with a teasing grin.

“Not until he gets his license,” he said seriously, but his eyes sparkled with amusement.

“Oh, ha ha!” Vincetti deadpanned. “I let him drive before the state revokes his license due to advanced age. Besides, I like having a chauffeur.”

I laughed, enjoying the familiar banter. Vincetti reached into his pocket and started digging out some money.

"If you're back to pay for the coffees you guys grabbed earlier, I already paid. Kenny mentioned you'd been in, and I owed you for helping me with Jimmy the other night." They had been the ones who had "arrested" Jimmy when the woman called the police.

Stevens chuckled. "Nothing to pay back. He wasn't worth the paperwork to book him. But thanks for the coffee anyway."

"Hey, Jocelyn, what's with the dog?" Vincetti asked, nodding to a carefully watchful Mateo.

I shrugged, feigning indifference. "I got mugged on the way home the other night, and he bit one of the muggers, scaring them away. He wasn't wearing any tags and doesn't have a tattoo. When he followed me home, I figured taking him in was the least I could do for saving my butt. So far it's working out to be a pretty good deal for the both of us."

"Jesus, Jocelyn! Are you alright? Why didn't you call the station? You should come in and give a statement." Stevens was swelling up into a full-on protective tantrum.

"Easy, big guy. The missus would miss you if you had a heart attack," I said as I took a sip of my cooling coffee, trying to calm him down.

"He's right, Jocelyn. There's been an increase in muggings lately. You should have come in to the station to report it." Vincetti frowned at me with an uncharacteristically serious look.

"I didn't report it 'cause for all I know it was someone Jimmy was following trying to scare us off. Besides, nothing happened thanks to Teo here." I reached down and ran my hand over Mateo's head as he closed his eyes in enjoyment.

Stevens huffed out a breath and crossed his meaty arms over his bulging gut with a grunt. "That's a crap excuse and you know it. While I'm glad some stray came to your rescue, you still should've come to us."

"Guys, I'm fine," I said firmly. There was no way I was going in to make any kind of statement. Statements meant having my name entered into the system, and I liked to stay off the grid as much as possible. "Now what's this about muggings in our fair city? Any place specific I need to steer clear of?" This was exactly the type of gossip I was hoping to hear.

Vincetti pulled a chair over to sit across from me and looked up at Stevens before he spoke. "Nothing specific other than it seems to be only women who are getting attacked. And it's mostly in the Fremont area."

Stevens leaned against the low railing that surrounded the outdoor seating area. "Seems to be a couple of crazies in town. They never seem to take anything but are spouting off all kinds of religious crap and terrorizing the women. In one case they managed to cut off a fair chunk of her hair before they were interrupted."

Fremont. As in Fremont near the troll under the bridge, the troll I teased Mateo about. Did the Inquisitors really think the Sidhe were dumb enough to mark the entrance of the Troll Market with a giant sculpture of a troll? Mateo let out a low menacing growl at my feet, and I flicked his ear to remind him that he was supposed to be just a dog.

"Wow, must be a full moon or something," I said, faking disbelief and trying to swallow my own memories of a knife at my throat.

"You know you should have a collar and a leash on him, don't you?" Stevens said, eyeing the obviously irritated dog at my feet.

I snorted. "If you can get one on him, be my guest."

"I'm not writing her a ticket for an unrestrained dog." Vincetti rolled his eyes. "Between the muggings and the new kidnapping case, we're swamped." He ran a hand through his hair in frustration.

I sat up. "Kidnapping?" Kenny had said it was an attempted kidnapping. The weed must have scrambled his hearing along with his brain cells. I immediately thought of the missing kids from Occidental Park: Ray-Ray and little 'Shel.

Stevens sighed. "Yeah, just came in this morning. Nine year old little boy went missing somewhere up in Salmon Arm, Canada, a few weeks ago. Joseph James Andrews was on a rafting trip with his parents and disappeared into thin air. A tip came in this morning that he may have been sighted here in Seattle.

Vincetti pulled a missing poster out of his pocket and handed it to me. The picture of a smiling, happy boy stared back at me. He had dark brown hair and brown eyes and a brand new set of teeth that looked slightly too large in his young mouth. The kid should have been out having fun with his friends, not scared somewhere all alone.

I frowned as I handed the poster back. He was the same age as the others. It couldn't be a coincidence.

"Keep it. We have others and the more eyes on the streets the better," Vincetti said.

I nodded and slipped it in my messenger bag. "I'll keep my eyes open. Where was he sighted?"

"That's the strange part. He was seen down in the East Industrial District; not sure why a kid would be there. We're not sure it was a credible lead, but we're keeping our eyes out just in case," Stevens said.

As I fiddled with my mother's ring, rolling it up and down my ring finger, out of the corner of my eye I saw Mateo look up at me. I was sure we were both thinking the same thing – the East Industrial District was close to where the Inquisitors were beating the Dark Elf and the Triangle Pub: the entrance to the Troll Market. Peter had said the ones who had tried to take Jackie were preachy types, so it *had* to be the Inquisitors that were responsible for the muggings and the kidnappings. But why would they be taking human children?

"Well, I'm hardly ever in that area, but I'll keep my eyes open if I go. You may want to talk to some of the homeless around Occidental Park. I heard something about religious nutjobs trying to lure some of the younger street kids into a van. Things are serious enough that they are voluntarily going back into the system," I said, careful to keep my tone even. "I'll ask around and see if I hear anything about your muggers too."

Stevens levelled a narrow look at me, the 'stache twitching into a frown. "I know you know people who won't talk to us, but I want you to be careful if you go sniffing around on this one. This isn't one of your cheating husband cases; these guys are nuts. I don't want to be called to a crime scene and find your body because you went after some muggers. If you hear anything, great, let us know. But let us handle it, okay?"

I grinned at him cheekily. "I'm just a receptionist, Stevens. What do I know about chasing bad guys?"

"I thought you were an assistant?" he said sarcastically.

They both rolled their eyes at me when I simply smirked and sipped my coffee.

"Well, gentlemen, it's been fun, but I have errands to run." I stood and gathered up my things. Mateo stood and waited patiently at my side.

Vincetti stopped me with a hand on my arm. "We're serious, Jocelyn. Be careful, okay?"

When Mateo growled at him, he dropped his hand and stepped back with raised eyebrows. "Protective."

I laughed. "I feed him steak; he's protecting his meal ticket."

"Uh huh." His face said he didn't doubt me. "Thanks for the tip about the homeless kids. We'll head over there and ask around."

A few minutes later and we were back in the Jeep.

"Well, that was a productive morning," I said.

"Pull into an alley and let me out. I'll fly over to the Nandis' and pick up the kid's stuff," Mateo said.

I nodded, turning on my signal. “But at least now I know where I need to be concentrating when I scry. Something tells me we’re going to find more than just the Nandi kid when we track them down.” I hoped to find Peter’s friends too.

“That’s what I’m afraid of,” Mateo said as I pulled into a sheltered alley and stopped the Jeep.

“I’ll see you at home?” I asked as I opened the door for him.

“Yes. Stay there until I get back,” he said and then jumped out. He stopped and looked back at me. “Be safe.”

“You too.”

I watched as he trotted behind a dumpster. Seconds later, a huge bald eagle flew up between the buildings and into the sky.

“So cool,” I whispered and then put the Jeep in gear and drove away.

Chapter Eleven

It was weird coming home without Mateo. In only a few short days, he had become so much a part of my life I had a hard time remembering what it was like without him. As I walked in the house and into the upper kitchen, I froze.

There was something different.

I looked around the sunlit room, not quite able to place what the problem was. Something nagged at me. I cautiously took a few more steps, careful to walk softly. As I looked over the counter, I realized there should have been dirty plates and cutlery in the sink from our breakfast yesterday. They were gone, and the chrome faucet glinted in the sun. The stove had been cleaned, and the windows looked like they had been polished. My red and white checked curtains around the window over the sink looked freshly laundered. The egg encrusted frying pan was missing, and the red kettle on top of the sparkling stove was placed precisely in the center. Chairs were pushed into the table at exactly ninety degree angles, and a rose from the garden was in a bud vase in the center.

What the hell?

I frowned as I walked further into the house. The living room, which should have been slightly dusty because I so rarely used it, was gleaming; the vintage wooden flooring looked like it had been sanded and refinished, it was so shiny. My wooden coffee tables had been polished, and the windows were cleaner than I had ever seen them; the decorative sage green drapes hung in perfect pleats. The throw pillows on the couches had attractive Vs in the tops. Everything was immaculate. It was like coming home to June Cleaver's house.

I could see the deadbolt and safety chain on the front door were still securely fastened, all the windows still firmly locked. I had to unlock the back door when I had come in from the garage, so I knew the house had been secure.

I backed out of the room quietly and left the house to sit in the backyard. I didn't know how long I had been sitting there staring, contemplating why someone would break into a house to clean without taking anything, before Mateo's dog form trotted out of the bushes leading to the park. He had a fairly large bag in his mouth, and he set it down beside me.

He looked at me then at the house and then back to me as I studied the house with narrowed eyes. "What are we doing?"

"Watching the house," I said absently, still thinking.

"Okay." He sat down beside me. "Why?"

I chewed on my lip in thought, my mother's ring chiming quietly as it rolled up and down my finger. "Because it's clean."

"It's clean," he repeated, clearly confused.

"When I came home and went inside, things weren't the same. Everything was clean."

"Isn't that a good thing?" he asked.

"Not when I didn't clean it and all the doors and windows were still locked," I replied.

I could practically feel his realization. His body stiffened next to me, and the hackles on his back stood up. "Stay here."

I snorted. "Yup."

He trotted away, nose to the ground. He circled the house once before disappearing. I assumed he was using the tunnel in the front to enter the hidden basement.

Long minutes later, he came back around the house, his hackles down but he was still clearly angry. "You can come inside. It's safe."

I stood and brushed myself off before gathering all my stuff and the bag from the Nandis. When we went back into the strangely clean kitchen, he turned to look at me.

"What?" I asked. He looked like he was mad at me again.

"A Brownie."

"A what?" Was he hungry? Wasn't chocolate bad for dogs? What did that have to do with our house being clean?

"We have a Brownie. A Boggart, a..." he struggled to explain "...a type of house-elf...thing."

I stared at him for a long moment. "You're telling me a creature just moved in here and decided to clean?"

He huffed out a frustrated breath. "I'm guessing the fairy clan you invited to live next to us had a Brownie living in the house that was being demolished. All I can think is the thing decided to move in here when the fairies moved to the park. Brownies only live in houses."

"Well, how do we get rid of it?" I asked with a squeak.

Mateo barked out a laugh. "You don't! And besides, why would you want to get rid of something that cleans your house when you're not looking?"

I threw up my hands. "Because I already have a roommate!" I huffed out a breath, releasing all the stored tension from my tense afternoon in the backyard. "Wait." I looked up. "It *likes* to clean?"

Mateo chuckled. "That's what Brownies do. My guess is it's made a home for itself somewhere in the house. All you have to do is leave out some honey or milk and the occasional loaf of fresh bread. The house will never be dirty again. You won't even see it. Brownies are almost never seen and work mostly at night or when the home owners are out."

"That's..." I thought for a minute. "That's kinda creepy. I don't know how I feel about something sneaking around the house while I sleep."

"Well, genius, there's nothing you can do about it now. You can't get rid of a Brownie once they move in, not without having serious damage done to the house. You would have to insult it repeatedly, after which it would trash the house in retaliation before leaving the mess to go and clean someone else's house," he said, almost sounding smug.

I sat down at the immaculate kitchen table and dropped my head in my hands. "My life used to be so much simpler." Three days ago I hadn't ever heard of

Brownies or Thriae or Trolls or Kitsune or...whatever Mateo's bar-owner-spider-man friend was. I shivered at the memory. Now, every fairy tale I had ever heard turned out to be true. I lived with a talking dog/cat/leopard/horse Shifter who was my new best friend; I have Unseelie Fairies for neighbours; I was hit on by a Satyr; I saved the life of a Dark Elf, only to learn he probably won't be too happy about it... I pulled at my hair, needing the world to slow down.

After rubbing my eyes, I peeked out from under my fingers. "Anything else you should be telling me before I die of shock?"

"It can probably be bribed to do light laundry duties if you leave chocolate lying around." The smug tone was still present.

Growling, I narrowed my eyes at my smartass protector. "I meant important stuff. *Big picture* kind of stuff."

He sat down and narrowed his eyes in thought. "Sidhe are ruled by a governing council. Each species has a representative on the council allowing for the peaceful mediation of disputes and negotiation of trade treaties. In the event of interspecies altercations, they can serve as a non-biased jury."

I sat up straighter. "That sounds reasonable."

He nodded. "In theory. But like in any political arena there are occasional backdoor deals and favoritism. Some species hold more power than others because of the goods they trade in. Some species hold a seat but rarely send a council member to attend, preferring to keep to themselves."

"You're talking about the Dark Elves."

He nodded. "As far as I know they haven't sat on the council in a few thousand years. Relations between the Light and Dark Elves became strained. I don't know much about the details, but there were implications of some kind of profiteering and exploitation. Battles broke out and a valuable resource was stolen. The Dark Elves were accused of betrayal. Whatever the circumstances were, it almost caused a war. The Dark Elves have rarely been seen since, refusing to align themselves to anyone or participate in trade."

"But how do they get the things they need?"

"They seem to need very little that they can't produce themselves. Outsiders aren't allowed within their borders, so very little is known about them."

Now I knew why Mateo had been so angry over wanting to help the Dark Elf and why he was worried about the possibility that elf was looking for me. I had a million more questions I wanted to ask but my yawn made it impossible to form anything resembling coherent speech.

"Come on." Mateo pulled at my jacket before padding off down the hall to the small reading room where the entrance to the hidden basement was concealed. "We can continue your history lessons another time."

I trudged behind him mechanically. "Where are we going?" I opened the bookcase and followed him down the stairs.

"You're going to bed to take a nap."

I rubbed at my eyes. "But the Nandis—"

He used his now larger leopard body to push me towards the bedroom. "Can wait a couple of hours. You've only had two hours sleep, and you need to be rested before we go out looking for trouble. Plus, I want to hear from Shido about the situation with the Dark Elf before we go anywhere."

Chapter Twelve

"Jocelyn."

A loud rumbling purr and the feel of something furry bumping against my cheek brought me out of sleep. I curled deeper into my bed, wanting nothing more than to go back to sleep.

"Jocelyn, the message from Shido is here."

I took a deep breath and cleared my throat. "How long was I sleeping?" I blinked my eyes to see Mateo, beautiful as a leopard, sitting beside the bed staring at me.

"Three hours. It's five-thirty." He grabbed the corner of the pillow I was using and started to pull.

"Nooo," I whined, trying in vain to keep it. "Five more minutes."

He laughed at my childish whining, pulling the pillow out from under me and dropping it on the floor. "Come on, sleepy, we have kids to find and Inquisitors to kill."

I sat up with a frown. "I don't kill people, Mateo."

"*You* might not, but I do." Satisfied I was up, he turned and padded out to the kitchen with his long tail flicking behind him.

Groaning, I dragged myself out of my warm cocoon of blankets, hoping he hadn't been serious about killing people; self-defense was one thing, but actively hunting people down in order to kill them was something else entirely. I was still smoothing back my hair as I walked into the kitchen to see one of Mr. Shido's foxes sitting in the empty area between the kitchen and living room. His small black eyes missed nothing as they darted around the room, the red bib standing out brilliantly against his snow white fur. The mischievous animal let out a happy yip when he saw me and gracefully scampered to sit in front of me.

I crouched down to see a roll of paper tucked into the red bib. "How did he know where to find us?" I asked Mateo as I pulled it free, keeping a wary eye on the fox. I had no desire to get bitten, no matter who sent him.

Mateo was focused intently on the small fox. His leopard eyes were unmistakably predatory as he ensured the furry messenger behaved himself. "The witch stone pendant Inari gave you. Part of the protection is making sure he can find you."

I sighed but it made sense. I unrolled the paper and began to read aloud.

Jocelyn-san,

I arrived at the discussed location to find it vacant. The guest there had apparently felt well enough to leave on his own. Despite a thorough *search, I could find no evidence that neither you, nor he, had been there.*

I will continue to make inquiries and inform you when I have answers. Until then, I would encourage you to be vigilant but assume he means you no immediate harm.

来

The note was signed with a Japanese character written in beautiful brush strokes that I assumed was Mr. Shido's name.

At Mateo's deep, angry, feline growl, the small fox scampered out of room and out the tunnel that led to the front porch.

Mateo snarled angrily. "*No immediate harm*? We waited all day for this?"

I sat for a moment watching his angry pacing. I was just as dissatisfied as he was but figured that Mr. Shido must have taken so long for a reason. "He was probably looking for the guy, Teo. He wouldn't have left us hanging all day for nothing." My next thought was that the elf couldn't have been as injured as I had thought if he was already up and gone, apparently under his own power.

Yawning, I stood up to make myself some coffee. The elf was not the immediate concern. "Where's the stuff from the Nandis? I want to get started on scrying so we can find those kids sooner rather than later."

Mateo was still growing but went to the cupboard that concealed the front tunnel where a large canvas shopping bag sat. He picked it up and brought it to me. Taking it from him, I went to sit on the couch so I could use the large, low, chest table in front of it to spread out the contents of the bag while I waited for my coffee to brew.

The Nandis were definitely serious about finding their child. The bag was pretty heavy, and looking inside I couldn't help but ask Mateo, "How in the name of the Goddess were you able to carry this all the way back from Guemes Island?"

He had a twinkle in his eyes and yawned widely, showing off his impressive fangs as if bored. "Because I'm amazing."

I laughed and threw one of the smaller decorative pillows at him. He of course batted it out of the air playfully, looking every inch the feline predator he was, albeit a more massive version.

I turned my attention back to the contents of the bag. Reaching in, I pulled out a plastic bag that held an abundance of silky red hair that looked to have been pulled from a hair brush. Another bag held a baby tooth. An envelope revealed the picture of a smiling red-headed child with a gap-toothed grin as he playfully peeked around the trunk of a large tree. The back of the picture read, "Dawen, age two," and must have been taken fairly recently. A plush stuffed cow that was missing one of its button eyes sat on top of a large, folded, well-loved patchwork quilt and was the reason the bag had been so heavy.

It was everything I had asked for and more, and as I gazed at the picture of the happy child, it brought tears to my eyes. It had probably killed Mrs. Nandi to pack all her little boy's favorite things and send them off to a complete stranger in the vague hope it might lead to getting her child back.

Mateo saw my tears and padded over to me, bumping his big head in my lap and purring. "We'll find him, Joss. We'll find them all. I can't see them keeping the children separate. If we find one, we'll find them all."

"What if they're already dead?" I voiced my fear in a choked whisper. "What if this is all she has left of her baby and I've taken it?" My thoughts drifted to the little girl I hadn't been able to find. I couldn't fail this time; my heart wouldn't take it.

"We'll never know unless you look." He used one of his paws and sharp claws to pull the throw blanket into my lap so I could wipe away my tears. "Faith and trust in the Lady. These children would not have been put in your path if *She* didn't want you to help them."

I nodded, not able to say anything just yet. I used the time it took to go to the kitchen and pour my coffee to compose myself. Stalling, I made some willow bark tea. My bumps and bruises were healing, but I was still sore. I needed to be calm and clearheaded to do the magick required for the location spell; emotional turmoil and physical pain would only distract me.

I stopped at the cupboard to the left of the open fireplace, which held my spelling supplies. Pulling out a wooden box, I returned to the couch. I reached around my neck and removed the simple silver chain I wore every day and placed it on the table. Nestled in the wooden box, surrounded by the cleansing energies of moonstones, was the quartz crystal pendant I used exclusively for pendulum scrying.

I opened the bag holding little Dawen's hair and carefully withdrew several long strands. Focusing solely on my desire to find the missing boy, I took the crystal pendant from the box and threaded it onto my silver chain before winding the long red hairs around the crystal and securing them to it with knots.

Matco watched as I placed the crystal on the table where I would leave it to charge with the boy's energy while I prepared for the rest of the spell. "You do this often?" he asked.

I shrugged. "More often than I like. The night we met I was coming home from trying to find a little girl named Toncsha Johnson. She was only nine years old." Pausing, I looked at him, almost pleading for answers. "I don't know what went wrong. The spell didn't *work*. I even hit the streets to do my searching the old fashioned way. It's the first time I've ever failed. Normally, I can at least find a body..." My voice trailed off. I couldn't think about my failure right now. I needed to be focused on this child.

Mateo's voice brought me back to the present. "What else do you do?"

"Usually, I start with a world map if the child has been gone long enough to be smuggled to another country. From there, I use map after map until I narrow it down to the general location I need to search. Since we know Dawen Nandi is likely here in the city, I'll start with the Seattle map right away," I explained as I opened the drawer in the chest table to pull out my world atlas and a huge stack of maps.

"You don't use any other magick than the pendulum?" he asked.

I looked at him in confusion. "No. Is there something else I could be doing?"

"Try scrying in a protective circle. Include an appropriate offering at your altar. The magick will be stronger with the attention of the Lord and Lady."

I grew excited; it had taken me almost two whole days to get the location of the last person I had successfully looked for. Anything that sped up the process was a definite bonus. "What would be appropriate?"

"You need aspects of the Gods that bring about truth, prophesy for the location, and wisdom. There is a possibility of danger..." His whiskers twitched as he mumbled his thoughts. His eyes narrowed as he made his decision. "Bay or laurel leaves and olive oil would be acceptable offerings."

Before I did anything, I needed to set up the second half of my evening. If we got a location as quickly as Mateo seemed to think we would, I wanted to know everything I could about what we would be walking into. After filling my cauldron with fresh rainwater, I started the fire underneath it. Laying my hands on the side of the still cool pot, I whispered:

"Herbal potion, cauldron brew
now be charged with magick true.
With intent I speak this charm,
that all be blessed and none be harmed.
Ever minding the law of three,
this is my will, so mote it be."

Reassured that my intentions were good, I added my usual three parts rose petals, one part cinnamon, one part nutmeg, one part bay leaf, and one part mugwart to the water, leaving it to boil while I hopefully got a location through the pendulum. I could come back to this later.

Instead of spreading the maps on the coffee table as I usually did, I followed Mateo's directions and set everything up in front of my altar. I spread Dawen's blanket on the floor to kneel on during the spell and placed his picture in the center of the altar. It was more cramped than I was used to, but if it worked it would be well worth it. After pouring a salt circle, I knelt in front of the altar reverently and requested the attention and protection of the Gods. Reaching forward, I first lit the green candle on the left and then the red one on the right before lighting a cone of incense on the seashell in the center of the table. Picking up the quartz pendant by the silver necklace in my left hand, I smoothed out the Seattle city map on the baby blanket between me and the altar. As it began to gently swing and then settle into a circling motion, I began to speak.

"Sun and Moon, dark and light,
guide my hand to what is lost this night.
Forth and back, right and left,
locate the child, a family's heart bereft.
Help me find that which is lost,
the innocent life valued beyond any cost."

I focused on the memory of little Dawen's smiling face as the pendulum started to circle gently above the map. I let out a relieved sigh; he was here. It wasn't like last time when the pendulum had only swung back and forth, indicating a negative response to my query. Pushing aside my relief, I concentrated. I refused to think of the tip we had gotten from Stevens and Vincetti earlier. I didn't want the possible location to influence the magick in any way. There was no way of knowing if that information was correct or if the two cases were connected; I had to remain centered and completely unbiased. Nevertheless, the pendulum started pulling towards the East Industrial District. As I followed the movement, the circles began to get smaller and smaller, the quartz pendulum rotating ever faster as it homed in on the location of the person it was charged to find. In seconds the crystal stopped abruptly on a street corner deep in the seediest part of the area, right on the docks. I dropped my hand with a sigh and heard Mateo let out a growl. Whether it was in anger or anticipation, I wasn't sure.

"The incantation is good," Mateo commented absently.

I nodded. "I only use it for lost children. It took me forever to get the wording right, but I have better luck with that one than any of the others I've tried. The circle helped though. I've never gotten a location this fast before."

We studied the map for a few more minutes before I placed my offering of a few drops of olive oil and a fresh laurel leaf on the offering plate. I whispered my thanks to the Lord and Lady for their assistance before snuffing out the candles and breaking the circle. I gathered the map as I walked to the kitchen. It was time to find out what I would be up against at the warehouse.

Mateo padded after me. "What's the cauldron for?" he asked.

"I like to get an idea of what I'm up against when I go looking for trouble," I said. And I wanted to see if Dawen was alive, although I didn't voice that particular thought.

Mateo shifted from leopard to tabby cat and gracefully jumped up on the counter beside the fireplace so he would have a better view. "Hydromancy," he stated.

"Yup," I said as I turned off the now boiling herb-infused water.

"What, no crystal ball?" he teased as he flicked his tail.

"Are you kidding? Those things are like six hundred bucks for a decent sized one! I don't need to spend that kind of coin when a bowl of water works just as well." I snorted and rolled my eyes. Freaking crystal ball! How cliché!

"I'm truly impressed at your depth of knowledge, Joss. I have never seen a Danaan of your age doing such advanced magick. Taking into account that you should be virtually untrained, it's staggering."

I felt myself blush under his praise. "And yet you had to teach me a kindergartener's cloaking spell."

"Gaps, Joss." His tail flicked as we waited for the water to boil. "You have gaps that are easily filled. The magick you're performing on your own is normally stuff a century's old Danaan is proficient at. The rest will come."

As the water started to boil, Mateo suggested I wear the scrying pendant around my neck and hold the quilt, both objects further anchoring me to Dawen's energy.

Pulling a teaspoon from the drawer, I scooped out a mouthful of the now bubbling water. After blowing on it to cool, I drank it as I cleared my mind. Repeating the process twice more, I added a single strand of Dawen's hair to the steaming brew.

"Stygian Sisters, Swan Maidens of sight,
the use of your eye is required this night.
Children stolen, subjected to horrors untold,
mirror my water with events as they unfold."

As I spoke, I gazed intently into the still, black water. The steam danced over the surface, teasing me with shadowed glances of fuzzy images. Then the images began to clear.

A child cried as he lay curled at the bottom of a cage. I forced myself to focus as I watched him shiver and pull his gangly calf legs closer to his body, one hand rubbing the silky hair of his tail back and forth over his nose as he sucked his thumb and tried to soothe himself. The image pulled away and around him I saw more cages containing more children. A faintly-spotted feline child hissed and spit as a man with a scarred face banged on its cage while the man beside him frowned. It looked as if he hadn't liked his companion's taunting of the child.

A human boy in the cage next to it looked shell-shocked and cried silently beside a much tinier little girl who clung to him. The last cage held a fiercely scowling little boy with chin length black hair barely concealing his pointed ears and dark olive complexion. It had to be the elven child. He was chained in addition to being caged and looked as if he had put up quite a fight if the black eye and bruised cheek were any evidence. I got the feeling the little warrior would be pacing if it weren't for the chains around his ankles and wrists that were attached to a metal collar. The kid was trussed up better than most convicts.

I was disheartened to see that the human children missing from Seattle weren't anywhere my vision could reach. My heart ached at the conversation I would have to have with Tonesha's parents as well as Peter. They would need to know that Tonesha, Ray-Ray, and little 'Shell weren't ever likely to come home.

Refocusing on my vision, the warehouse was dark and dingy with the evening light barely filtering through dirt blackened windows. Unused machinery lay scattered around. A man paced on a catwalk high above, his hands holding some kind of gun. From my love of action movies, I knew it was something like a machine gun and would let out a hail of bullets with the squeeze of a trigger. It was in sharp contrast to the crucifix he wore around his neck and the monk's tonsure haircut.

A man lay on a cot, injured, while another prayed at his side. They too had guns within easy reach. A large crucifix hung on one wall. Two more men sat around a table, studying a map of Seattle. One of them held what looked like a rock in his hands. The only one without the weird haircut was the one with the rock. It was Scripture Guy, the short one who had gotten away the night I was attacked and again when Mateo and I had saved the elf. He seemed to hold the rock with reverence and would gesture to it and then point to places on the map as he talked to the other man. What was it?

"What do you see, Joss?" Mateo's voice was slow and sounded so far away.

My words felt thick in my mouth as I described the scene and the location of the kids. Before I could get to the strange rock the *priest* was holding, I stopped, feeling dizzy. My eyes began to water, and I took a deep breath before pulling back from gazing into the cauldron. Blinking a few times, I squeezed my eyes shut, rubbing at them as they stung.

"How long was I out?" I asked, my eyes had never stung and watered like this before.

"Almost an hour."

Well, that explained the watering eyes. Staring and not blinking for an hour would dry out the eyeballs. "I've never seen that much detail before. And I've never been under for that long."

"Magick is like a muscle. The more you use it, the stronger it gets. You have been given the gift of sight, walked among the Sidhe, drunk of their wine. You may have been strong before, but now you've been awakened. Your powers will only strengthen."

I opened my stinging eyes to see Mateo, still perched as a cat on the counter, staring at me. "I don't know what that means."

"For now, all it means is that you're getting stronger. Details and answers will come as you need and are ready to hear them." His explanation was cryptic, and I didn't like the sound of it.

"What aren't you telling me?"

"A lot. But if I were to tell you everything I know, we would be sitting here for years. I'm not deliberately hiding things from you, but as I said, baby steps. You can't expect twenty years of the knowledge you're behind on to just be handed to you. Some things have to be revealed in context, otherwise they're too unbelievable and fantastic to be true." He jumped down from the counter, turning to a leopard mid jump. "Come on, I want to know everything you saw."

He was right. If someone had just sat me down last week and told me everything I had seen so far, I would have called the men in the white coats. I had to see to start to truly *believe*.

Getting comfortable on the couch, I told him everything. When I got to the part about the rock, Mateo growled.

"What is it?" I asked.

His tail flicked violently as he started to pace. "It's a witch stone. It has to be, but I can't figure out how they would have gotten their hands on one."

I fingered the one around my neck. I thought about how the priest had held it almost reverently. "They were looking at a map while they held it. Could it be how they're finding the children?"

Mateo growled something that sounded positive. "Have you felt how your stone seems to vibrate when you get close to something or someone Sidhe?"

Thinking back, I realized he was right. When Shido had handed it to me, it had vibrated. It had happened again when we went to see the fairies and again when we went to the Troll Market. "*Lord and Lady*," I whispered. "What do we do? Won't it warn them if you and I show up?"

He stopped pacing and I could tell he was thinking. "I'm hoping they haven't figured out exactly how it works yet and they will think it's because of the kids."

"That's a thin hope." I felt cold and clammy all over. For the first time in my life, I was running *into* a dangerous confrontation. The concept was completely foreign to me. I would have to face down the same men that had been trying to kill me my whole life. There would be no calling the police to have them save the Sidhe children, no more running away. I felt sick.

"I don't know if I can do this." My voice was a whisper.

"You can't," Mateo said. When I looked up at him, he continued. "*We* can. It's not just you anymore, Joss. I have been in battle many times before. You're not going in there alone. I *will* protect you and we *will* save those kids."

I took a deep breath and nodded.

"But you need to realize those men have to die." My head shot up at his statement, immediately shaking in denial. "Don't shake your head at me. They know too much, Joss. They have somehow gotten their hands on a powerful Sidhe talisman and have figured out what it means and how to work it. They likely know where the Troll Market is and are only taking kids because they're the easiest to pick off."

I stood up and practically ran to the kitchen. I began to clean up my mess to keep my hands busy. I felt like I was ready to rattle apart. "I can't... *We* can't." My chest was tight, and I felt like I couldn't breathe. "The Goddess doesn't..." I spun to look at him. "By the

Goddess, Teo! I can't be responsible for killing someone!"

"You won't be. I'll take care of it." He sat calmly on the floor between the living room and kitchen, watching me freak out. "How many Sidhe do you think they've killed? How many innocent humans? Danaan? People you're related to, if only distantly."

He had a point, but I couldn't do it, couldn't be a part of it. "I'm not like them! If we do this, it makes me no better than they are. I can't be a part of that."

His head cocked to the side as he asked, "So you would rather walk away and let the children die?"

I threw up my hands at his obviously ridiculous question and went back to cleaning. "Of course not, but there has to be a better way. I won't commit murder." The kitchen was spotless as I looked around for something else to clean. Damn it! The place was immaculate. Why the hell had I been so happy that a Brownie had moved in?

He growled and started to clean and chew on his claws. He looked as frustrated as I felt. I got the feeling that chewing at his feet was his answer to my frantic need to clean something. We were deadlocked, neither willing to budge, and I knew he had the upper hand. I couldn't stop him from doing it.

I leaned against the counter, staring unseeingly at the immaculate sink. "I thought you believed in the Goddess?" I asked over my shoulder. "I thought you followed Her? I thought She sent you to me?"

He sighed. "My relationship with the Goddess is complicated. While I have faith in the Lord and Lady, I don't always agree with Them. My own experiences have left me feeling...very angry and at times resentful towards Them."

I turned and opened my mouth to ask why, but he shook his head, forestalling my questions. "I don't want to talk about it, Joss. Suffice to say that my first and only concern is for you and your safety. Killing may not be the way of the Goddess, but it is the only way to keep you safe and save those kids."

Tears welled up in my eyes. I may not have known why, but I understood his crisis of faith. Gods knew I had been there before. "There has to be another way. There has to be a way to make them see that blind bigotry and hatred aren't the way."

He stilled, looking thoughtful.

"What?" I asked. He seemed to have thought of an alternative.

Mateo shook his head. "No. No, it wouldn't work."

My fingers started to move nervously, the tinkling sounds of the three bands of my mother's ring sliding up and down my right ring finger filling the silence. "What wouldn't work? Teo, if you've thought of an alternative, I want to hear it."

He sighed and looked at me intently. "It would be kinder to kill them."

"Teo, please." If he had thought of an alternative to murder, I was all for it.

He closed his eyes briefly in resignation. He opened them and looked at me intently. "There's a spell. It does exactly what you've suggested. It will make them see and feel everything they're doing."

"But that's..." my mouth fell open at what he was suggesting "...it would mean using magick against someone. I would be doing *harm*." It went directly against the Wiccan Rede.

An it harm none, do what ye will.

"Yes...and no," Mateo said. "If they were doing nothing but good things for others, it would only make them feel the goodness they were doing. It's the three-times rule personified."

"But they're abducting and killing people..."

He gave the feline version of a shrug. "It's their actions that direct the spell. The spell itself is benign."

Confusion and horror warred within me. "But I *know* it will hurt them."

Again, he simply shrugged. "It will likely drive them mad, but you wanted an alternative to killing them."

Remembering the man in the vision who had frowned when his companion had tormented the Kirata child, I made my decision. "I'll do it. Teach me the spell."

If there was even a slight chance that one or more of the Inquisitors wasn't one hundred percent committed to their horrific and misguided beliefs, I had to try. If I stood by and allowed Mateo to kill them all, I would be betraying all the tenets I lived by.

Mateo's whiskers twitched as he looked at me in concern. "Are you sure about this?"

I nodded, not completely convinced, but it was the only alternative. "Yes. Let's do it."

We spent the rest of the day going over our plan of attack and preparing the new spell that would make it all happen.

Chapter Thirteen

Pulling my Jeep into a shadowed parking spot, I pulled the parking brake and shut off the engine. We were in a deserted part of the industrial area of Seattle, down by the docks, just around the corner from the warehouse where the Inquisitors had set up shop. Mateo and I had argued about the best time to hit the warehouse and save the kids. He had wanted to go early to catch the Inquisitors all in one place, but I had argued that if we went around midnight they might be out looking for more victims. While I didn't want them to hurt or kidnap anyone else, it meant there would be less of them for us to deal with and a better chance for us to save all the children.

I wanted to be able to do a thorough search of the warehouse to see if, by some small chance, my magick had been wrong and Ray-Ray, little 'Shell, and Tonesha were there. Plus, there was a lesser chance of roaming humans. Mateo agreed to it as long as he could stay behind to clean up the returning strays while I got the kids out of there. I didn't ask him about the clean-up. I didn't want to hear his answer.

"Are you ready for this?" Mateo was in his dog form in the seat beside me.

I nodded but didn't say anything. I pulled up the deep hood of my most comfortable hoodie, adjusting my long braid over my shoulder and zipping it inside to keep it out of the way. Mateo had wanted me to wear my cloak, but if there was a chance of me fighting at all, the cloak would become a weapon that could be used against me. We compromised on a hoodie to conceal my features just in case.

Reaching for the handle, I opened the door and jumped down out of the jeep. Mateo followed silently and waited while I pulled my bag from its place in the milk crate behind my seat. Pulling the strap over my head and across my chest, I closed the door, looking down and nodding at him. "Okay. I'm ready." Taking a step towards the warehouse across the street, he let out a low bark to get my attention.

"I *will* protect you." The pointed ears and sharp features of his shepherd form looked fierce in the shadows cast by the nearby street light.

Switching my mother's ring from its usual comfortable loose fit on my right ring finger to the tighter fit of my middle finger so I wouldn't lose it, I shook my head. "No, your first priority is those kids. They need to go home to their parents."

"Joss—" he growled but I interrupted.

"No, Mateo! I'm not kidding with this. Those kids *will* be going home to their parents. Promise me." I stared at him, willing him to agree.

His ears flattened out and his eyes narrowed. "No, my job—my duty—is to protect *you*. More than that, you're my friend. I will not watch something happen to you to save a bunch of children. You can't make me promise you something like that." The hair on his neck started to stand on end, and his lips turned into a half snarl.

I opened my mouth to argue further, but Mateo's head snapped to the alleyway closest to us and snarls erupted from his mouth. His body took on an aggressive stance. All the hair on his back stood on end, bristling. I tensed behind him, ready for an Inquisitor to attack, when a tall, dark shadow separated from the rest.

"Perhaps I can offer an alternative." The voice was low and slightly rough, coming from the depths of a hooded and cloaked figure.

Recognizing the Dark Elf, I took a nervous step back.

He held up his hands as if in surrender. "I mean you no harm, milady." His voice was just as I remembered it from the Gorgon's Head, if not a little rougher because of the beating he had taken.

Mateo growled in a continuous deep grumble and took a step forward.

The elf took a half step back. "I speak truly. I wish to help you, milady Danaan."

Apparently, that was the wrong thing to say. Mateo stalked forward, growing larger as he did, spots morphing into stripes as the fur changed into that of a Bengal Tiger. Knowing him as I did now, I knew he was truly pissed. Exposing his fangs threateningly, he pinned his ears and hissed. "You won't take her! I will not allow you to turn her into a slave for your political games, elf!"

"Ease yourself, familiar. I mean her no harm." He was speaking faster, trying to convince Mateo of his sincerity, his hands still visible as he took another step back. "I am only here to free my young Prince; I didn't come here for her. I owe her a life debt."

That gave Mateo pause. He stopped stalking the elf and backed up against me. I was shaking. I wasn't sure what Mateo meant about the elf not taking me or his talk of slaves. Mateo had told me that my kind was rare and valuable, but did that make us valuable as a commodity? The thought hadn't occurred to me before. Then I thought about the lengths we went to keep my face hidden, his insistence that no one know what I am, his worry at the Troll Market. My fingers tightened in his fur, scared suddenly that I was in a whole new type of danger.

"What does that mean?" I took another step back; Mateo matched it. "Teo," I whispered and felt his tail curve around my legs as if to reassure me.

"He means you saved his life," Mateo growled, his attention not shifting from the elf in front of us.

"I owe you," the elf stated and nodded deeply.

This felt like it meant more than I understood. "Well, you're welcome." I took another step back, my instincts urging me to get in my Jeep and get as far from here as possible, the mention of slaves still fresh in my mind. He was a lot bigger than I thought, now that he was on his feet, and I remembered Mateo arguing with me about helping him. How he said Dark Elves were ruthless and untrustworthy, the accusations of exploitation.

"Honestly, you don't owe me anything. It was nothing."

The elf frowned under his hood. "My life is not nothing," he snapped but calmed down, quickly raising his hands in a placating gesture when my hand went to the door of my Jeep. "I'm sorry. Don't go. On my honor, I swear I am not here to hurt or use you in any way. While I meant to find you eventually to acknowledge the life debt, my first duty is to my Queen. I came here to save the boy and return him to his mother. Our meeting is a fortuitous coincidence."

My heart was in my throat. It was all too much to take in. I had never let myself get in any kind of situation like this before. "Who are you? What do you want?"

He cautiously brought his hands to his hood and lowered it, revealing his face. The bruises were almost gone. The nasty cuts were now puckered pink lines as if having healed for weeks rather than only a day. Mateo let out a huff and flicked an ear at me. I was sure he was just as surprised as I was at how quickly the elf had healed.

"My name is Caelan. For the moment, I want only to save my Prince and return him to his parents. As we have the same goal, it would be prudent to work together." With the hood back, I could see he was armed to the teeth. A sword hung at his side, a quiver of arrows on his back, the tip of a bow showing over his shoulder, and leather braces on his forearms and shins revealed the hilts of daggers.

Mateo's head tilted to the side as he considered the elf for a minute. To his credit, Caelan stayed still as a statue. I wondered what Mateo would decide. I sure as hell wasn't saying anything.

The answer came as Mateo took a step forward, his fur leaving my fingers as he shrank back into his more public persona as a shepherd. "Fine. But as soon as this is over, you leave and forget all about her and your life debt. The best way to repay her is by forgetting she exists at all."

Caelan shook his head. "You know I can't do that."

"You don't have a choice. If she is brought into the open, she'll become a target. Every race in the known worlds will be hunting her." Mateo was growling again, irritated that the elf wasn't agreeing with him.

My thoughts were whirling through the snippets of information revealed in the last few minutes as well as the history lesson Mateo had given me earlier. Slaves, a target, every race in the *known worlds*? By the Gods, what was going on?

"I won't let that happen." Caelan shook his head.

Mateo snarled and stepped forward again. As his anger grew, so did his size until he had shifted to a leopard, his tail thrashing in agitation. "You won't be able to stop it! She's not ready! She's not even thirty years old. She's—"

My fear slipped to irritation and the volume of their currently pointless argument was getting loud enough that the Inquisitors were bound to hear them. It was obvious this was dissolving into a pissing match and could go on all night.

"*She* is right here! If you two don't shut up, we won't have to worry about who finds out about me 'cause I'll be dead!" I snapped. "Sweet Circe, you two are terrible! We're here to save a bunch of kids, not fight about something I may not live to see."

Throwing up my hands, I started walking towards the warehouse. This obviously wasn't something that would be resolved in the next few minutes. They could stand there and argue all night for all I cared. I would not stand there and let another child disappear.

"No!" Mateo whisper-shouted behind me.

"Wait!" Caelan half yelled.

Their respective attempts at getting me to stop overriding each other were urgent enough to stop me. I turned to look at them, the panicked looks on their faces almost comical.

"Are you two coming or am I going in there by myself?" I asked, propping a hand on my hip in irritation.

They shared a commiserating look, as only males could, and turned to join me.

Caelan stepped forward and reached out to grab my arm, but Mateo leaped in between us with a fang showing in warning.

Caelan held up his hands. "I just thought we should come up with a plan first. I meant no harm..." he looked at me "...milady—"

I huffed at him, interrupting whatever it was he was going to say. "My name is Jocelyn. *Just* Jocelyn. I'm sure where you come from titles are important, but here I'm just plain Jocelyn."

I caught Mateo's frustrated eye roll out of the corner of my eye.

Caelan smiled and nodded respectfully. "As you wish." He gestured back to the shadows of the alley. "I merely thought it prudent to discuss tactics before storming the gates, so to speak."

"We have a plan," Mateo stated.

As we walked to the alley, I frowned at Mateo. He was being stubborn in refusing Caelan's help. I wanted to smack him but wouldn't in front of Caelan. "What Mateo *means*," I said with a half-growl of my own and a pointed look at my furry friend, "is that we have a pretty good idea what we're up against, and we made a plan. Now that you're here, we should re-evaluate."

As I explained the layout of the warehouse and the number of Inquisitors that could be inside, Mateo paced in front of me, keeping a wary eye on Caelan, who, for the most part, looked unconcerned about the agitated leopard.

"What is your biggest concern?" Caelan asked.

I looked at Mateo, deferring to his experience.

"The guns on the catwalk. We're not sure exactly how many are going to be up there, and I'm worried about Jocelyn exposed on the floor by herself," Mateo admitted grudgingly.

Caelan smirked. "Well, that is no longer a concern. I'll take care of the men and ensure their guns are no longer a problem."

Mateo tensed when Caelan pulled a long, ornate, but lethal looking knife from the sheath at his calf, handing it to me hilt first. “If you get to my Prince before I do, make sure you give him this. His name is Ares.”

I looked at him in disbelief. “You want me to give a knife to a child?”

Caelan chuckled and even Mateo seemed momentarily amused. “He may be young, but don’t underestimate my Prince. Young Ares can be quite formidable. And when he sees it he will know to trust you.”

While that made sense, I wasn’t too keen to hand a weapon to a kid no matter how *formidable* he may be. “We have a spell that should incapacitate the Inquisitors, but we have to get the kids out before I can perform it.” Thinking, I realized that with him there he would be subject to the dangers of the spell as well.

Mateo looked up at me, easily following my train of thought. “Dig into your carpet bag and get him an amulet as well.”

I rolled my eyes at his continued abuse of my bag and started fishing around inside it for one of the sachets I made in case I couldn’t get the kids out before casting the spell. “Knock it off. It’s not that big.” Sticking out my tongue and glaring at Mateo when I found it quickly, I handed Caelan a pouch of pungent dried herbs on a string. “Tie this around your neck. Try to get it close to your nose where you can smell it easily. When I cast the spell inside, you do not want to breathe in the smoke or you’ll be subject to its effect.”

As he did so, he studied me, wrinkling his nose at the smell. “Neither of you have one?”

I shook my head. "I'll be inside a circle, and as my familiar, Mateo isn't subject to my powers." At least if what Mateo had told me was true. I had to admit I was really worried about that part.

Caelan took a large square of fabric from the folds of his cloak and fastened it around his neck. "I can pull this up over my face when you cast the spell."

I nodded. "That will work. Just make sure the herb pouch is under it as well so you can't smell any of the smoke."

He nodded. My mouth opened as if to ask a question but I hesitated. I needed his help but they were humans. Would he be willing to help them? Mateo's warnings about Dark Elves caused the words to dry up in my throat. Would I be putting them in more danger if he did help? Closing my mouth, I swallowed. The risk would have to be worth it. I wouldn't be able to search for them all on my own, not without getting caught. "There may be more children hidden in the building somewhere, separate from the others. Three human children have also gone missing in the past month. Two girls and a boy. I couldn't see them with my magick but I'm hoping. I know they're not Sidhe but–"

He held up a hand interrupting my nervous rambling. "All children are precious, and I will look for them the best I can. If I find them, I will free them just as I would any child of my world."

The look on his face was earnest. I nodded, giving him a small smile. "Thank you."

A few more particulars were discussed before we split up. I shook my head as I watched Caelan literally melt into the shadows, all but invisible unless you knew what to look for. Without being told, I *cloaked* myself. Mateo slinked from spot to spot, keeping up with me, but now looking like nothing more than a stray alley cat. Waiting the agreed upon five minutes, I made my way to the nearest door. As Caelan promised, it was unlocked. Easing it open a crack, Mateo slipped inside. Before long, he was back, and with a glance I knew the coast was clear. Quickly ducking behind a large wooden crate, I strained my ears.

The warehouse was rank with the metallic scents of old oil, dirt, and hydraulic fluid barely masking the smell of human waste. Furious, I noticed the assholes weren't even allowing the kids the use of a bathroom. I could hear one of the kids crying as another tried to offer comfort. I realized my being quiet really wasn't necessary because of all the sermonizing going on. Peeking over the edge of the crate, my blood ran cold. There were *way* more Inquisitors than the six I had seen in my cauldron. In between old pieces of machinery, I had a view across the warehouse. It looked like a small service at a ghetto monastery.

No less than twenty men, all wearing the same crappy tonsure haircut, knelt in front of the goriest crucifix I had ever seen. Apparently, they hadn't been satisfied with the regular amount of suffering Jesus usually depicted. This one looked like he had been bathed in blood, and rather than serene acceptance, his face was contorted in agony, a silent scream coming from his mouth.

The *priest* I had seen holding the stone in the waters of my cauldron, the one I thought of as Scripture Guy, stood on a small raised dais and was all but shouting sanctimonious bullshit that sounded like nothing more than pure bigotry worthy of the most fanatical Klan member. I flinched, my heart racing, when something brushed against me. I looked down to see Mateo, his emerald green eyes blazing in the dim light. His paws were flexing, and I got the impression it was taking everything he had to keep from shifting to something deadly enough to kill them all.

As I listened to the sermon, I felt my face blanch.

"We are the servants, the tools of our Lord! In His name we will smite down the threat to the righteous!" He held up an ominous looking package. Wires and electronics covered the outside along with another image of the gory crucifix and an ornately decorated cross.

Maybe it was the completely unreal situation I found myself in or the proximity to real danger. Maybe it was the adrenalin causing my endorphins to go into overdrive. I had a totally inappropriate mental image and snorted back a laugh, unable to help myself.

Mateo looked at me incredulously, obviously wondering what I could possibly find funny in these circumstances.

"Sorry, but he's got a *Holy Hand Grenade,*" I whispered, my eyes wide and a bit blurry with tears that I wasn't sure were from fear or laughter. At his blank look, I rolled my eyes, taking a deep breath to calm the conflicting emotions and the tension in my chest. "If we get out of this, we are *so* having a Monte Python marathon." I turned my attention back to the Mass of destruction, trying to stifle the hilarious thought of Mateo shifting into a white bunny and ripping people apart. The priest's next words wiped the humor from the situation.

"We must remember the sacrifice of Samson, my brothers." The priest raised his hands, gesturing wildly to prove his points.

"Judges 16: 23-31 says the rulers of the Philistines assembled to offer a great sacrifice to Dagon, their heathen god. Blind, weak, and forced into entertaining his captors..." Scripture Guy staggered a bit, leaning against his pulpit, acting as if he was Samson, squinting his eyes shut and mimicking blindness. "Samson waited, biding his time until the temple was crowded with men and women; all the rulers of the Philistines were there, and on the roof were about three thousand men and women watching Samson perform. Then Samson prayed to the Lord." He threw his head back, his eyes squeezed shut as he fell to his knees in supplication, palms raised to the heavens. "'Sovereign Lord, remember me. Please, God, strengthen me just once more, and let me with one blow get revenge on the Philistines for my two eyes.'"

Scripture Guy exaggeratedly climbed to his feet as if it took enormous effort. "Then Samson reached toward the two central pillars on which the temple stood." Arms wide, he pantomimed grasping the pillars of the temple and acted out his words. "Bracing himself against them, his right hand on the one and his left hand on the other, he pushed with all his might, and down came the temple on the rulers and all the people in it. Thus he killed many more when he died than while he lived, sacrificing himself while doing the Lord's work."

The priest turned his attention back to his captivated congregation. "From this we see that in order to serve the Lord our God, sometimes the ultimate sacrifice is necessary and just. Our crusade will be swift and decisive. We will smite the wicked, purging the streets of Seattle and the world. We will attack on two fronts. First, will be the market where the evil congregates. Brother Ezekiel has earned his place in paradise, and like Sodom and Gomorrah, *God's justice* will rain down upon those whom the Devil has sent!" The last was said with an enraptured yell. Every sentence was dramatically stressed with emphatic gestures.

A chorus of "Amen" rose from the captivated men.

"Second, will be the drawing out of surviving demons. We will use the spawn captured to entrap those who remain. None will escape God's glorious cleansing." He looked out with a falsely sympathetic face. "I know there are those among you who may be feeling uncomfortable with the deaths of these *children.* Do not be fooled by the image of their innocence. Demons are masters of lies and deceit. They are the seeds from which evil grows."

He said the word *children* as if it were poison in his mouth. "Our Lord and Maker has provided us the reassurance of His Path in Samuel 15:2-3. 'Thus sayeth the LORD spare them not; but slay both man and woman, *infant and suckling*, ox and sheep, camel and ass.'"

Studying his audience carefully, he enforced the genocide he was promoting with another quote. "Ezekiel 9:5-6. 'And to the others he said in mine hearing, Go ye after him through the city, and smite: let not your eye spare, neither have ye pity: Slay utterly old and young, both maids, and *little children*.'"

The congregation was nodding in agreement now. Scripture Guy had made his point. I felt sick. How could anyone blindly follow such obviously horrific teachings? Tears spilled over my cheeks at the enthusiasm displayed by the men in front of me. Nothing about this was right. I was too appalled by the blatant savage bigotry to even form a prayer for strength.

The priest raised his hands and voice, shouting to the audience. "The righteous shall rejoice when He sees the vengeance. He shall wash his feet in the blood of the wicked! Happy shall he be, that taketh and dasheth thy little ones against the stones!"

All the men were on their feet now, cheering and throwing their hands back in adoration.

Mateo made a noise beside me that was reminiscent of a cat hacking up a hairball. "I'm going to see if I can find the keys for the cages. You try to get in position."

Wiping the tears off my face and tamping down my fear, I nodded. With a glance at the ceiling to make sure the guards on the catwalks were actually gone, I ducked down, darting from place to place to get closer to the children's containment area. Before long, I was backed against a large wooden crate nearest to the kids. My pendant vibrated under my shirt, and peeking around the corner, I tried to figure out who to free first. As my eyes darted from one cage to the next, a quiet gasp drew my attention. The tiny girl had seen me.

Putting my finger to my lips, I motioned for her to keep quiet, hoping she would understand. If she made too much noise, this rescue attempt would be over before it started. She blinked and nodded but tugged on the sleeve of the boy she was curled up against. When she whispered to him, he turned to look at me, and I recognized the Canadian boy Stevens and Vincetti had told me about. Why the hell was he here? I shushed him as well before ducking back behind the crate.

Movement beside me made me look down to see Mateo sidling up to me—I think.

I whispered around my hand, which had flown up to cover my mouth. "A ferret?"

He sat up and handed me a ring of keys in his furry paws. "Shut up. It worked, didn't it? And you try carrying keys without..." he looked down at his paws, and his whiskers twitched "...hands," he finished lamely.

I choked back a giggle and peeked around the crate again. *So not the time to fall over laughing*.

"Try to slip the keys to Ares if you can. He can free himself and the other kids while you perform the spell." His voice was deeper now, and I glanced back to see he had shifted back into his more dignified shepherd form.

I nodded. "You realize I am *never* going to let you live this down, don't you?" I whispered before slinking out towards the cages, not waiting for his answer.

Keeping an eye on the men clearly still caught up in their adulation, I crouched as low as I could, using my hands for balance. I was in plain view of the kids now, and they had clearly realized I wasn't there to hurt them.

Reaching Dawen's cage, I pulled the battered plush toy his mother had sent me from my bag. As the youngest, he was most likely to give us away. "Hey, buddy. Your mom and dad sent me to get you." His eyes lit up when he saw the little cow and his chin quivered. "Hang on to this and be brave. You'll be out of here soon, okay?"

He nodded and pulled the toy to his chest shyly. "I wanna go hom-m-me. I want M-m-mommy." Tears welled up in his beautiful big brown eyes as he looked at me.

"I know, sweetie. Stay quiet and do as you're told, and it'll all be over soon, alright?" He nodded and I ruffled his hair before moving on. When I got close to Ares, I pulled out the dagger Caelan had given me. Seeing it, his eyes took on a wicked, almost bloodthirsty look. When his chains rattled, I shushed him.

"I'm going to get you out of here. When you get out, you're going to take this dagger and the keys and free the other kids," I whispered.

He sneered at me as only a tough little boy could. "I can fight."

Huffing in frustration, I levelled my best "*mom*" look at him. "I'm sure you *can*, but what you're *going* to do is free the other kids and get them out of here. There's a green Jeep around the corner—that's your goal."

A stubborn look took over his face. "But—"

Interrupting him, I glared. "No, Ares! I need you to protect the other kids while Caelan, my friend, and I take care of these guys. Tell me you understand me."

Defeated, he slumped slightly. "Yes, milady."

Tapping on the bars to get his attention, I waited for him to look at me. "What are you going to do?"

Swallowing, he looked me square in the eyes. "I'm going to take the keys and the knife and I'm going to unlock all the other children. Then I'm to escort them out those doors to the green Jeep parked around the corner," he said, nodding to the doors far behind me.

"Good man." I nodded and got to work on the locks. There were a lot of them to restrain what was essentially a pre-teen. Irritated at my limited vision, I pushed my hood back. "Sweet Circe, how mad did you make them?" I muttered.

He let out a very evil sounding chuckle. "I wasn't going to make it easy for them."

"Just watch my back," I whispered with an eye roll at the kid's smart ass remark. Apparently, teenagers were the same no matter what the species.

The door squeaked a bit when I managed to swing it open but no one noticed. While Ares got to work behind me, I grabbed the supplies out of my bag to set a circle. I wasn't happy about what I was about to do, but it was the only way to take on so many Inquisitors at once.

The thought of their plans for the city if I couldn't stop them spurred me to go through with the spell.

I was almost ready when our luck ran out. Dawen stumbled as he tried to maneuver his gangly calf-body out of the too small cage. The resulting clang drew way too many pairs of eyes in our direction. Without my hood, I was easily spotted.

"WITCH!" The cry went up from the priest as he recognized me from the night they had tried to take my hair. Pointing a finger at me, he screamed, "Kill Her!"

Pandemonium broke out.

Chapter Fourteen

Screams of pain echoed as arrows rained down from above. Men scrambled to pull out their guns. Others rushed towards me, intent on taking me barehanded. The scene was reminiscent of the alley just the night before, and once again, I threw up my hands instinctively, wanting to stop them from reaching the kids. Just like before, they forcefully hit an invisible barrier and fell back.

Caelan jumped from somewhere up above me and landed in the gap between the attacking Inquisitors and the half-freed kids. "The spell!" he yelled over his shoulder, his body looking like a blur as he used his bow like a staff, swinging it in a deadly arc and disarming any Inquisitors he could. Bullets pinged off metal as they ricocheted around the warehouse.

Mateo joined in the fray, the appearance of an irate tiger causing a pause in the action as the Inquisitors tried to process the new element of danger.

Ares appeared at my side looking fierce in a defensive stance. Grabbing his arm, I pushed him at the cage, still holding the human boy and tiny girl. "Get them out!"

"No, I can help," he said, jumping in front of me, eager to fight as the Kirata cub clutched at a bawling Dawen nearby.

I gripped his upper arm, turning him to look at me. “We don’t have time to argue about this. I need you to—” A scream of outrage stopped me and had me looking up over Ares’ shoulder.

“Satan’s whore!” The head priest drew a gun and pointed it in our direction.

Without conscious thought, I swung Ares’ small body around as the sound of a gunshot echoed through the warehouse. I placed myself between the exposed kids and the approaching bullet. Ares clutched protectively to my chest. Fire tore through my shoulder, and we were knocked to the ground. Mateo let out a roar behind me loud enough to shake the building.

Looking over my shoulder, I watched as if in slow motion as Mateo’s massive claws raked across the priest’s neck, blood spraying and the head nearly being torn from his body. Bullets ricocheted around me as the corpse reflexively squeezed the trigger, and I laid my body on top of Ares, holding his head down. Looking up, Mateo’s eyes gleamed with bloodlust, and he was so intent on his kill, he didn’t see the Inquisitor behind him with an axe.

“Teo!” I yelled with the remaining breath in my lungs. “Behind you!”

Mateo whirled around in time to avoid the axe that was aimed right at his spine, but he was still sliced across the ribs. His feline roar was filled with pain and rage, and he swiped the axe out of the man’s hands with ease, almost removing the arm in the process.

My attention was brought back to my own problems as Ares struggled out from beneath me. I worked to catch my breath from the pain raging through my body.

Caelan yelled as he caught a glimpse of our problem. "Ares!"

"He's alright!" I called out. Caelan's eyes burned with black fire as he quickly assessed us, but seeing we were indeed alive, he nodded and went back to the battle he and Mateo were only marginally keeping up with.

The boy in question was sitting dumbfounded in front of me. "I-I'm s-sorry," he stuttered out. His tunic had a dark stain on it that I was very afraid was my blood.

Wincing, I tried to sit up. "Get my bag."

He handed it to me and I looked at him seriously. "*Now* will you do as you're told?"

He nodded and I could see tears in his eyes.

"Good, go and wait by the Jeep. Protect the others."

He scrambled off, and in what seemed like seconds, all the kids were hightailing it out the door. Gathering the smudge stick Mateo and I had prepared, I quickly repaired my protective circle. Kneeling in the center, I shook the pooling blood off my hand and wiped the rest on my jeans. I lit the stick with fumbling fingers. Blowing on the braided grass and herbs hurt my chest, but I needed more smoke.

"Can we hurry this up?" Caelan grunted at me as he swung his bow hitting several Inquisitors, keeping them from getting near me. His words were muffled underneath the fabric drawn up over his face and mouth, robber-style. I could barely hear him over Mateo's furious growls and the screams of the Inquisitors brave enough to take on a tiger.

"How about I take a nap and you do the spell," I growled. I got that we were working on a time crunch here, but damn it, I was pretty sure I had been shot. My one hand was numb and the fingers were all but useless.

"Wolf and horse, old signs of might,
lend your strength to me this night.
By the Goddess' laws of three times three,
their sorrow or joy paid back by She.
The pain and grief they so easily give,
must be returned so they may live.
To know and feel what they have done,
and change their ways with harm to none.
As the seasons turn from seed to snow,
what you reap is what you sow."

The effect was almost instantaneous. As the Inquisitors breathed in the smoke, they started to drop to their knees screaming, some clutching at their heads, others their chests. Caelan looked a bit stunned as his opponents writhed on the floor in front of him, crying. The one nearest to me kept murmuring, "What have I done? God, forgive me! I'm sorry, so sorry!"

Mateo appeared at my side making a strange noise that sounded almost like he was trying to clear his throat. He was sniffing me all over and panting. "You're bleeding." He sounded strange.

"Are you alright?" I asked, swaying on my knees as I touched his neck, smearing it red with my blood. The orange of his fur was stained dark red with blood as it ran down his side where the axe had caught him.

"Am *I* alright?" he asked incredulously. "Joss, you've been shot!"

I grimaced as I looked down at my soaked hoodie. Carefully, I pulled down the zipper. The green top I was wearing underneath looked black. "Yeah, looks like it." My chest hurt but my arm was numb.

Caelan crouched at my side, his eyes bright behind his masked face as he cursed in a language I had never heard. He pulled another square of fabric out of somewhere and quickly wadded it up over the wound in my shoulder. Glancing at my back, he frowned. "The bullet went all the way through. It's not a fatal wound, but we need to get you to a healer."

There was no way I was going to a hospital. Fingering my mother's ring, I thought fast. I looked at Mateo. He wasn't going to like this plan. Switching my gaze back to Caelan, I asked him, "Can you go and get the kids and bring them just inside the door, away from the smoke? I have a plan."

Eyes hard, he looked between me and Mateo before nodding and jogging off.

"Joss," Mateo growled.

Palming his huge face, I looked into his eyes. “This is the only way to tie up all the loose ends with the humans.”

He sighed. “I’m going to hate this, aren’t I?”

I winced as my shoulder gave a throb but nodded. “Yup.” Pulling my bag closer, I tried not to get too much blood everywhere. “I’m going to call my friends at the police station. I have a location on the kidnapped little boy and the religious muggers. But they need to be careful because there’s a captive tiger and all the bad guys are heavily armed.”

Mateo was already growling, but I spoke louder, ignoring him. “Caelan can take me and the other kids to Mr. Shido’s. I can get bandaged up there, and you can meet me once you *escape*.” I looked at him with a plea in my eyes. “Please, you need to stay here with the Canadian boy. He deserves to get back to his parents.” I nodded to the carnage around us. “We can’t clean this up by ourselves, and there needs to be a reason that some of these guys look like they’ve been attacked by a wild animal. An escaped tiger fits the story.”

Mateo let out a frustrated roar and shook his head. I slumped back against the wooden crate I was propped next to as the door clanged open. Hauling myself to my feet, I leaned heavily on Mateo as he hurried to help me. We moved away from the lingering smoke to stand with the kids, machinery and wooden crates shielding them from seeing the worst of the battleground behind us.

“Everyone alright?” I asked, looking them over.

The Kirata cub was shaking and mewling as her eyes darted around, terrified at the sounds of the now all-but-insane Inquisitors. The Dwarf girl was still clinging to the Canadian boy she had been caged with, and Dawen was shivering, looking a bit shocked. Other than mental trauma, and needing a good bath and a hot meal, they appeared to be relatively unharmed.

Ares sidled up to me, his bruised face looking sheepish. "I'm sorry I didn't listen, milady. I only wanted to help."

"I know, kid. Next time, though, stick to the plan, alright?" I sighed.

Drawing a deep breath, I turned to a now unmasked Caelan. "Were there...?"

He shook his head with a sympathetic look before I could finish asking the question. "I was able to search quite thoroughly. There are no other children in the building. I'm sorry."

My heart sank. My last hope was gone. I swallowed past the lump in my throat and nodded. "Before you take Ares back to his parents, can I ask you to take me and the other children to a safe place? I need to arrange for them to get back to their parents and get patched up."

"Of course," Caelan agreed immediately. "It would be my honor."

"Wait!" Ares looked up at Caelan. "They have my pendant." He pointed in the direction of the moaning and crying Inquisitors. "That's how they found everyone else."

Caelan frowned but explained. "Ares was given a witch stone when he was allowed to journey here." He looked down at the child-warrior. "How were you captured?"

Ares suddenly looked every bit the chastened boy. "I was playing down by the river. The rocks were slippery."

"Would that be the river your guard Camulus told you to stay away from?" Caelan asked, quirking an annoyed eyebrow, his muscular arms crossed over his chest in disapproval.

Ares nodded, toeing the ground. "I fell in. When I finally got close to the bank, a human pulled me out. When they were pulling at my ears and calling me names, they found my pendant and said it looked like some guy named Jesus?" Ares looked puzzled but continued. "When it vibrated reacting to me, they said it was a sign from their God. They started using it to collect us to use as bait for our parents."

Mateo padded off and before long came back to drop the blood-stained rock the priest had been praying over. He had been right when we guessed after my vision in the cauldron; it was definitely a witch stone. Wiping it on my ruined jeans, I studied it, spinning it a few times, tilting my head back and forth before I finally saw it. Snorting a laugh before realizing it hurt too much, I held it up for Mateo to see. "Remember the *Jesus Toast*?"

Mateo's chuckle was a deep grumble.

Seeing Caelan's confusion, I explained. "Humans have been known to see images of deities in their food or other objects. Most of the time it's either a case of the person seeing what they want to see or someone deliberately creating the image so they can sell it for exorbitant amounts of money."

"Selling the image of your God, how mercenary...and irreverent," Caelan said dryly.

I nodded and handed the stone back to Ares. "But at least it explains how these bastards were able to kidnap so many kids and find the Troll Market." I looked at the kid wryly. "Have we learned to do as we're told *now*?"

Ares nodded seriously as Caelan smothered a grin.

I looked over at Joseph, seeing him in a new light. There were only Sidhe children here. I exchanged a speaking glance with Mateo, looking from him to the Canadian boy and back again. "Well, whatever. It's time for everyone to go home," I said, turning my attention to Caelan once more. "You and I will go to Inari Shido and get his help to deal with the Sidhe children; Mateo is going to stay to help Joseph."

The dark haired boy looked up at me with hope on his face.

Kneeling down painfully, I waved him forward, putting my hand on his shoulder. My suspicions were confirmed when my own witch stone vibrated softly under my shirt. "Can you be brave for just a little bit longer?"

A tear rolled down his cheek, but he nodded. "I'm really gonna see my mom?" he whispered.

I reached out with my good arm and ruffled his hair. "You bet." Narrowing my eyes at him playfully, I asked him, "Have you ever touched a *real* tiger?"

His eyes were wide as they darted back and forth between me and Mateo, who was standing protectively over me. "N-no."

"No?" I asked. "Well, then you're in for a treat! This is my very special friend Mateo. He's going to stay with you until the police get here, okay? But I need for you to do something for me."

He looked intently at me but nodded.

"I need for you to keep a *big* secret. Can you do that?" I levelled a serious look at him. When he nodded emphatically, I continued. "I need you to forget that all these other kids were ever here. And me...you can't tell them about me either. You can't tell the police or your mom or dad. They wouldn't understand."

He looked around and I saw the comprehension on his face. He turned back to me and nodded. "They wouldn't believe me anyway."

"Good man." I pulled him in gently for a hug and whispered in his ear. *"Someday soon, your very own special friend is going to come and find you, and this is all going to make sense. If you ever need help again, you and your special friend can come and find me, okay? Mr. Shido knows how to contact me. My name is Jocelyn Matthews."*

When I pulled away, he looked at Mateo and reached out a hand. Mateo obligingly pushed against his palm, accepting the petting.

"Can you stay with him and be brave a bit longer?" I asked. "Mateo will be with you every second till the police come and get you."

Joseph hugged me around the neck and nodded. "Thank you, Jocelyn."

My eyes teared a bit, only partly from the pain of his hug. "You're very welcome, sweetheart."

He released me and went to stand beside Mateo, holding onto his fur for comfort. I looked up at Caelan, not sure I could stand on my own. "I think I'm going to need a little help getting to my Jeep."

Almost as soon as I had finished speaking, I was weightless. For the first time in my life, I was in the completely unfamiliar position of be held bridal style in someone's arms—not someone, a *man's* arms. My heart seemed to skip a beat, and I felt breathless. I hoped it was the blood loss. Looking up into his eyes, I knew that wasn't entirely the case. His near-black eyes were actually the deepest darkest brown and had the tiniest flecks of chocolate brown with echoes of gold. Cradled gently against the warmth of his chest, I felt small and oddly safe.

Blinking, I tried to regain some sense of self. "This wasn't exactly what I meant."

His lips pulled back into a sensuous and slightly teasing smile. "Maybe not, but I'm enjoying it."

A deep rumbling hiss came from my right. Mateo's ears were laid back and his eyes were fierce—furious. He was snarling with every tooth and fang on display. Poor Joseph looked terrified.

"Mateo, it's fine. As much as it pains me to admit it, I think I'm too dizzy to walk straight anyway." I breathed through my nose and blinked as the world seemed to slide sideways, proving me right. "I need my bag."

Ares ran to get it and pulled the strap over his shoulder. "It's heavy."

Mateo snorted but I cut him off, growling through clenched teeth. "Shut it."

"Just get her to Inari and get lost," Mateo growled, not looking any less angry for the inside joke. "If she disappears, I will hunt you down and kill you."

Caelan smirked at Mateo but didn't answer. Turning, he carried me with no sign of effort out the door and onto the darkened streets, the Sidhe children following behind like ducklings after their mother. Caelan settled me in the passenger seat gently before opening the back and helping the kids inside. It was a very tight fit with Dawen's calf body taking up the majority of the area, but the girls were small and able to fit on the wheel wells. Ares perched himself in the gap between the two front seats, holding on to Caelan's quiver and bow, eager and seemingly fine after his abduction, despite the bruises he still wore.

As Caelan got in my usual seat behind the wheel, I looked at him dubiously. I had paid extra to get the automatic transmission, but still, driving didn't strike me as a skill for an elf to have. "You do know how to drive, right?"

He chuckled, the deep sound making me want to smile despite the circumstances. "Shouldn't you have thought to ask me that before now?"

"Just answer the question." I winced as the Jeep rumbled to life. This ride was going to suck.

He smoothly pulled the gear shift and put the transmission in drive. "Yes, I know how to drive. I've been doing it for several decades now."

We hit a bump and I grunted, the world spinning. It was suddenly darker; a curtain was falling, and I knew I was close to passing out. I needed to hurry. "Ares, get my phone out of my bag, please."

Feeling it pressed into my hand, I blinked hard as I pulled up the contacts.

"Ares, put pressure on her wound. She's losing too much blood," Caelan commanded.

I cried out as the little demon actually did as he was told and pushed hard on the now soaked fabric. "Sweet merciful mother..."

"Easy, milady. Caelan will have us there soon," Ares whispered.

Refocusing, I pressed the entry for Stevens. As I held the phone to my ear, it only rang once before it was answered. "What the hell are you doing up at this hour, Nancy Drew? You should be home in bed sleeping like decent people."

I chuckled. "Who ever said I was decent?"

"Don't give me that. You're trouble but only because you think you're some kind of superhero."

"Please, spandex isn't my thing," I joked, trying hard not to let the pain in my shoulder creep into my voice.

"So, what is it this time? Drug deals in the park? Drunk driver? Domestic violence?"

Crap, did I call him *that* often? "How about an *anonymous tip* on your missing Canadian kid?"

"You found him?" Stevens sounded excited.

"Yup, but you're gonna need the whole team for this one. And animal control...like the zoo kind. Oh, and the bomb squad."

"BOMB SQUAD?" he barked out. "What the hell did you get caught up in this time?"

"Well, it looks like your abductors and the muggers are one and the same. From what I could find out, those religious wackos mugging people around the city are into some bizarre crap. Some kind of weird cult. There are about fifteen or twenty of them. They're in a warehouse in the industrial area planning an attack on the city. They've got the kid and a bunch of huge cages for holding animals in them, like exotics. Apparently one of them has a tiger in it. It might be some kind of trafficking racket or terrorist cell."

"Wait, a tiger? Like a live, breathing, snarling, man-eating tiger—*tiger*?"

"What's the matter, Stevens? Scared? I told you to bring animal control." I grunted as we hit a bump, and Caelan's eyes shifted in my direction worriedly. Breathing through the pain, I shook my head.

"How did you find the boy so fast?" Stevens asked.

"Oh, honey, you know good girls never tell tales," I said coyly.

"Riiight." I could hear him typing away and things bashing around. It sounded like he was getting the ball rolling. "If this is everything you say it is, I may need you to testify."

I shook my head, forgetting he couldn't see me. "Not a chance. This is anonymous. You know our deal. Besides, you'll have plenty of evidence to work with."

He grunted but I knew I had him. We'd been doing this dance for a while now. "Fine. Give me the address."

I rattled it off and then hung up, gulping for air. The pain was getting to be too much.

"We're almost there, milady. Hold on," Ares said, his voice cracking slightly as the Jeep hit another bump.

"Stay with us, Jocelyn." Caelan's voice sounded like it was coming from far away as I lost the battle to stay conscious and everything went black.

Chapter Fifteen

The dimly lit room was blurry, and I blinked several times, trying desperately to bring it into focus. The surface I was lying on was comfortable, a sharp contrast to the ache in my upper body. Rolling my head to the side, I saw cleanly organized shelves filled with various items both familiar and unrecognizable. Shido's shop. The events of the night came back in a rush, and I relaxed back into the softness that cradled me.

The comfortable surface turned out to be a good sized cot with fresh scented linens pulled up over my shoulders. I was a bit self-conscious to realize I was pretty much naked under the covers; only my black boy-short panties remained in place. The rest of my clothes were likely too dirty and blood-stained to keep. Feeling constricted as I took a deeper breath, I used my right hand to gently raise the sheet covering me. A relieved sigh escaped me as I realized my chest and left shoulder were tightly bandaged, providing me with a bit more modesty than I had assumed. I wasn't sure I wanted to know who had the task of stripping me down. Dropping my head back, I fought against the dizziness and the dryness of my mouth, wishing desperately for some water.

"Ah, Jocelyn-san, you are awake. Good."

I rolled my head to see the concerned face of Mr. Shido. "You gave us quite the scare, young woman."

"Sorry." My voice sounded more like a croak. "Where are the kids? Are they okay?"

He put a softly restraining furred hand on my uninjured shoulder when I tried to get up. "They are just fine. Sleeping now after a good meal."

Swallowing back the nausea that threatened to overwhelm me, I concentrated. "How long have I been here? What time is it?"

"Water," he said as he offered me a cup with a straw. "Only a little over an hour. Everything is fine."

He took the water away far too soon for my thirst, but it tasted heavenly and helped me clear the cobwebs from my throat. Looking around, I didn't see the one face I wanted. "Mateo..."

"Will be back soon, I am sure. Drink this now. It will help you regain your strength and reduce your pain." He brought me a small ceramic cup and held my head up so I could drink. It was bitter and I tasted something floral that only barely tempered the sour bite of willow bark.

"But he was hurt. He should've been back by now." He was out there, somewhere in the city, hurt, and I was lying in a bed. Tears filled my eyes.

Mr. Shido placed a rough padded palm on my cheek, gently wiping away a tear. His beautiful blue eyes held an almost paternal softness. "Do not fear for your familiar, young one. He is much tougher than you think. He will be back with you soon, I promise."

I nodded and relaxed back into the pillow, still worried but reassured.

"Is she...?" a low, smooth voice came from my left.

I looked over to see Caelan's large form slipping through an ornate curtain serving as a door. Seeing my eyes open, he smiled. *Lord and Lady, the man was handsome.* Stripped of all his weapons and the concealing cloak, he was sporting a few new bandages of his own, although nothing that looked too serious.

"Good to see you awake, milady." He came and crouched by the cot I was on. "You had us worried."

My eyes flicked to Mr. Shido, and I forced out a small smile despite the ache. "So I've heard. Sorry."

Kneeling beside the bed, he searched my face with a concerned expression. He gently smoothed back some of my hair that had escaped my braid and tucked it behind my ear, the gesture sending butterflies through my stomach. "No apologies. You're safe now."

Licking my lips, I asked, "Where's Ares?"

Caelan chuckled, shaking his head slightly. "Doing as he's told, apparently." At my questioning look, he smiled. "You told him to look after the other children. He's standing guard over them with my knife doing 'what Lady Jocelyn commanded.' I have the feeling he will be the model child from now on."

I smiled. "Well, for a while at least."

His lips twitched into a smile. "You're probably right. He'll be happy to hear you're awake."

He sat at my side, gently petting my hair as we enjoyed the silence that comes after a battle; the sense of calm that comes from knowing everyone came out of it with their lives, if not entirely unscathed. As I thought about the battle, a question occurred to me. He had been every bit the warrior he appeared to be against the Inquisitors. "How did you end up in that alley outside the Troll Market? I mean, you don't seem like the type to let a few humans get the jump on you."

He frowned and his eyes seemed to darken. "While you were able to alert me to the other card players' cheating, you didn't see them slip something into my drink. The bastards took my good knife and all my money before dumping me in an area where Inquisitors had been seen," he spat out under his breath. "Cowards!"

I silently agreed with him. Breathing deeply, I closed my eyes and felt the tea Mr. Shido had given me starting to work.

"Are you alright?" Caelan asked, resuming his comforting petting of my hair as he searched my face for signs of pain, his forehead showing his worry.

"That feels nice." I nodded and hummed an affirmative, cracking an eye to look at him. "Just tired. I haven't gotten much sleep in the past couple of days." Closing my eye, I breathed slowly, feeling myself drifting a bit.

"Some of that is due to me, I suspect," he murmured.

I smiled and opened my eyes, shifting my head slightly so I could see him straight on. "A bit."

"I haven't thanked you for that."

Raising my eyebrow, I smiled. "I figured that's what all the talk about a life debt was."

"While I have an obligation to you now because of it, I am truly grateful you thought to put yourself at considerable risk to save me." His eyes seemed to see deep into me, as if he had never come across someone who was willing to take chances for the sake of others without some kind of compensation. "You are a rare woman, Jocelyn."

I got nervous at the mention of my rarity, Mateo's talk of slavery coming back to me, and I cringed away from him.

"Shhh...not like that. That's not what I meant," he soothed, seeing my fear. "There are very few who would go out of their way to help another if it puts them at risk. Fewer still who would help a Dark Elf. I cannot imagine anyone in your particular position that would risk exposing themselves at all, let alone for the sake of a complete stranger. You have a beautiful heart."

Relaxing, I took in his rumpled state. His clothes had splatters of blood on them, a new bruise decorated his jaw, and the sleeve of his tunic was torn. "Why are you still here? I thought you would have wanted to get Ares back to his parents as soon as possible?"

"I won't leave you until your protector returns," he said simply.

"I'm completely safe with Mr. Shido," I said.

"I have already failed to defend you once tonight. I won't do it again by leaving you before you are adequately protected," he stated with a tense set to his mouth that hadn't been there before.

"What are you talking about?"

"You were shot. You were shot protecting my Prince, who not only ignored your express command after being presented with the dagger representing my authority, but you were shot after I had acknowledged the life debt. I failed you," he said, sounding bitter and self-reproachful. He shook his head in disgust, his shoulders slumping making him look defeated.

"*I* failed her." The familiar deep voice of my best friend sounded out of the shadows, and seeing his emerald green eyes staring at me as if there was no one else in the room, a tightness in my chest I hadn't entirely recognized loosened.

"Mateo!" I breathed out his name in an exhalation of relief. Even after Mr. Shido's assurances, I had carried my worry like a burden. Seeing him walking towards me, the remaining tension in my body dissolved and tears came to my eyes.

Caelan stiffened but as Mateo padded over, he relinquished his position at my bedside. I rolled onto my side, not caring about the pain that shot through my chest. I needed to touch him, to know he was real, that he was okay. My good arm reached out, and he bumped his leopard head into my palm. "I'm so happy to see you."

His deep rumbling purr relaxed me, and in a new gesture of affection, he pushed his head into my neck, rubbing his face on my cheek. "I thought I lost you, *paulo dea,"* he whispered in my ear.

Hugging him with my good arm, I breathed in his comforting scent, his purr resonating through my body. "Never." We rested our foreheads together for a long moment, reconnecting as we stared into each other's eyes. Now that he was back, I felt safe again, stronger. Separated, the two of us injured, I had felt incomplete—like a piece of me was missing. Now we were together and I could relax. Nothing bad could happen now. "Are you alright?" I pulled back and tried to look at his flank where he had been caught by the axe.

He turned his body obligingly. "Good as new." And it was, except for the crusted bloodstains on his fur. You would never know he had been hurt. "Perks of being a familiar."

"I was worried," I whispered.

"I'm never leaving you, Joss. Promise." With a final gentle head bump, he pulled back to look at Caelan. "Thank you for bringing her here safely."

Caelan nodded respectfully, his eyes seeming to study the two of us. He leaned back against the wall and crossed his arms over his chest, taking up a watchful position.

"You're free to leave and take Ares back to his parents. Your obligation to her is over," Mateo said in a firm voice.

"I beg to differ. The scales have tipped even farther in her favor after tonight. You won't be rid of me that easily," Caelan said with a lift of his eyebrow, which seemed almost challenging.

Their brewing argument was interrupted by a ball of excited energy running through the curtain. "Lady Jocelyn!" Ares came to a sliding stop at my side, not even thinking of the possible danger of shoving a leopard out of the way.

I chuckled painfully as Caelan chided him. "Careful, Highness. Lady Jocelyn is still injured."

Mateo stepped quickly out of the way with a dirty look for the kid but didn't show any aggression.

Ares looked at me with a worried expression. "Are you alright, milady?"

I smiled at him. "I'm alright, kid. A little sore and a whole lot tired, but I'll be good as new before you know it." Of course my shoulder picked that moment to twinge, and I winced at the pain.

"It's all my fault. I'm so sorry, please don't die!" he cried out, seeing my pain and dropping to his knees beside the bed.

I chuckled. "Relax, kid. I'm not dying."

He looked up at me, his face stained with tears. "Really?"

Caelan stood and dropped a reassuring hand on Ares' shoulder. "Really, Highness. Lady Jocelyn will be fine."

Mateo moved to the foot of the narrow bed I was on and crawled up carefully to lie alongside me. Feeling the silky fur around his ears under my hands gave me something else to focus on besides the pain.

Movement drew my gaze as Mr. Shido came through the curtain. I hadn't seen him leave. "Of course she will be fine! I would not let my favorite *human* die!" Mr. Shido scoffed as he shuffled into the room. He exchanged a serious look with Caelan, who pursed his lips but nodded briefly.

Something had been decided. Mateo relaxed slightly upon seeing the silent agreement. I would be asking him about it later.

"Now, I believe she needs her rest, and I am quite certain you have an anxious Queen desperate to have her son returned to her," Mr. Shido said, his brilliant blue eyes twinkling while his long whiskers twitched with amusement.

"But I have to protect the kids!" Ares protested as he stood with his hand on the hilt of Caelan's large dagger sheathed at his waist.

Mr. Shido's tails swished. "And what am I, a carbuncle?" He was playfully indignant.

"What is a carbuncle?" I whispered to Mateo.

He chuckled. "A kind of squirrel with a ruby in the middle of its forehead. They're harmless."

Ares stammered, embarrassed that he may have offended the wise Kitsune. "N-no! Of course not. I..."

We laughed at his blushing attempt to recover. I took pity on him. "Relax, kid. Between Mateo and Mr. Shido, the kids are well guarded. You're off the hook. Although, I'm happy to see you're doing as you're told."

Ares nodded emphatically. "I promise, Lady Jocelyn, I'll never disobey again. *Never*!"

Laughing really hurt so I tried not to give in to the urge too much. "Easy on the promises, kid. Just do your best."

Caelan smiled at me over Ares' shoulder. "Come, Highness. Shido is right. Your mother is eager to have you back." Taking my good hand in his, he kissed my knuckles slowly as he stared into my eyes, his thumb caressing my fingers. "Lady Jocelyn, you have my eternal thanks. I am in your debt and look forward to our next meeting." He glanced down at his prince and then back at me. "And I'm sure my Queen will wish to extend her thanks for all you have done as well."

Mateo growled low in his throat, his body stiffening. Caelan acknowledged the veiled threat with a nod. "Concessions will be made for your safety and comfort, I assure you."

Mateo didn't look impressed, but I was too tired to ask the questions necessary to unravel the complex silent conversations taking place over my head.

"Goodbye, Lady Jocelyn," Ares chimed in. "I'll see you soon."

Caelan bowed with a soft smile and a wink before following his prince out the curtained door.

"Life is never boring around you, young woman." Mr. Shido chuckled.

After a few hours' sleep, Mr. Shido agreed I was strong enough to drive home. The children would be waking up soon, and Mateo wanted to keep my direct contact with them to a minimum. Mr. Shido agreed. He would be contacting the parents of the still-sleeping children for their reunion at the main square in the Troll Market that night, and I was determined to be there to see it, if only from the sidelines. Lending me a pair of his linen pajama outfits, Mr. Shido pressed a sack of herbs and candles into my hands, making me promise to perform the necessary healing spells when I got home. I knew Mateo was worried about me when he picked up my bag without a single smart-ass comment on its size.

I was thankful for my automatic transmission even more as it would have been impossible to drive a standard with only one arm. Each bump and jar from the stiff suspension caused me to grit my teeth, and I felt Mateo's watchful shepherd gaze on me from the passenger seat.

"Unless you can shift into an animal that can drive this Jeep better than I can, you're going to have to deal with the fact that this hurts like hell," I grumbled when I couldn't stand the staring anymore. Glancing at him, a flash of pain went through his eyes.

"I only wish I could," he whispered.

The moment was uncomfortable as I remembered his abrupt declaration that he couldn't take human form. There was definitely more to it, but I wasn't willing to pry into what was obviously a sore subject.

Searching my mind for a new topic, I asked one of the million questions that had come up over the past twelve hours. "Why did Mr. Shido call me his favorite human when Caelan knows what I am?"

Mateo looked thoughtful for a moment. "Caelan may know, but Ares doesn't. Inari was reminding him that your safety rests in your ability to remain...human. None of the children know more than your first name and didn't see you do anything a normal human woman wouldn't do."

I winced, holding my breath as the Jeep hit a bump. "Somehow I don't think Caelan will keep my secret from his Queen."

"Likely not, but we'll cross that particular bridge when we get to it."

"Did Joseph make it to the police alright?" The boy had been pretty shaken up last time I saw him.

Mateo nodded. "I went in one of the cages and clawed my way out to reinforce the story you planned to tell the police on the phone. By the time they got there, I had convinced Joseph to sit with me in the cage they had locked him in, leaving the door open. As soon as the police came, I slipped through the bars as a cat."

Distracted by his story, I stared at him in disbelief.

"Joss! The road!" he barked, and I jerked the wheel to avoid hitting a median. "What the hell?"

"You made a traumatized little boy go back into the cage we broke him out of?! Are you *crazy*?!" I shouted.

"That's what you're so upset about?" He growled. "First of all, it was *your* crazy plan in the first place. Did you really think I was just going to climb in a cage and wait for them to tranquilize me? Secondly, how were we supposed to explain how he got out of his cage? And thirdly, I kept the kid well distracted by answering his questions and turning into pretty much any animal he asked for. Do you know how exhausting that is?"

We were silent but for the sound of the road under our tires. He was right. It was an off-the-cuff plan. He'd done what he could to fill in the gaps and everything had worked out for the best. “Did you turn into a ferret?”

His disgusted snarls mixed with my restrained giggles the rest of the way home.

Chapter Sixteen

Getting home at sunrise was becoming a habit I would be happy to break. Streaks of grey and gold were lightening the sky when we pulled in the driveway. The jeep was securely tucked away in the garage as Mateo and I made our way to the back door. At first the buzzing noise didn't register as a problem until I saw the hair on the back of Mateo's neck stand on end and my witch stone vibrated, alerting me to the presence of someone Sidhe.

"Oh, what now?" I groaned. Could the bad guys of the world cut me some slack for one day? I had been shot, was wearing someone else's pajamas, and was in desperate need of a meal, a shower, and some sleep—in that order.

Out of the grey shadows of early morning flew a fairy. The same nasty little twit who had escorted me to see Baron Blackthorn.

"*Human*," he sneered.

"Hello, Nettle. What do you want?" I wasn't wasting any energy on manners with this one.

"You will come with me. My Lord demands to speak with you," the little bastard spat, his hand fingering the tiny bow over his shoulder.

My head tilted to the side as I appraised him. Nothing in my dealings with the leader of the local

Unseelie Fairies had led me to believe he would be so rude. Bracken, his son, had been the image of courtesy.

"Does he now? Is that really how he put it?" I asked.

"How dare you question me? You disgusting—" He was working up into a fine tantrum as I cut him off.

"Careful," I sang. "You wouldn't want to be sent to the mole hills."

In a flash he had drawn his bow and Mateo had shifted into a small falcon taking flight and chasing the irate fairy around the yard. Someone must have been watching because Bracken flew out of the trees, one of his father's guards at his back. "Enough, Nettle!"

Tired, I slumped down to sit on my back steps, too exhausted to deal with the drama. Mateo landed in front of me, his feathers ruffled, and let out a high pitched cry.

"Cage him. My father will want to deal with him," Bracken commanded the guard, who nodded and dragged a still-screaming Nettle off into the trees.

"My apologies, Lady Matthews. My father hoped he had learned some humility and would be grateful enough to request the audience without letting prejudices color his actions." Bracken was red-faced and I wasn't sure if it was from embarrassment or anger as he watched them leave. Likely both. He looked at me and seemed to actually see me for the first time. "You're injured."

Mateo shifted into the grey tabby cat he seemed to favor when we were in the yard. "She was almost killed by Inquisitors last night."

"They found you?" Bracken asked, landing on a plant pot looking concerned.

"We found them. They won't be bothering anyone around here any time soon," I explained as I rubbed my eyes with the hand Mr. Shido hadn't strapped to my chest. Bracken was a nice guy, but I really didn't want to get into the specifics right now. "Now, what is this about your father wanting to see me? I really need to get some sleep."

"In light of your injuries, I feel the meeting should not wait. However, under the circumstances, it might be better if my father came to you. Provided you are comfortable with that?" Bracken offered.

I looked down at Mateo to see what he thought. I wouldn't make the mistake of inviting them into our home without his input again.

Seeing our hesitation, Bracken offered, "We owe you a debt."

Great, more debts.

Mateo seemed to be appraising the young fairy before he said, "Tell your father we would be happy to receive the two of you in an hour. Your guards will not be necessary. You may use the tunnel to avoid the harsh effects of the sun."

My jaw dropped open. Mateo was letting them use the tunnel? My jaw snapped shut as Bracken looked to me for confirmation. "Yeah, sure. Ummm...see you in an hour."

"Thank you, Lady Matthews." Bracken bowed low and then flew off.

"What the...?" Mateo looked up at my disbelieving tone, but instead of continuing, I held up my hand stopping the conversation before it started. "You know what? I don't want to know. If we're going to have visitors in an hour, I need a shower and some food."

The house was spotless when we entered, which was becoming the new normal, but at least I didn't have to worry if the house was fit for guests. I knew if I wasn't going to fall asleep before our guests arrived, I would have to hurry.

I could have stayed in the shower forever. The hot water felt heavenly as it washed away the remaining dirt and blood. I had a hard time washing my hair one-handed, and I had to be careful of my wounds. I probably shouldn't be getting them wet at all but figured with the rushed time frame, it couldn't be any worse than the dirt.

My favorite plaid flannel pajama pants and a large black t-shirt were the limits of my abilities with only one arm. Probably not protocol when meeting a fairy Baron, but again, concessions would have to be made. I had no sooner finished my sandwich and milk when Mateo padded in from the bedroom. His emerald green leopard eyes were calm as he led Baron Blackthorn and Bracken into the kitchen.

"Lord Blackthorn, thank you for agreeing to meet us here. I'm sorry for the inconvenience," I said as I leaned heavily against the kitchen counter. "Can I offer either of you anything to drink?"

The Baron shook his head, worry written on his face. "Thank you for the offer, but no. Please, Lady Matthews, my son tells me you have been injured; why don't we sit somewhere so you can rest?"

I nodded, appreciating his concern, and gestured to the living room.

Sinking into the couch was lovely and drained off much of my remaining tension. Mateo sat in front of me, calmly eyeing the fairies now standing on my coffee table. "What can we do for you, Lord Blackthorn?"

"Actually, it is us that owe you. Not only did you save the tribes, but you have provided us a safe place to shelter. And Bracken tells me you may be willing to allow us to make a permanent home there despite the perceived risk of having neighbors with the reputation of the Unseelie in such close proximity." He studied me with a veiled mix of emotions, respect and admiration at the forefront. "My people owe you a life debt, Lady Matthews. Not only for warning us of the destruction of our previous property, but for future generations who shelter in the shadow of your home. It is a heavy obligation."

I hadn't seen my actions in that light as they were happening, but I saw his point. Knowing a bit more now than I did then, I understood where he was coming from. "You understand I didn't do it to deliberately place you in my debt?"

He nodded. "That is what makes you so singular. And what makes my offer easy to extend. I propose a partnership. You allow us to stay in the shelter of the tree caves you so helpfully pointed out, and you will have the protection of my tribes over your lands. We will endeavor to protect you from any attack whenever you are at home. I would offer you more, but as fairies we are somewhat restricted to distance and hours of travel. I'm sure you understand."

"And her...identity?" Mateo didn't need to finish his thought.

"Will not be spoken of outside of the coastal tribes," he reassured us.

"I have a concern." I paused, trying to frame my thoughts. "It's obvious by the...reaction...from Nettle that not all of your people will be as grateful to me as you and your son are."

Lord Blackthorn's face darkened in anger. "I cannot tell you my embarrassment over his actions towards you both. He is being dealt with, I assure you. As for your concerns, they are valid but unwarranted. Nettle is the exception and is blinded by past run-ins with humans. My Chiefs have spoken with their tribes and, as a whole, they are grateful for their lives and their new home."

Bracken stepped forward. "When word got out about his attack upon you, the general feeling among the tribes was outrage at his actions. Many felt you would be justified to refuse us sanctuary. We have never had anyone outside of our own people offer us anything more than derision and mistrust and, on occasion, attacks on our home. They are calling you a gift from the Goddess." He looked to his father for permission. When he received a nod, he pushed forward a small canister I hadn't noticed before. It looked to be made from a reed and was no bigger than a test tube. "When I told them of your injury, our healers offered you one of our stores of Thriae honey."

Mateo shifted his weight slightly, and I remembered him saying the honey had healing properties.

"That is very generous of you," I murmured. Anything that got rid of the ache in my upper body would be welcomed.

"It is a small thing compared to the lives of my people," Baron Blackthorn offered. "Do we have an accord?"

I nodded at Mateo when he looked at me, indicating he should handle the negotiations.

Turning to the Baron, he nodded to the cupboard where the front entrance was concealed. "We would ask that you post sentries at the other three entrances to our home. One is under the front porch, and I'm sure you noticed the tunnel you used branched off in two other directions. One leads to the garage and the other to the neighbor's shed."

Bracken and Blackthorn shared a speaking glance but it was Bracken who spoke. "Posting sentries would enable us to expand our territory."

"Keep the areas tidy and you can house a family or two if there's room. Just keep in mind the front entrance under the porch is Mateo's main way in and out," I offered.

"These are acceptable terms," Blackthorn said, looking pleased. "We will leave you now to rest. Add the Thriae honey to your tea and when you wake you should be fully recovered."

They left quickly with plans to discuss the finer points of our new relationship in the future, but overall Mateo seemed pleased.

When Mateo came back from seeing them out, I was in the kitchen preparing some herbal tea. If the honey had healing properties, I wasn't going to waste any time hurting. "That went well."

He nodded and jumped onto his favorite barstool, shifting to a tabby cat mid leap. "I'm satisfied. It's a measure of protection I could never provide for you on my own. Hundreds of eyes watching over the property day and night means we don't have to worry about coming home to an ambush."

As the water heated, I rolled my mother's ring up and down my finger, the repetitive noise and motion somehow soothing. "Why does everyone hate the Unseelie so much? And the Dark Elves? In both cases you said they were vicious, ruthless, and untrustworthy."

Mateo was thoughtful. "I told you I didn't know all the details about the accusations that were leveled so many millennia ago. What I do know is hearsay. Most history is written by the victors. The conquered are depicted in the worst possible light. Eventually, the conquered people lash out in retaliation and almost prove the tales being told of them. Perhaps the very nature of the Unseelie fairies and Dark Elves, both who thrive in dark harsh environments, project an image of evil or danger where there isn't necessarily one. Over centuries past, I have kept out of the political games, keeping my Danaan charges safe through secrecy and isolation. I may not be as informed as I thought."

I finished making my tea and eagerly added the honey. "This is too deep a subject for me right now. I'm going to drink my tea and crash. When I wake up, I want to go to the Troll Market and watch the kids reunite with their parents."

"Are you sure?"

I knew Mateo was worried about possible exposure. "I need to. After all the crap we've had to deal with over the past week, I need to see something pure and happy come from something I did."

He nodded in understanding.

Drinking the tea was like nothing I had ever tasted. Fruit, flowers, summer rain, and sunshine—the flavors burst over my tongue, and my body felt warm all over. It was like lying in the sun on a spring morning while you were lulled to sleep by the warmth surrounding you. I barely felt Mateo guiding me to the bedroom before I collapsed in my warm, comfy bed. The last thing I felt was Mateo's deep purring as he lay against my side.

Chapter Seventeen

We made sure to arrive at the Troll Market a good hour earlier than the time Mr. Shido had arranged to meet the frantic parents. I wanted to find a good vantage point that wouldn't be too obvious. I was amazed at how good I felt. The honey had done its job leaving me completely healed if a little tired. Mateo said the honey healed injuries but couldn't make up for blood loss. Only time would fix that.

Making sure the hood of my cloak hid the majority of my face, we casually wandered through the Market. I was used to blending in and being inconspicuous. It was my job to watch without being seen. It was all new to Mateo though. He was tense and watchful, confused at my random wanderings and unnecessary shopping. We stopped at the shop where I had seen the candles with the shifting smoke, buying one whose smoke looked and smelled like blooming flowers. A quick stop at the vegetable market filled my canvas bag with fresh ingredients for a salad.

"I don't see the point in this. We should have come, watched the happy reunion, and then left," Mateo grumbled.

Keeping my head down, I paid the vendor for a handful of beautiful apples that looked perfect enough to have been painted. "The point is to be just another bystander. Someone who acts like you want us to stands out. People remember lurkers. Their behaviour isn't normal. Surveillance is blending in, being one of the crowd. Today, I'm just another shopper about to unexpectedly witness a happy event. You need to relax. You're drawing attention to us looking like someone is about to start a shooting rampage."

A kiosk outside the Apothecary had a miniature decorative gong that I quickly bought thinking it would make the perfect fairy doorbell for when one of the Blackthorn tribes needed to visit. Mateo admitted it was a good idea.

This time I got to linger a bit around Lapis Lane to admire the jewels in the windows. Rings and necklaces so ornate it seemed impossible they could be made at all; stones cut into shapes the likes of which I had never seen or thought possible—some of them clearly never having been seen or heard of by humans. Some glowed, some changed color, and some affected the wearer's mood—*true* mood rings.

When Mateo realized no one was noticing us specifically, he relaxed somewhat. While still watchful, he no longer looked suspicious. He even helped me pick out a new lightweight cloak from another kiosk selling fabrics and clothes. It was a beautiful dove grey/green with a huge hood. The color would blend in perfectly on a foggy morning in the forest. The vendor didn't even blink an eye at my reluctance to lower my own hood.

"Many beings feel the need to remain covered for a variety of reasons. Some are self-conscious while others worry about the effect their faces will have on the public." When I looked at him with a question on my lips, he explained. "Think Medusa."

We wandered down to Bootes Road where Mateo said they had a pet store. I got to see my first Carbuncle. There were also Ink Monkeys whose tails could be milked for ink, but they made helpful pets and could have easily worked as service animals to the humans if they were allowed to know of their existence. Glow worms were sold to fairies to be used as living lanterns, silk worms for clothing, all in quantities small enough for them to be easily looked after.

I was tempted to buy something called Grout Munchers. The ugly little bugs liked to feed on the dirt and slime that accumulated on tile floors and shower walls. Mateo pointed out I had acquired a Brownie and he or she would most likely be offended at the unintentional suggestion that they weren't keeping my tiles clean enough.

While I was enjoying my leisurely shopping trip, it was getting close to the time for the children to arrive. The main square by the fountain had several small groups who were obviously the parents and families of the missing children. The Kirata family drew my notice first, the father pacing as if caged. His muscular, striped, tiger upper-body, almost rippling with leashed tension, blended seamlessly with human legs that looked like they belonged to a bodybuilder. His leonine wife was being consoled by another female who I recognized as my waitress from the Gorgon's Head.

Mrs. Nandi stood nearby with her husband, a powerful looking bullish figure. Horns grew out of the sides of his head above his large ears, his steel grey body towering over his much smaller wife. Where she reminded me more of a red and white spotted milk cow, he conjured images of the huge Brahma bulls cowboys rode in the rodeo.

Mateo and I wandered to a cart that sold a variety of beverages and snacks, and I bought an herbal tea and some kind of fish-bar for Mateo. Settling ourselves under one of the trees on the same bench we had sat on after our run-in with Silvani, the randy Satyr, we had a perfect view of the area around the signpost where Mr. Shido would be bringing the kids through the main entrance to the Market.

A small group of Dwarfs hurried into the square, their rotund figures easily clearing a path despite their short stature. It looked to be the parents as well as both sets of grandparents, although admittedly it took me a minute to differentiate between the males and females, the only real difference in appearance being the lack of real facial hair on the women. Although, that was somewhat debatable as well.

Watching the anxious parents, I was struck by the diversity in their species. Looking around, I saw a dozen other species going about their errands. Something Mateo had said to Caelan floated through my mind.

'If she is brought into the open, she'll become a target. Every race in the known worlds will be hunting her.'

Known worlds.

My breath caught in my chest. "None of these people are from this planet, are they?" I whispered.

Mateo looked up at me appraisingly. “Remember when I said some things have to be revealed in context, otherwise they’re too unbelievable and fantastic to be true?”

I nodded. I took note of the signs around us. “The street names...they’re constellations.”

“The names of their home galaxies,” he confirmed. “If I had told you you were surrounded by *aliens*, what would you have thought?”

Gazing into my tea, the answer was obvious. “I would have been afraid.”

He nodded. “You needed to see for yourself that things are so much bigger than the narrow view humans take. They believe their God created the earth but refuse to entertain the thought that other planets were created in the same way, that other species could be created in God’s image. God can create something as strange as the platypus, but the thought of other planets being inhabited is blasphemy.”

“It’s not that I never thought about it,” I offered.

Mateo smiled. “I’m not surprised with the movies Hollywood puts out. Not very believable.”

“No kidding. If they don’t look like green men, they must not be aliens.” I chuckled and took a sip of my tea.

Mateo growled out a laugh, his leopard tail twitching. “Oh, there *are* green men from outer space.”

I choked on my tea. “What?!”

“Well, their heads are green anyway. Their hands are blue,” he explained, as if that cleared everything up. Seeing my incredulous look, he took pity on me. “Magellans are celestial sailors. They have a monopoly on interstellar travel and trade. If it moves about the universe, the Magellans ship it."

"Like Fed-ex."

"More like American Airlines, Fed-ex, Boeing, and the Longshoremen all rolled into one. Their galaxy is one giant shipping port. Picture the Port of Seattle with all the stacked containers ready to be loaded on ships, only the port is the size of an entire planet. Another nearby planet or moon is strictly for the transport of traveling Sidhe, some only vacationing while others are immigrating to another system. Another planet is strictly for the quarantine and transport of livestock. Their galaxy is one of the largest and richest in the universe." He levelled a serious look at me. "If you ever see one, walk away. They don't take kindly to *your* kind."

He meant Danaan. "Why?"

He looked around to see if anyone was paying attention. "The only other way to travel around the universe is through Danaan Dhoras Glass. *Dhoras* literally means doorway. They're travelling mirrors." Staring at me, he finished, "They're *rare*."

Dhoras Glass. Witch…Danaan-made travelling mirrors.

Seeing my comprehension, he nodded. "The fees attached to Magellan shipping are exorbitant. The worlds that have Dhoras Glasses don't need to pay for shipping or passenger fares. Worlds that have the ability to *make* Dhoras Glasses could effectively reduce Magellan profits or put them out of business entirely.

Travelling by Glass is virtually instantaneous and costs nothing, as opposed to months on a Magellan ship."

My breath was short. Bits and pieces of conversations we'd had over the past week flashed through my head. "So the means to make Dhoras Glass..."

"Is very competitive," Mateo finished.

That was why he was so worried about me staying hidden. I would be hunted for something I didn't even know how to do. A small voice whispered in the back of my mind. *Not yet.*

'*Every race in the known worlds will be hunting her,'* Mateo had shouted at Caelan. Caelan knew I was Danaan. He would tell his Queen.

"Breathe, Joss." His head bumped against me, and he started purring, trying to calm me. "You're safe."

I looked down at him, pulling my hood farther over my face. "For how long?" Suddenly, I felt incredibly exposed and the urge to cry was choking me.

He rested his head on my knee. "At least for today. Tomorrow will take care of itself. You are meant for great things, Joss. Your magick is instinctual. You know things without being taught. The Goddess has gifted you far beyond any other I have ever seen. Trust in her to take care of you. Trust in me."

"I do, but I'm scared." I felt tears well and then spill down my cheeks.

"There's nothing wrong with being scared. Courage is being scared to death and saddling up anyway." He had a small smile pulling at his mouth, a hint of fang showing.

I blinked at him. "Did you just quote John Wayne?"

He gave the leopard version of a shrug. "I love The Duke." His ear twitched and it drew our attention to the mounting excitement in the crowd.

Wiping away my tears with the edge of my cloak, we watched as the doors to the Troll Market opened and three small children were ushered forward by Mr. Shido and his foxes. Excited cries came from the assembled families as people ran forward to scoop up their children. More tears welled in my eyes—this time happy ones—as I saw parents holding their most precious possessions. Small arms wrapped around grateful necks, and tears flowed freely as small bodies were passed around from family member to family member.

Mr. Shido's eyes somehow found mine, and he nodded with a smile, enjoying the reunion every bit as much as I was.

"You were right," Mateo said. He looked up at me. "You were right to want to see this. It was worth it."

I nodded, looking back at the happy display. "I don't get to see this often. I needed it after everything."

We watched as Mr. Nandi approached Mr. Shido, embracing him gratefully. Then he handed him an envelope. It would contain the required payment I was loath to collect but that Jimmy would demand. A few words were exchanged and then Mr. Nandi handed over a small wooden box.

Soon the other fathers went to Shido and the routine was repeated, expressions of thanks given before handing over a small box. Strange.

Before long, the families were ready to leave, anxious to take their children home and have them safe in their own beds. It was a quiet ride home, both me and Mateo remembering the happiness and revelling in a job well done.

Still tired, we made it an early night. Well, early as in we made it to bed before sunrise.

Chapter Eighteen

Waking up without the urgency that had ruled my life for the past week was a relief. There was no urgent phone call, no waiting messenger. The missing children were safe at home in their beds.

Well, most of them. Tonesha Johnson still hung around my heart like a weight. I wished I could have at least given her family closure, some kind of answers as to what happened to her. Then there was Ray-Ray and little 'Shell. Peter would be worried sick, and I had no answers for him either. I knew thousands of families lived with uncertainty all over the country, but these ones were *my* failure, families I knew. I wasn't sure I would ever get over it.

Forcing myself to leave the bed, I went to have a shower so I could start my day.

My hair was still wet as I took my first sips of my coffee. Only nine in the morning, it was nice to get back to a more normal daily routine. Selecting one of the beautiful apples I had bought at the Market, I made my way to my altar to give thanks. Kneeling, I went through the familiar routine of lighting candles and incense before cutting the apple to expose the natural pentagram within as an offering. Bowing my head, I prayed.

"Lord and Lady, this woman thanks you for the gifts you have bestowed upon her. She would also give thanks for the guide and friend you have sent in Mateo. The recent tests and challenges were some of the hardest ever faced, but the good that came from them was some of the most rewarding. This woman is but a child, still learning Your ways and is in need of Your guidance. There are many questions that remain unanswered, but this woman has faith You will show her the way. She will attempt to walk the path with grace and humility, ever mindful of the Rede of Three. Blessed be."

Blowing out the candles, I stood and turned to find Mateo waiting for me, his long leopard tail curled around his feet. "Good morning."

Stroking his large head as I passed to go to the kitchen, I smiled. "Good morning. Sleep well?"

He padded after me. "Yes, actually. It was nice not having to get up to patrol every hour."

As I cracked some eggs, I raised an eyebrow at him. "Every hour?" He nodded. "Wow. Well, it looks like being neighbors with a fairy tribe is going to work out well for all of us then."

I looked around for my dish cloth. Not finding one, I was forced to take a clean one out of the drawer. "Sheesh, even the laundry is done. The Brownie is thorough, I'll give it that."

"She," Mateo offered.

"What?"

Leaping onto his barstool, shrinking to a tabby cat mid leap, he repeated. "She. Your Brownie is a she. I caught a glimpse last night. Cute little thing for a Brownie. Shy. She whispered her name before running off. Bobbin."

Suddenly, I felt a bit jealous. "Bobbin. Well, crap, I'd like to meet her."

Mateo snorted. "Good luck. I haven't seen hide nor hair of her since. I think she lives upstairs."

Mentally shrugging, I continued to make breakfast, resolving to leave her some milk and honey before I went to bed later.

As we were finishing up breakfast, one of Mr. Shido's foxes scampered in through the front tunnel.

Mateo hit the ground, jumping off the stool, full-sized once more. His irritation showed as his heavy paws made more noise than usual as he crossed the floor.

The little white fox came to a bit of a sliding stop at my feet, a small canvas bag in his mouth. He really was cute, so I offered him the last bite of my bacon. He took it nicely, swallowing it in one gulp before giving a happy yip and scampering right back out again, his job apparently done.

Mateo huffed out a growl as he rolled his eyes. Laughing, I took the bag to the living room to open. Inside I found the three wooden boxes Mr. Shido had received from the fathers as well as a larger flat velvet box and scroll. As I unrolled the scroll, another one fell out. I chose to read the first. It was from Mr. Shido.

Jocelyn-san,

As you saw, the parents were very happy to have their children back safe and sound. They wished to express their gratitude in person and acknowledge their debt as is Sidhe custom. However, out of respect for your wish to remain anonymous, I suggested an alternative to the verbal discussion, which they happily accepted.

They presented to me, as your proxy, a charm representing their family Should you ever find yourself in a position where you need to call in the debt, simply present the charm to the family, and they will do everything in their power to assist you. I have taken the liberty of including a silver bracelet so you may keep the charms close to you at all times.

Stay safe.

来

The letter was signed with the same Japanese character as before.

A post script was hastily scrawled underneath.

Jocelyn-san,

This was delivered to me this morning. I can make a reasonable assumption as to the contents. I offer my home as a central place to meet and will make a personal guarantee of your safety.

I.S.

Wanting to put off any anxiety, I chose to open the boxes instead of reading the other scroll. The larger flat box held a beautiful thick silver bracelet with a very secure barrel clasp that stood no chance of breaking easily. It was lovely.

Setting it aside, I opened one of the three smaller boxes. Inside was a small silver circular charm. On one side was the raging bull of the Taurus zodiac symbol. I didn't need to flip it over to know it was from the Nandi family, but on the other side was engraved: DN. Dawen Nandi.

The next box held what looked like an iron bead. It had the zodiac symbol for Gemini on one side and the other had the initials DV. A small slip of paper read the name Dori Volund. I gave an inquiring look to Mateo and held it out so he could see.

He took a quick look before explaining. “Dwarfs and Gnomes come from the same galaxy. They will deny it unto death, but they are actually related. They come from the Gemini constellation. Twin planets in the same solar system, two sides of the same coin.”

“If they hate it so much, why represent themselves by the constellation? Why not establish themselves as separate entities?” I asked.

Mateo chuckled. “The Magellans. They’re the ones that set the star charts and mapped the universe. It’s been that way for untold millennia. It’s too late to change it now.”

The third box held a stalking tiger with tiny rubies for eyes. It was beautiful and fierce, a perfect representation of the Kirata family. The clasp that would thread on the bracelet had tiny initials: T.T. An accompanying paper read, “Ta-Miu Tigris.”

Such a big name for such a small cub. She had been adorable, despite being so scared. “I was expecting another zodiac symbol.”

Mateo shrugged. “More than likely that family has been here on earth for generations and identifies more with this planet than the one they originally came from.”

It made sense. I sighed and picked up the only thing left to open: the scroll. I had received an acknowledgment of debt from each Sidhe family except the rulers of the Dark Elves. Sharing a nervous glance with Mateo, my hands shook as I broke the wax seal.

The letter was ornate but impersonal.

Lady Jocelyn Matthews,

Their Royal Majesties wish to mark by this personal message their appreciation for the service you have rendered to the Crown. They are cognizant that to this unselfish task you have sacrificed much of your own comfort and wellbeing. By your sympathy, you have earned the gratitude of those to whom you have shown your heroism, and by your readiness to right a wrong, you have helped the people of Dokkalfar.

Their Royal Majesties request the honor of your presence at a meeting place to be determined by you within the next month to discuss matters of the Crown.

We await your hasty reply,

Sigurd

Correspondence Officer to the Queen

I dropped the parchment in my lap and looked at Mateo. “Well, shit.”

Excerpts from a translation of the Mallaeus Malificarum or Witches Hammer

In passing sentence the Judge or priest may use some such method as the following in conjuring her to true tears if she be innocent, or in restraining false tears. Let him place his hand on the head of the accused and say: I conjure you by the bitter tears shed on the Cross by our Saviour the Lord JESUS Christ for the salvation of the world, and by the burning tears poured in the evening hour over His wounds by the most glorious Virgin MARY, His Mother, and by all the tears which have been shed here in this world by the Saints and Elect of God, from whose eyes He has now wiped away all tears, that if you be innocent you do now shed tears, but if you be guilty that you shall by no means do so. In the name of the Father, and of the Son, and of the Holy Ghost, Amen.

And it is found by experience that the more they are conjured the less are they able to weep, however hard they may try to do so, or smear their cheeks with spittle. Nevertheless it is possible that afterwards, in the absence of the Judge and not at the time or in the place of torture, they may be able to weep in the presence of their gaolers. And as for the reason for a witch's inability to weep, it can be said that the grace of tears is one of the chief gifts allowed to the penitent; for S. Bernard tells us that the tears of the humble can penetrate to heaven and conquer the unconquerable. Therefore there can be no doubt that they are displeasing to the devil, and that he uses all his endeavour to restrain them, to prevent a witch from finally attaining to penitence. But it may be objected that it might suit with the devil's cunning, with God's permission, to allow even a witch to weep; since tearful grieving, weaving and deceiving are said to be proper to women.

The hair should be shaved from every part of her body. The reason for this is the same as that for stripping her of her clothes, which we have already mentioned; for in order to preserve their power of silence they are in the habit of hiding some superstitious object in their clothes or in their hair, or even in the most secret parts of the their bodies which must not be named.

About the Author

James Ramsey is a devout book worshipper who can be found in the wilds of British Columbia, Canada, with her husband and a menagerie of animals. When she's not glued to her laptop she enjoys travelling with her husband, having fun with her friends, and riding her horses. Currently she is working on the sequel to Andromeda Rising and the next book in the Celestial Series. Check out her website for information on the upcoming *Sagittarian Scandal.*

You can follow her on Twitter @jamesramsey09, Facebook and Goodreads under James Ramsey or subscribe to her website at www.james-ramsey.com for outtakes, teasers and fun character information.

23627460R00162

Made in the USA
Lexington, KY
17 June 2013